# Five Wishes

# Five
# Wishes

KARIN M. GERTSCH

*To Karen*

*With Best Wishes,*

*Karin*

*atmosphere press*

Published by Atmosphere Press

Library of Congress Registration Number: TXu 2-359-974

Cover design by Senhor Tocas

atmospherepress.com

Dedicated to my beloved daughter
Elizabeth Gertsch
1972 - 2014

# Matilda and Delbert MacInnes

Matilda, known as Tilli to friends and family, laid down her pen and closed the book. Almost five o'clock, and Delbert, known as Bertie, would be rising and looking for his breakfast. She padded over to the tall bookcase and put the journal back among her gardening books.

In front of the mirror, she stood straight as a sunflower and frowned. Coarse sprouts had appeared on her chin. She pursed her lips, noticing a fuzzy mustache. With a swipe of the comb and a bobby pin to control loose strands, she neatened her thinning hair. Ready to face the new day, she wore elastic-waist jeans, air-cushioned sneakers, and her favorite blue mock turtleneck.

As she tied on the navy blue apron, her thoughts turned to her daughter, Amelia, who friends and family called Mel. She had worked, one summer during high school, at a nuns' retirement home. The kitchen staff had cleaned out closets and drawers, and this apron was taken out of circulation. The nuns had given it their blessings, so she would never burn anything in the kitchen. Hah! Certainly, this blessing hadn't applied to Tilli. She'd scorched a few potatoes, blackened the bacon, or steamed green beans until they'd run out of water before they were supposed to be tender.

She smoothed the front of the apron and smiled. Mel was coming for dinner this evening, and so was her so-called Irish twin, Caitlyn, whose nickname was Lyn.

Though Mel was born eleven months before Lyn, it was Lyn who always took the lead, charged forward into adventure, and dominated the conversation whenever the girls were together. In contrast, Mel was cautious, more thoughtful, and a good listener. Tilli wished they'd visit more often.

Bertie entered the kitchen, wearing the clean work clothes Tilli had put out for him. He sat down and reached automatically for his perfectly steeped cup of Darjeeling tea. Picking up a dunker, whole wheat bread carefully toasted, buttered, and cut into strips for him, he smiled.

"Morn, Tilli."

"Morn, Bertie," she replied, sitting down opposite him.

Tilli tried not to be obvious as she studied Bertie. Should she ask him or not? After all these years, he'd grown shorter and more rotund. As she eyed him over the rim of her cup, she wondered: what had attracted her to such a bow-legged man? Maybe twenty-five years of riding on Hamlet's fire engines had done that to him. Bertie's hair had thinned but was still brown, and he parted it cleanly on the right. She couldn't help smiling as she thought about how pleasant his voice could sound and how excitedly his eyes could glow. Would they glow with enthusiasm when she asked him what was nagging her this morning? Her husband was no ordinary man: opposite her sat Hamlet's former fire chief, a man many considered a hero.

She noticed Bertie was almost finished with his dunkers. Any minute now, he'd be pushing back his chair. She thought about all the years Mr. Buxton, his best customer, had given him a Quechee wall calendar to hang inside his shop. Bertie loved the colorful photographs taken during the annual Hot Air Balloon Festival. She wondered if he'd ever consider lifting up in one such balloon. Had he imagined how it might feel to drift over the landscape and fly with the birds? Knowing his fear of heights, her thoughts returned to earth, and she sighed.

Bertie looked up from his breakfast and noticed Tilli sipping her tea. "What's on your mind, Tilli?"

"Oh, just thinking about nothing in particular."

"Nonsense, I've been 'round you long enough to know when something's a bother."

"Well, I just don't know how to put it to you."

"Why don't you give it a try?" He popped the last bit of dunker into himself.

"Okay," slowly she began, "remember how many times we said we'd take Lyn and Mel 'cross country to visit one or more National Parks? We thought we'd travel with our girls, see something new, do something different. Well, lately, I've been pondering what we might have missed by not taking *any* of those trips. You know I love living in Hamlet. You were born here; but even if I lived to be a hundred—and I've been here forty years now—they'll never consider me a native!

"That's what's been on my mind. Life is good, and don't get me wrong, I'm not complaining. Forget it; it's nothing." She bit into her toast, sipped the last of her tea, and regretted that she'd spoken. Nothing would come of this, so why had she bothered to voice her innermost thoughts? She should know by now Bertie could never be made to do anything he didn't think was his idea. Once again, she'd opened herself up, knowing he'd never change.

"Tilli, I'll tell you what. I don't need to remind you

that I have my workshop and my customers who depend on me *every working day.* I've never closed the shop and put a *Gone Fishing* sign on my door, but if this is nagging you, we should do something about it, don't you think? Certainly, we can afford it. The mortgage is paid; our bills are up to date. What's keeping us? Why don't you plan where you want us to go, and I'll be your willing escort? Pick a park. Maybe the AAA office downtown can help. Just remember that my eyesight isn't what it used to be, and with my heart condition, I can't drive hundreds of miles across this country. Perhaps we could fly somewhere, then rent a car? What d'you say?"

"Really, Bertie? What about those customers? What about your fear of heights? Ah, sorry to have mentioned it, but I never imagined your feet leaving the ground."

"My dear Tilli, when a man reaches seventy-six, his perspective is long on looking backward and short on looking into the future. And you're right; the highest my feet have been off the ground is when I'm up on that stepladder pruning your climbing roses or the wisteria growing on the pergola Woody built. But we can still get around, and we're pretty healthy for our ages. Go to AAA then let me know the plan."

"Oh, Bertie, you're the best." She rounded the table and gave him a head-and-shoulders hug, tears welling up as she considered how little faith she'd had. To think she'd assumed it would be another *no-go* sort of conversation. Her thoughts flashed back to another time when she'd asked Bertie about going away. All she'd wanted then was a weekend on Cape Cod or a trip to the Berkshires, but he'd replied, "If I want to see a different view, all I need do is look out another window!" That remark had made her clam up for months. And now, this—at last, a vacation!

Soon after she'd waved goodbye at the front door, she started to hum a little tune contemplating her afternoon visit to AAA. She scanned the April sky and saw the dark clouds. Perhaps it would rain, so she turned her thoughts to housework until it cleared up. Her attention focused on the bookcases in the den. Those shelves needed a thorough dusting, and certainly, not everything would go back on them.

Every spring, Tilli tackled the rooms in the house, and no nook or cranny was safe from her keen eyes. Today, the den; tomorrow, the living room, and so on until the house shined in all its corners. Over these many years, she had often wondered how others could live in houses never scrubbed, with closets packed full of needless belongings, corners uninvestigated, dust bunnies forever blowing about, and windows unwashed—cleanliness was definitely better than its alternative.

She got a couple of paper bags from the kitchen closet and set them on the rug in the den. This room used to be Mel's bedroom while she was growing up. And even though it was an upstairs room, because of all the built-in bookcases, it was the perfect place for a den, while Lyn's room became the guestroom, although hardly anyone ever spent the night.

Shelf by shelf, Tilli scanned the books' spines, and about a third were put into a bag. *Peyton Place*, *The Wind in the Willows*, *The Complete Works of Edgar Allan Poe*, and *Silent Spring* went back on one shelf, while contemporary paperbacks were culled. Dusting made her feel lighter, and soon she began humming a tune. Creating space for new books had cheered her, and those in the bag would go to the Hamlet Library for their Spring Book Fair. The ones patrons didn't buy went to a third-world country. As she hummed, she wondered how many people in third-world countries read English; perhaps it was what the library wanted patrons to think when the books actually were sold for pulp. At any rate, they made money for her favorite charity, and wasn't that what mattered?

# Peach of a Sole

Meanwhile, Bertie headed to his shop. He walked the distance from his cozy six-room Cape-Cod-style house every morning in about ten minutes. As he walked along, he whistled a little marching tune, something from Souza or perhaps a Strauss waltz. He mimicked the sounds birds made in the hedges along the sidewalks, and they replied from hidden perches. He could walk it blindfolded: he knew every house, every tree, and all uneven surfaces on the sidewalks, the curb cuts, and every street crossing by heart. After all, for seventy-six years, he had breathed the clean air of this tidy New England town.

He thought back to a day when he was still in school. His mother told him: "An apple doesn't fall far from its tree." He wasn't sure what apples had to do with him, but since then, he'd learned that she had meant—him—he was that apple, and he certainly hadn't gone far from where he was born. In fact, he was as much a part of Hamlet as the very oak tree he was standing under. He remembered swinging on one of its limbs—long ago removed—when he was young. He scanned the trunk to where the limb had been. The wound still visible, where bumped-out, puckered-up bark clearly marked the spot. He recalled when the tree was much smaller and thought how tall it was now, and wide in girth. The cement sidewalk at its base had been lifted up by the power of this tree's roots. He tried to see the topmost branches and heard a flicker tapping in the canopy, perhaps scouting for insects in the grooves of the bark. This oak was a reminder that he had grown old, even though a small boy remained inside him.

Bertie loved the early morning, when the day was new and the light in the sky was a lemony shade of yellow, unlike the golden sky before sundown. It was quiet, with little traffic, so he crossed streets on his way to the shop without having to stop at every corner for cars to go by. The traffic never used to be so busy and more people used to walk. He looked at his watch and knew, even as he checked, that it was almost five-forty-five, and certainly, at least one customer would be waiting in front of his *Closed* sign. Customers could be picky; well, some of them.

Bertie knew the commuters loved his early opening time when they could drop off their fine leather dress shoes before getting on the train to Boston, and the horsey set got personal attention for expensive riding boots, as well as repairs for harnesses. Ladies came to him with fine leather handbags, and he repaired straps and handles, zippers, and toggles. New Englanders were thrifty folk who wanted to keep their favorite leather goods working as long as possible. Bertie loved the feel of supple boot leather and sharp tiny tacks. He got shivers of delight after a shoe had been re-soled.

As he approached the final yards to his shop—Peach of a Sole—wouldn't you know, Bertie recognized an old-time customer pacing on the doorstep. Bertie chuckled when he considered all the people who had approached his shop for the first time while thinking it was a restaurant. How they pushed open the somewhat unyielding door, then heard the loud buzzer, set off by a sensor under the doormat. They took one whiff of shoe polish and adhesive before looking around, totally perplexed. He would explain, once again, his repair shop was named after his favorite dessert: peach cobbler. "Well, they just don't get it," he said aloud to no one in particular.

"Morn, Mr. Buxton."

"Good morning yourself, Delbert. Are you running late?"

What impertinence! Buxton always suggested Bertie was late. As Bertie unlocked his shop door and turned his *Closed* sign around to read *Open*, Buxton was already inside before Bertie had a chance to flick on the light switch.

Buxton knew, from Bertie's years of working with machinery, that Bertie had become somewhat deaf and needed to have things said loudly or repeated twice, so he raised his voice, "It's my elk-hide L.L. Bean slippers, Delbert, the stitching's come undone, and I don't want to return them to Bean's because they don't make this style any longer. They're the best damned slippers I've ever had: soft, warm, and roomy. Can you have them ready later today so that when the six o'clock arrives in Hamlet, I can pick them up?"

"Mr. Buxton, you're my best customer"—he tells every customer this—"and I will be happy to have them ready. I hope the train's on time today, 'cause Matilda and I've dinner plans this evening. Our daughters are coming over, a rare occasion, Mr. Buxton, as you know. Rare, when children have time for parents these days."

"Oh, you've got that right, Delbert. Stacie and I rarely see our offspring: one's in California, has some high-tech kind of job, while our son shadows a politician down in Washington, D.C. Sometimes I wonder if *anyone* knows what's going on down there. If we see each offspring twice a year, we're fortunate. Well, got to get to the station ahead of the train. See you this evening, Delbert."

"Have a good one, Mr. Buxton."

As Buxton left the shop, Bertie thought about why Buxton always yelled at him. He's not being rude. Maybe I do need a hearing aid. He reflected on a recent conversation with Tilli when she had scolded him about needing a shoehorn to pry open his ears so she wouldn't have to holler.

It was quiet, and no one else was coming, so Bertie had a chance to look at his familiar surroundings. On the wall facing the customers as they entered the shop was a sign: *I'm a Doctor in a Shoe Hospital.* One of his customers had it made for him when he had celebrated thirty-five years in business.

A large color print, copied from the painting by Horatio McCulloch, depicted Kinlochaline Castle on Morvern in Scotland—the MacInnes castle—hung in a simple brown frame on the wall nearest his cash register. This cash register was actually a forty-year-old calculator set on top of a cash drawer. Delbert MacInnes still hand-stamped his customers' receipts: no electronics here. Next to his register was a round glass dish filled with wrapped butterscotch candies. Lots of shoelaces—all lengths, widths, and colors—hung on a rack. The longest laces were 108 inches for hockey skates, while regular laces were 72 inches long. A hand-written sign, *Special 25 Cents,* drew attention to a shoebox filled with assorted cotton laces.

Several sizes of wooden shoetrees were in a pile. And shoes, boots, and handbags to be worked on were piled on a shelf. Items ready for pickup were in plastic bags, ticketed, and neatly stacked. Boar bristle brushes for sale and jars with shoe cream in several colors, also mink oil paste and glycerin leather cleaner, as well as Nu-Life Color Spray cans, filled his shelves. Containers of Barge All Purpose Cement were also stacked in a pile. Gel Comfort Center insoles hung on a rotating stand; boxes marked "soakers," which were used to put over ice skates after skating, stood nearby. When skates were cold, they gave off moisture as the blades warmed up; the soaker absorbed the moisture from the skate blades and helped to keep them from rusting. As soon as the skates stopped perspiring, the soakers were supposed to be removed.

Inside another frame, on a sheet of plain paper, was written, "Happy Sixty-fifth Birthday, Delbert MacInnes." In the middle of the paper was a picture of Delbert taken in his youth, and all around this picture were signatures and well-wishes from members of the community. Delbert MacInnes smiled, proud to have owned his business for nearly forty years.

Several American flags decorated the walls, as did a framed certificate indicating that Delbert MacInnes had been a member of the local American Legion for thirty-five years. Pictures of family and customers, as well as their children and grandchildren, hung on one wall. A framed picture of Delbert, flanked by firefighters clad in yellow slickers, with Hamlet's Engine One in the background, and a small brass plaque on the bottom of the frame read: *Hamlet is Thankful for Twenty-five Years of Service*, was in plain view. A certificate Tilli had given to him a few years ago, on their thirty-fifth wedding anniversary, hung proudly behind his cash register. Engraved in gold letters, it read: *Thirty-five Years of Dedication and*

*Devotion.* Customers thought the certificate commemorated his years in business.

His upright vacuum stood in one corner with its cord neatly wrapped. Everywhere Delbert looked, his shop appeared orderly.

Bertie had two old clippings. One was taped to the customer side of his register:

*Dear Customers,*
*I will heel you*
*I will save your sole*
*I will even dye for you.*

The second clipping hung at eye level nearby:

*The difficult age has come and lit*
*I'm too tired to work*
*and too old to quit.*

Upon entering Peach of a Sole, his customers heard classical music playing on the old portable radio, even though Bertie couldn't hear the music due to the earplugs he wore now to drown out the whirring and grinding noises of his machinery. In addition to a good cup of tea, he appreciated well-brewed music.

Some customers thought he was weird because a stuffed cat sat on one high shelf. Bertie loved cats and dogs equally; heck, he loved all animals. When his beloved cat, Mr. Hugg, died, one of his customers, a taxidermist, stuffed Mr. Hugg so he could be with Bertie forever. Poor Mr. Hugg was eighteen years young when a careless driver ran over him—right in front of Peach of a Sole. The taxidermist didn't charge Bertie a dime for his services. "It's on me, Mr. MacInnes," he had said kindly. Now Mr.

Hugg sat proudly on this wooden shelf, which Bertie had made himself.

The stuffed Mr. Hugg on this shelf had led customers to give Bertie cat memorabilia. Every available spot in his shop without shoe-related merchandise was filled with cat curios. Whenever the shelves in his shop got too crowded, Bertie went to Harmony Hardware and bought lumber and nails to build new shelving.

Though a golden retriever wagging its tail bit him in the rump when he was a little boy, it hadn't stopped Bertie from having three dogs of his own. Of course, since Tilli never wanted animals in the house, he'd had to keep the dogs in his shop. He thought back fondly to his beagle named Peachy, then his Labrador retriever named Glow, and his best and most dear pet, which was the last dog he owned, named Pansy. He never knew what had made him get a golden retriever, but everyone loved Pansy. Children would come in and tussle with her on the floor while their mothers looked around the shop. Adults would come in and scratch her behind the ears and pat her silky fur. He thought back to the day when one lady remarked, "Why, Pansy, you've helped me stop awhile and relax today."

"Enough reminiscing," Bertie said aloud to the four walls. He knew Mr. Buxton might be his only customer today. How times had changed since World War II. When he had finished his hitch in the Navy aboard the aircraft carrier USS *Ticonderoga*, he came home to Hamlet and worked for four long years as an apprentice to another shoe repairman. One Friday, when Bertie couldn't stand the curmudgeon another week, he had taken a leap of faith and gone into business for himself. He and Tilli were a young married couple with a baby on the way, a new mortgage, and … "Jiminy Cricket! What was I thinking?" he said aloud.

Of course, at the time, how were he and Tilli to know she'd have a miscarriage? He'd never forget how distraught they were—she especially—and then she lost another one. Thank goodness Mel came along in January that year and then Lyn eleven months later. At last, they'd been blessed with so-called Irish twins, no less!

When he was young, he never gave failure a thought. Succeed he must for himself and his family. After World War II, people were thrifty, and they repaired their shoes. He thought back to those years when he might repair one pair of shoes four times! He was always busy. By the 1980s, he sometimes worked on thirty pairs a day. These days he was lucky if he repaired five. Maybe he'd fix fewer than that. Plastic was the culprit. These days, shoes had a lot of plastic and were harder to repair than the leather shoes of an earlier time. Now that it was spring, he would be busier than during the winter months, when he sometimes sat in his shop for days waiting for people to bring him work.

Last winter was a rough one. On slow days, he sometimes made seventy phone calls to people to come and pick up their repaired shoes. After all the dialing, maybe seven people showed up. So, he gave up calling and decided it just wasn't worth it. Times were different now. People had too much stuff, and they threw things away rather than getting them repaired. By golly, come to think of it, there were people who rented storage containers for their overage, then never visited their belongings until, finally, the storage facility sold off the forgotten contents because these people hadn't paid their rent. What foolishness the world was coming to! Bertie couldn't grasp the sense of it.

He remembered the '90s when he charged people twenty percent down when they dropped off their shoes for repair. If they paid fifty percent down, or the entire amount, he'd given them a slightly better price. Supplies were so expensive that he barely made enough to scrape by. For five years, he and Tilli had tried to sell this hundred-year-old building, but no one had made an offer yet. This old place had once been a school, then a church, and afterward, his shoe repair shop. To the four walls, he whispered, "I've spent my life restoring soles."

As Bertie continued to ponder the history of shoe repairing, he was jolted by his own loud buzzer, which had been activated by someone stepping on the *Welcome* mat.

"May I help you?" Bertie asked the young man.

"Hello, are you Mr. Delbert MacInnes, the cobbler?"

"Yes and no."

The young man looked perplexed, but Bertie's response did not put him off. "Mr. MacInnes, I'm with the *Hamlet Weekly*, and I thought you might let me interview you for a story I'm preparing for next week's edition; the theme is local businesses, and someone told me you've been here a long time. Do you have a few minutes to spare?"

"First of all, young man, I'm not a cobbler; I'm a shoe repairman. I'm a rarity in these throwaway days, when few people seem to want my services. When economic times are good, shoes are cheap enough; tossing the old and buying new seem to be what folks do. A cobbler makes shoes; a shoe repairman repairs them. There's a big difference; make sure you get it right when you do your article."

"Yes, sir, Mr. MacInnes," said the young man while

scribbling on his notepad. "Do you have any funny stories you think our readers might enjoy?"

"Young man, you know my name well enough, but I don't know yours. Is this the way they teach you at the newspaper? Just go right into a shop and start asking questions? Do you have a business card? How do I know you're not trying to sell me something?"

"My name is John Brewster, and I'm apprenticing with the *Hamlet Weekly*. I'm a senior at Salem State in their journalism program; I live on Maple Street."

"Well, John Brewster, you must be related to Mary and Tom Brewster?"

"Yes, sir; they're my grandparents. Do you know them?"

"As you've just said, I've been around for a few years, and it just so happens I went to school with your grandfather. Maple Street is near where I grew up. Tom and Mary are good customers, but I haven't seen you since you were a baby. It's your lucky day, John! I'm in a good mood, so go ahead. You asked if I had a couple of funny stories for your readers?"

"Yes, sir, I think the *Hamlet Weekly* readers would enjoy that."

Delbert began, "Once upon a time, a man left a pair of shoes for re-soling. After he walked out of my shop, I put my right hand into one of the shoes and pulled out a banana. Guess what I did?"

"You ate it?"

"You bet! And it was just the perfect ripeness. The guy never mentioned his banana when he picked up his shoes.

"Another time, there was a man who left a pair of work boots for new soles and heels. I did the work, and those boots sat on my shelf where I put all the repaired shoes ready for customer pick-up. Those work boots remained on that shelf for a long time before I put them in my dead pile. I have a pile in my basement of unclaimed but repaired shoes. The work boots were down there two years! One morning, a poor man walked in. Threadbare clothes, worn-out shoes. I asked him what size he wore, and when he told me, I knew immediately that those work boots would fit, so I gave them to him. He was very happy. Well, guess what happened then, John?"

"Don't tell me the owner came in looking for his work boots after two years?"

"John Brewster, the *Hamlet Weekly* should be proud they have you as an intern. You guessed right!"

"What did you do, Mr. MacInnes, when the owner showed up?"

"I did the only thing I could; I told him the truth. And he just stood right where you're standing and laughed! He wasn't angry. He said he'd recently moved, and in the process, he had found his claim stub behind a bureau."

"So, Mr. MacInnes, do you still have a dead pile in your basement?"

"I do, John. Each spring, I look the claim stubs over, and if the dates on the stubs are two years old or older, I donate those shoes to the Salvation Army. Over the years, I have donated hundreds of unclaimed shoes. And it's one of the biggest frustrations in this business: people who do not come back to pay for and pick up their shoes."

"Mr. MacInnes, is there anything else you'd like me to write in my article?"

"John, the only thing I can add is Matilda, my wife of forty years, looks after me, and we've got two healthy, independent daughters. I've pretty much lived the life I imagined when I was a young skedaddler right out of Hamlet High, about the age you are today. Have I been anyplace? No. Have I missed anything important? I don't think so. Regrets? Nope! Life's been good."

"Thank you, Mr. MacInnes. The article will run in next week's edition. And I'll be sure to come by and bring you a tear sheet."

"Now you're talking another language. A *tear sheet*?"

"Well, Mr. MacInnes, that's just a fancy way of saying I'll give you a copy of the newspaper page where my article about you and Peach of a Sole will be printed."

"Here, John Brewster," Bertie held out the candy dish. "Have a candy for the road, and you might want to add this to your article: Peach of a Sole is for sale, so if readers decide they want to try their hand at shoe repairing or if they want to buy the building for any business purpose, it's available. Oh, and I don't need that *tear sheet*; I've been subscribing to the *Hamlet Weekly* since long before you were born."

John scribbled something on his pad, put the pencil behind his right ear, and unwrapped the butterscotch candy before popping it into his mouth. "Thanks again, Mr. MacInnes."

As John left the shop and pulled hard on the door to close it fully, Bertie watched the young man stuff the candy wrapper in his coat pocket, cross the street, and get into a vintage, somewhat-dented Subaru. The young man reminded him so much of himself at that stage in life. And John had been brought up right; the young man didn't litter, and he was polite. Why did moments like this sneak up on him? It was all those questions. Why was he thinking—now—maybe, after all, he might have missed some-thing important? He remembered his mother telling him that a man shouldn't spend too much time thinking; it leads to trouble. Bertie went into his workshop and got busy.

# Matilda's Passion

Tilli was excited Mel and Lyn were coming for dinner, but first, she had to prepare Bertie's lunch, which she did every day. He'd be home at noon and expect it to be ready. "I'm glad he takes a two-hour break every day," she thought aloud as she pulled the blue apron over her head and tied it on.

Thinking back to breakfast that morning, Tilli was still in shock that Bertie had so quickly agreed to a vacation. After all these years, why hadn't she pressed him sooner? She moved about the kitchen, opening and closing cupboards to gather the ingredients for lunch. She took the salt pork out of the refrigerator, all the while thinking back to an article that she'd read a couple of weeks ago in the *Hamlet Weekly* describing the different communication styles of men and women. One point had stayed with her: if the woman didn't spell out clearly to the man exactly what she wanted, he would definitely not be able to guess what was on her mind by the process of osmosis. A point quite revealing to her because she'd spent years keeping thoughts to herself and then wondering why Delbert didn't know what was important. How silly she'd been!

She hummed as she prepared New England-style codfish chowder. She started by frying out the quarter pound of cubed salt pork in a large saucepan until it turned golden brown. After draining off all but about a tablespoon of the fat, the little cubes were put on a plate for later. With a flick of the wrist, she turned on the stove's blower before she put a cup of chopped onions into the pan. "Don't want the entire house to smell of onions," she said aloud.

When the onions were tender, she added some peeled and cubed Yukon Gold potatoes, then laid the pound of fresh cod filet on top. Next, whole milk went into the pot until it almost covered the fish. And, just before the boil, she lowered the heat and simmered the fish and potatoes until they were tender and the fish flaked easily when poked with a fork. At this point, Tilli put the brown cubes of salt pork back into the pot, along with freshly ground pepper and a generous pouring of half-and-half. Bertie loved her fish chowder, and she made sure to have plenty of cornbread on the side. Cornbread made with Vermont maple syrup in the batter, never sugar.

After lunch, Tilli put on her going-to-town clothes and headed to AAA. She had no idea where they would go on vacation. There were so many places they'd never been. Where to start? She thought back to the days before she got married. After secretarial school, she got a bank job in Boston. She always dressed nicely, loved helping the customers, and even had a little money left over to travel occasionally to New York City to attend an off-Broadway show or a concert. She had especially enjoyed her annual trips to Radio City Music Hall for the Christmas extravaganza with those high-kicking Rockettes. Those were the days when she didn't have to think about another person before deciding what to do or how to spend her money. She had had a taste of spreading her wings and taking flight— then. "It's been much too long," Tilli whispered.

Anxiety began to settle on her shoulders as she neared

the AAA office and questions began to form. Twice, she almost turned back, thinking she'd made a mistake to press Bertie about her traveling bug. Maybe they could just watch another one of those programs on the local PBS station. Or, sometimes, the Hamlet Library had guest speakers who traveled extensively and came back with slides and presentations about their trips. She and Bertie could travel vicariously through the experiences of others. All the while, she kept putting one foot in front of the other and soon found herself pulling open the door at AAA.

"May I help you?" A friendly young woman had looked up as Tilli entered.

"I need help planning a vacation for my husband and me."

"You've come to the right place. Where do you want to go?"

"I don't know." As soon as Tilli said this, she imagined a pinched expression on the woman's face, and Tilli realized her answer must have sounded silly.

"Okay," said the woman kindly. "Let me show you our travel destinations, and perhaps something will speak to you." She indicated Tilli should come behind the counter and sit at a desk while the woman brought colorful brochures from a wall rack to spread in front of Tilli.

"We have a special eight-day cruise to the Eastern Caribbean, which includes Antigua, the island with three hundred and sixty-five beaches, one for every day of the year. There's a five-day Panama Canal cruise, stopping in Panama City, which continues through to the Pacific, with a flight back to Boston. This one's a brochure with a fly-and-drive trip to San Francisco, including excursions to vineyards, redwood forests, the Spanish mission at Monterey, and artistic Carmel." She paused briefly. "But, if you want something closer to home, there's a three-day cruise, including a car rental to Nova Scotia and Cape Breton Island. We've got lots more opportunities, something for everyone. When were you thinking of traveling?"

All of these *opportunities* left Tilli dazed. "I'm not sure."

"Well then, might I suggest our annual three-night coach bus trip through southern Vermont and New Hampshire? We stop in Quechee and Woodstock and go to Keene and the Mount Monadnock region. Great bed and breakfasts, shopping, and sightseeing. If you and your husband would like a hot-air balloon ride, we will be in Quechee during their annual festival, which is held every year in June on Father's Day. The trip is very popular, quite reasonable, and you don't need to fly or drive, just sit back and relax. You'll be pampered and come back wanting more."

"I'll give that one some thought, take these brochures home, and get back to you."

"Don't wait too long; if you're interested in the Quechee trip, it fills up fast. You don't want to be left behind in Hamlet."

Tilli started walking home from the AAA office, and along the way, she began to think about the various trip suggestions. "Thousands of people have gone on trips. Why can't Bertie and I? The woman said the bus trip didn't go far from Hamlet, so if we don't like it for some reason, we'll return before we know it. It's not expensive, but that's not an issue. We've never been on a coach bus. Maybe we'll get motion sickness." Tilli had heard about this happening to people, and it certainly didn't sound like a pleasant thing by any means. What about bathroom stops? She didn't want to embarrass herself. These were definitely concerns, and she would have to think things over very carefully because if this vacation didn't turn out to be a good experience, she'd never hear the end of it from Bertie. She imagined him saying, "'I told you so, Tilli!'" And she didn't want to be made to feel guilty. Suddenly traveling seemed complicated, and she considered dropping the whole thing.

"I know what the matter is; living for years inside my comfort zone has made me afraid to venture into new directions." Tilli looked around as she said this aloud and hoped no one had heard.

She reached her front walk and decided to put the brochures away. If the rain held off a little longer, there were still a couple of garden chores to do before starting dinner. A smile spread across her face as thoughts turned to her daughters. "I've missed them so much!"

Through a low gate in the white picket fence, Tilli entered her garden. On the gate was a sign: *Weeds Not Welcome—All Others May Enter.* She scanned the sky with its dark clouds, ready to let loose. Next to the path was her pet rock, decorated as a hedgehog, which Lyn and Mel had given her for a birthday years ago. The girls had begged for a cat or dog, but Tilli was of the mind that animals belonged outdoors and not in the house. She thought back to that day when Lyn and Mel tried to sneak Peachy into the house. Tilli heard Peachy's soft bark and her daughters' laughter, and the dog went back to Bertie's shop. The girls weren't happy, and now Tilli wondered if she'd been wrong not to give in. Who liked dirty paw prints on polished floors and dander blowing about? And who was the crazy person with the idea to keep animals *inside* a house?

Tilli's passion was *Hemerocallis.* In May, she would be able to poke her nose into Hyperion and breathe its fragrance: how marvelous! She'd planted Strutters Ball next to Mary Todd because they were going to make a bold statement in the border beginning in June; the purple next to yolk-yellow would be a showstopper.

"Daylilies are so rewarding. No pests that I've found. Hardy as can be. I must be patient and wait for these ladies!" Tilli talked to her plants as she moved about the garden.

At the end of last season, she'd planted a new variety, Mardi Gras Parade, and was awaiting its flowers with great anticipation. The catalog had described it as having "ruffled bright rose-lavender blossoms, with an unusual double wine eye, and a green throat, surrounded by a medium lavender band, which blended into a darker wine-purple eye."

"What a sight it will be, blooming in my garden for the first time this year."

Since it was still April, her daylilies were just green blades erupting from the cool earth, and some tips hadn't even emerged yet. What she especially liked about daylilies was that they bloomed throughout the season, some early, others came later, and still some, like Rosie Returns and Stella D'Oro, bloomed more than once in a season.

As she walked, Tilli deadheaded tulips and narcissus already gone by. The minor bulbs, grape hyacinths, *Chionodoxa,* crocus, and Siberian squills were blooming in the borders along her path. A forsythia shrub was ready to burst into flower. Here and there, perennials were just green clumps, low to the ground, but they had made it through another winter and would enliven the garden in their season.

"There you are, my pretty Veronica Crater Lake Blue; you made it through another cold, wet winter. Oh, and my iris Jennifer Rebecca is coming up and looks like it's spread a little from last year. When I noticed your brown leaves, I thought I'd lost you for certain."

Tilli continued walking among her borders, greeting some favorites and looking pleased overall. She loved the early spring when everything looked tidy, and the buds on branches were in a state of suspension, just waiting for the right moment to burst forth with leaves or colorful flowers. Tilli knew the Latin and common names of her garden plants and always poked permanent metal markers into the ground near each newly planted clump until she'd committed them to memory. Plants held such promise of new life.

Tilli hummed and continued her stroll. Reaching down, she gently pulled some jonquils for a vase. "Day-lilies are so lonely by themselves," she thought. "It's why I've planted lots of perennials, biennials, and the occasional annuals to fill in the bare spots throughout the year. And, look at my David Austin roses, the divine Gertrude Jekyll, so delicately pink and fragrant. I can't wait for them to bloom. I love all the colors of the flowers. But not white; it isn't a color, in my estimation."

With a frown, she reached down and pulled out a young weed growing in her otherwise orderly and neat plot. She noticed her threadleaf *Coreopsis* beginning to shoulder its way into her *Centaurias*. If only plants would be content with occupying their designated spaces. These she would have to lift and divide before they infringed upon their neighbors. At times, the upkeep of her flower borders—all around the house, except on the north side where various ferns, English ivy, and hostas were low maintenance—could become overwhelming. But the off-shoots of plants made great gifts for friends, as well as donations to the garden club's spring and fall plant sales. She was grateful to have found a young gardener willing to come, when needed, to dig up plants for the sales since it now required more effort on her part to pot them up.

Just as the first fat raindrops splattered, Tilli took the three brick steps up to her front door and entered the small hallway. She never bothered locking her door whenever she went downtown. She hung her jacket on a wooden hanger in the coat closet. Wire hangers like those from the cleaners had no place in this house. Tilli had arranged all the hangers on the rod in the same direction, with Bertie's coats and jackets on the left side of the closet and hers to the right. She could open this closet in pitch darkness and reach for the exact item she wanted to wear. As she shut the door, she wondered—ever so briefly—why this level of order was so important to her.

She'd always liked the layout of this house, which was where Bertie grew up. They'd lived here with Bertie's parents when they were first married, so they could save money, and Bertie could start his own shoe repair business. Then he'd worked for four years for a cantankerous man, who was more demanding than Bertie could handle. Even though Bertie's parents were nice to be around—especially Bertie's father—it wasn't easy living under their roof. For one thing, she and Bertie had very little privacy. And Bertie's mother could be temperamental. She often frowned in Tilli's presence, causing Tilli to question her own ability to take care of Bertie. To everyone's benefit, Bertie soon agreed with Tilli that it would be best if they found a place of their own, so they moved across town to a four-room cottage. The place was small and primitive; something needed repairing or replacing constantly, but they could just manage the new mortgage. Bertie's good friend, Woody, often came to the rescue and exchanged carpentry projects for home-cooked meals.

After five difficult years due to two miscarriages, Mel came along, and they moved into a tiny house with two bedrooms—another fixer-upper. She thought of Woody and how many meals he shared with them after hours of sawing and hammering in their second house. Through it all, Woody was their lifesaver, the place got fixed up, he was always fair with the bills, and they became lifetime friends. It had been difficult those first few years, especially when Lyn came along eleven months after Mel. With two babies in diapers, Tilli was not able to work outside the house and help out with the bills. She thought back to one day when there was so little money and she had to decide whether to buy a new pair of ninety-nine cent pantyhose to replace the one pair she'd had to throw out or to spend that dollar on a cucumber and tomato for their salad.

Bertie was an only child, and when his parents passed on, she and Bertie moved back into his family home. This lovely Cape Cod-style house, with its central hallway, dining room on one side, kitchen behind, and the living room running front to back on the opposite side of the hallway, had a practical layout. A fireplace graced one wall of the living room, and a half-bath was conveniently located next to the kitchen. The stairs led up to two bedrooms and a den on the second floor, with a full bath at the top of the stairs. Tilli remembered how, at one time, the house seemed too small and crowded, what with four people living in it, as well as other people's children visiting after school. Those were good days, though, when Tilli baked for themselves as well as to raise money for different causes. She cooked extra helpings then, too, so the girls' friends could stay for dinner, but since Mel and Lyn moved away about thirteen years ago, the house sometimes seemed too big. She pondered how quickly the years had gone by.

Tilli laid the table with care; the daffodils were center stage in a vase that had belonged to her mother. She paused as she placed her mother's silverware and old Spode china together on the table with Bertie's mother's cut-glass wine glasses and lace-edged linen napkins. She thought of these women and how they had, in their time, done the very same things she was doing now.

Tilli's mother had been a good cook; her knowledge was embedded, and recipes unfolded from her unconsciousness, never prepared the same way twice. Bertie's mother, on the other hand, had cooked out of necessity. She had worked side-by-side with Bertie's father in their hardware store, Harmony Hardware, right here in Hamlet; it was now under a different owner. Those were long days on her feet, and when she came home, dinner was something to be put together quickly. The only time she fussed was on Sundays, her day off, when she cooked a big meal, hoping some of it would be left over for the next night. Bertie's mother was great at cooking meals in one pot, soups and stews, or casseroles, which could be reheated. For some reason known only to her, she often reminded Bertie that she had nearly lost her life giving birth to him, but that he had been worth the effort since he was her pride and joy.

After Tilli had graduated from a Boston secretarial school, her second job had been working at the hardware store as a bookkeeper. She met Bertie at Harmony Hardware one July afternoon. It wasn't common to have air conditioning everywhere, and when he saw her wipe the sweat from her forehead, he rushed over to her desk and plugged in a small fan to provide relief. Right from the beginning, she was impressed by his thoughtfulness.

Tilli worked at Harmony Hardware off and on for twenty years, even after the business was sold to the new owners. It was a great job because she could keep the books while the girls were in school, and if there was too much to fit in during the day, she could take ledgers home to work on in the evenings while the girls did their homework at the kitchen table. There were no computers in those days, just the double-entry bookkeeping system—paper and a sharpened pencil.

To this day, Tilli had kept the books for Bertie's shoe repair shop. Also, she prepared their business and personal taxes and managed the household budget. When she wasn't working in the house or garden, she found it relaxing to read books and fill in her favorite crossword puzzle in the *Hamlet Weekly*.

Now the air smelled of roasted rosemary potatoes, lemony green beans, and roast beef. Tilli had taken the roast out of the oven and set it on the carving platter to rest. Then she'd put her dessert in the oven to bake and afterwards the dinner rolls to warm. "Mustn't forget to take these out in a few minutes," Tilli thought to herself. Then, the doorbell rang, and laughter floated through the front hall.

"Why do the girls always ring that bell?" Tilli knew the answer even as she raised the question: they rang the silly bell because no one else did. Tilli had thought often, what a waste of time it had been to install it years ago, but back then, it seemed important to her to have a proper doorbell since they didn't have a dog in the house to bark when someone came. She thought about other priorities and how they'd changed over time.

"Hi, Mom." Mel squeezed Tilli and put a soft kiss on her cheek.

"Oh, it smells divine," Lyn said as she gently pushed Mel out of the way in order to get close to her mother. "I'm famished; it's been a long time since I've had a really good meal."

"Well, that's not my fault," Tilli responded in a good-natured tone.

"What can I do to help?" asked Mel.

"Hey, look who came to dinner!" Bertie had just come home from the shoe repair shop and caught them in the kitchen. Bertie loved having the girls just as much as Tilli did. The family around the dinner table: nothing was better! He gave his daughters a big hug, Mel in one arm and Lyn in the other, and tickled them in the ribs.

"Daddy, stop!" they exclaimed, wriggling out of his grip. But Bertie knew they loved it. Who else could he squeeze? He squeezed Tilli when he could catch her, but it wasn't the same.

"Here, Mel, take the roast into the dining room; Lyn, take the vegetables. Everything's ready. Oh, the rolls!" Tilli opened the oven door just in time to take the crusty Parisian-style rolls out before they burned.

"Mom, I see you have the blessed apron on. That's why the rolls didn't burn. Oh, yummy, it all looks so delicious." Mel had already sat down in her usual chair at the table.

"Mom, I've been looking forward to this all week," Lyn unfolded her cloth napkin and placed it in her lap.

"I know we never did this very often in the past, but I would like to say a few words before we eat. I feel very thankful we're together. I've missed you girls." Tilli nodded in Bertie's direction.

They paused and lowered their heads as Delbert prayed: "We give thanks to God that our lovely daughters are with us tonight and for this food, which Tilli has prepared for us. Amen."

"Pass the rolls, please." Lyn stretched her arm out in their direction.

"Oh, I forgot the butter dish; it's still on the kitchen counter." Tilli began to push back her chair.

"I'll get it," announced Mel. "Just relax, Mom; you've done all the work."

"So, what's new with you girls?" Bertie asked as he reached for the potatoes.

Lyn jumped in before Mel could answer first. "I've been busy installing a new exhibit at the Hamlet Community Arts Center with my staff and volunteers. We had fifty artists submit samples of their work, and it's a great mix of genres, from watercolor to sculpture and folk art. In a separate room at the center, we will exhibit amateur artwork as well as some drawings done by the Hamlet

High senior art students. The opening is a week from this Saturday, starting at ten in the morning; we'll have refreshments. I wish you'd come and see it.

"Since they made me director of programming, things have really taken off. It's been good to be busy. You know as well as I do that since Roger and I got divorced, I've been in a real funk. Thank God it's over! Picking up the pieces at thirty-three wasn't easy. Ten years I lived with that man. I'm so glad we didn't have any kids. Although you know I would have gladly had a child, but Roger was too busy to make babies. Those are his words, not mine!" Lyn stopped to eat some green beans but added: "Our relationship would never have improved with the passage of time."

"We all make mistakes, Lyn. Be glad you didn't wait any longer. Maybe you'll meet someone new. You never know when." Tilli began rubbing her wine glass as if it were a crystal ball. "I think I see a tall, handsome, and intelligent man coming into your life very soon," she said.

"Mom, the only man I want for the rest of my life is Daddy," Lyn quipped as she reached across the table and squeezed his hand.

"Mel, how are all your children doing in school?"

Mel laughed. "All my children: I think that was the name of a soap opera on television for many years. You wouldn't know, Mom, since I never saw you watch television, at least never in the daytime."

"I'd much rather read a good book," replied Tilli.

Mel continued, "Do you realize I've been teaching third grade at Hamlet Elementary for ten years? This year, I have three children who can't speak a word of English; it's been a challenge, but I do have an aide who comes in to help. Then there's one little boy who can't keep his bottom on a chair for more than ten seconds. I have one little girl who falls asleep at her desk and hasn't had a change of clothes for days. I know she doesn't eat breakfast, and I suspect no one ever thinks of giving her a bath. Otherwise, the other twenty children are doing great."

"So, what do you do about a neglected child?" asked Lyn.

"I bring extra fruit to school and share it with her at recess when the other children are busy so the little girl won't be embarrassed. In the meantime, I've spoken with the guidance counselor, asking him to contact the family to find out what's going on at home. Lyn, I have to be so careful. It's not like it used to be. People can come out of the woodwork to sue, but the law states if I see neglect or abuse, I must report it, and I do. I feel badly for this little girl; she's so sweet and shy.

"It's always bothered me that there are some parents I never get to meet the entire school year. Even though I'm not married and have never had a child, I treasure these children as if they were my own. I'm responsible to help them grow, not just in learning the required subjects and preparing for tests but in gaining confidence in themselves. Each year, they amaze me by the time they head off to summer vacation. Each one is precious."

"Any other news? How's the volunteering at the Hamlet Food Pantry?"

"Daddy, there's a fundraiser coming up in a couple of weeks. It will be great! Restaurants in Hamlet, as well as in surrounding towns, are donating prepared food for a delicious family-style dinner. Fifteen dollars per person, including salad and dessert; what a bargain! Every penny will go to stocking our pantry shelves. We're so low now."

"Maybe your mother and I will still be here when the event happens. We'll come."

"What do you mean, Daddy? Maybe you'll come? Are you sick? Anything I should know about? Don't make me worry."

Tilli laughed. "Mel, I think your father is referring to our upcoming vacation."

"Vacation? Wow! When? Where? You've never been on a vacation," exclaimed Lyn.

"Oh, I'm happy for the two of you. You deserve this so much. Please tell us about it." Mel finished her wine.

"If everyone's done eating, let's clear the table, and I'll share what I've learned from AAA. I need your opinions." Tilli pushed back her chair and began to gather up dishes.

"Oh no, Mom; Lyn and I will clean up."

"And I'm heading for the living room," Bertie stood up.

"Then I'll put the peach cobbler into the dessert dishes. Who wants ice cream on theirs?"

Everyone said, "I do!" The only choice Tilli ever offered was boring vanilla.

"Hey, Dad, when did you get the gas-fired unit installed in the fireplace?" asked Lyn.

Bertie eased himself into his father's old wing chair and answered. "Last month, I decided it was time to stop lugging heavy firewood and fooling around with trying to get damp wood going. It's too much like work."

Tilli added, "Besides, this way, we just shut off the switch and go to bed; no worries about dying embers. No sparks on the rug. No ashes to clean up, although I do miss the ashes to put on my garden." Tilli flicked on the switch before sitting down, and cheerful flames began dancing in the fireplace; a gentle warmth filled the room.

"So, Mom, tell us about your upcoming vacation. I'm really excited for you."

"Mel, the lady at AAA gave me several suggestions. Here, look at the brochures. What do you think? I'm drawn to the coach bus trip to Vermont and New Hampshire; it's not too far, and it's not exotic. No three hundred and sixty-five beaches, no canals, and no cruises to nowhere. I can't believe your dad has agreed, after all this time, to go on a vacation. And, since he said okay, I'm starting to fret about what could go wrong."

"Daddy," Lyn smiled at him, "the coach bus goes to Quechee, Vermont. Isn't that where people go up in hot-air balloons? I've read that if you're anxious, the balloon can stay tethered. Haven't you always wanted to go up in a balloon?"

"Oh no, you're confused, Lyn. I've always *liked* hot-air balloons because they're colorful, but actually lifting off the ground and going airborne in a little basket is not my idea of fun. Besides, if God had wanted me to fly, I'd be a bird."

"Oh, Daddy, I bet you'd love it once you're up there. One of my friends came back all taken in with the experience. She said the operator brought the balloon down just above the river so the basket splashed and lifted up again. Then they went up high over the waterfall at Quechee before hovering just above the treetops, where they came down a bit, so she could reach the highest oak leaves and grab a fistful. It was relaxing, peaceful, and great fun. The pilots are licensed; it's safe!"

"Well, then there's something else, Mel. I'm afraid the

bus trip will be too long a time sitting and not enough time for bathroom stops. And what about motion sickness? I do have some concerns."

"Mom and Daddy, today's coach buses are so comfortable, and they all have onboard lavatories, so I wouldn't worry. I think Lyn would agree with me; you should just go ahead and book the trip. It will be good to take time out and see new scenery; when you come back, you will most likely be ready to plan the next trip. You'll love it! And while you're gone, Lyn and I can look after the house, water the garden, and pick up the mail."

"This is not a trip to a foreign country, Daddy; you'd be going to Vermont. No exotic landscape with strange and unusual foods and unsafe drinking water. When will you start traveling?" asked Lyn.

"When do you plan to start living?" asked Mel.

Tilli had heard enough. "Okay, let's put the brochures aside; it's getting late, and your daddy got up early. I think he and I will go on the Father's Day weekend trip. There's still time to get used to the idea, but I'll have to go to AAA on Monday; they said it's very popular."

"I guess we've all had a busy week. TGIF! I can sleep in tomorrow." Lyn rose from the sofa, stretched her arms wide, and prepared to hug Bertie.

"Yes, I should be off, too. I'm helping to shelve dry goods and cans tomorrow morning at the pantry, so I'll be up early. Oh, Daddy, I have a pair of high heels needing some work. Can I bring them by the shop tomorrow morning?"

"You need to ask? Of course, Mel."

"Tonight's been great, Mom and Daddy. Oh, before Lyn and I go, I just had a thought. What do you think if

Lyn and I drove up to Quechee—it might take an hour and a half to get there from here—and we met you at the balloon festival? Lyn and I could join you for the ride, and afterwards, you could keep going on the bus trip as planned. Lyn, what do you think? Since the festival takes place on Father's Day, wouldn't it make sense for us to be there?"

Bertie beamed; he didn't have to think, "I like your idea, Mel."

After the girls had hugged good night, Tilli followed them to the front door and waved as Mel's car pulled away. She paused at the light switch and sighed; at times like these, her thoughts always turned to Jonathan. What if he'd been here this evening? She imagined him at the dinner table. What did his voice sound like or his laughter? It had been one more incomplete family gathering ...

# Caitlyn

Mel dropped off Lyn at her condo, which she had specially chosen because of its location within a ten-minute walk to the most necessary places in Hamlet: the post office, bank, and Hamlet Shopping Center. Also, the condo was only a ten-minute walk in another direction to the Hamlet Community Arts Center; this had turned out to be a great benefit because Lyn no longer needed to own a car.

"Hey, Mel, want to come in for a bit? We haven't been together, just the two of us, for such a long time. I've got a bottle of Riesling in the frig."

"Oh, Jeez! Lyn, I have to get up early. It's been a long week; maybe some other time."

Lyn got out of the car, "Aw, come on, Sis. How about a half hour, tops?"

"Okay, Lyn, but that's all." Mel put her SUV into reverse and parked it nearby.

Lyn's door stood open as Mel came up the stairs. "Nice place, Lyn. I remember we searched together for this apartment after your divorce from Roger."

"Of course, Mel. How could I forget? And, you know what? It's been the perfect place for me. My bedroom set fits perfectly, and there's lots of wall space for my modern art. Do you know, Mel, it's taken me two years to get used to being on my own? Have a seat, kick off your shoes and relax. I'm so glad you're here; it gets lonely at times. Before I moved in, I always had to think about what Roger would want, what Roger would like, what Roger would—yes, for ten years, Roger determined every step of my existence."

"Cheers, Sis," said Lyn as they clinked wine glasses.

"How's your love life?" asked Lyn. "Met anyone interesting lately?"

"Not since Mark." Mel kicked off her shoes and settled back into the soft pillows, letting out a sigh.

"Hasn't it been about five years? Do you ever wonder where he is, what he's doing?"

"Oh, he's probably married with a couple of kids by now. You're right; it's been about that much time since he and I went on our trip to the British West Indies. I've never had an affair with anyone before or since. I guess I like my space. I'm happy with my life. I've got the kids in school, lots of papers to correct to keep me busy evenings, and then the Hamlet Food Pantry volunteer work on a lot of weekends, unless I can find substitutes so I get occasional weekends free. You know, maybe spend a day in Boston, or go for a hike in the mountains with an outdoor group I belong to. Sometimes, I take the Acela to Penn Station and stay with Brigitte in Manhattan; she's from Sweden and is now a fabric designer in the garment district. New York's a great place to visit, but I've often told her I couldn't possibly live there: too much going on all the time. I met her online about two years ago. We really hit it off, and sometimes she invites me down. I haven't been able to convince her to come up to Hamlet yet, but I'm working on it. She's the city mouse, and I'm the country mouse."

"You're lucky, Mel; you never got mixed up with the wrong man. I've had plenty of time, now that I am in my own place, to wonder how I ever let Roger dominate my life to the degree where I actually became submerged to the point of drowning. It's been a long recovery, but I finally feel like I'm my own person." Lyn curled deeper into the sofa cushions and took a sip of wine before continuing.

"When I married him, I really loved him; but he killed my love by treating me like a second-class citizen. He wanted to be in charge all the time. He thought he had all the answers and never wanted to listen to anything I had to say. I felt as if he had built a moat around himself and pulled up the drawbridge to keep me from getting close to him. He's an enigma. And, to think, everybody who knew him liked him. They never knew the Roger I experienced behind closed doors."

Mel interrupted her sister. "Lyn, I can't believe I'm sitting here, late at night, listening to you go over the same story after you've been away from him for two years! How long 'til you're over Roger? You need to get out more. You spend too much time alone in this apartment—thinking. Find some hobbies, volunteer! Go on a vacation somewhere." Mel couldn't listen any longer. She stood up and slipped into her shoes, set her empty glass on the coffee table, and started towards the door. All this "Roger talk" was draining.

But Lyn wasn't finished. "When Roger and I divorced, all our friends sided with him. They thought I was to blame. Over the years, I have lost count of the times he called me stupid and told me how fat I was. Imagine? You're a teacher, Mel. You help your students grow in confidence. Whatever made me allow him to put me down, so damned low, for so long? What's my character flaw? I want to know what you think." Lyn emptied her glass, set it down on the small table next to her chair, and followed Mel.

"Jeez! Lyn, I'm no expert. I've never lived with anyone other than Mom and Daddy. I've dated some, but it's been a couple of years since I went out with anyone. I've tried those dating services, but I never told you about it because I've had some funny—well, in hindsight, funny—experiences, but while they were happening, there was nothing funny about them. Suffice it to say, I don't think there's a Mr. Right—at least not for me—and quite frankly, I've almost given up. I got tired of using those rehearsed introductions over and over again with guys I knew I'd most likely never see again. Lyn, it's this wine. It's loosened our tongues; time to call it a night."

"I know, Mel. Thanks for staying a little while with me. I'm relaxed now and could fall asleep on my feet. Let's plan on going out for dinner some evening after work. Remember how we used to talk for hours when we were growing up? We liked the same musicians: the Beatles and Elton John."

"Oh, Lyn, you used to make fun of me because I'd listen to music—turned way up—lying on my bed in the dark, with the streetlamp outside my bedroom window illuminating the bean tree next to the house. During my teen years, I spent a lot of time studying that tree. I learned, years later, the bean tree was actually a Catalpa; Mom told me."

"Say, Mel, I'd love to meet for dinner soon. How about we go to the Tally Ho Club next Friday at six o'clock?"

"It's a date, Sis." They laughed and hugged as Mel put on her jacket.

Once the apartment door closed, Lyn realized how much she'd missed Mel.

Lyn turned out the lights and headed for the bathroom. She got on the scale, something she did every Friday evening: it read 125 pounds, perhaps a bit high due to the lovely dinner with Mom and Daddy, but not bad for someone five foot five. After ten years of being told she was fat by Roger, she had become very conscious of weight gain. Now, why hadn't she found a man like Daddy? Mom and Daddy married for forty years and still happy—a rarity these days. How lucky they were.

After doing all the usual bedtime prep, she got her second wind and decided to read a chapter in her new page-turner; maybe it would help her to sleep better. She tried reading in bed, usually one of her favorite end-of-the-day things to do, but tonight she kept reading the same paragraph again and again. She put the book on the night table and turned out the light. She tossed around, her mind filled with thoughts. What had drawn her to Roger in the first place? Oh, yes, how could she forget: it was sex, that primal pull of man and woman. But, after the excitement had worn off, she had come to her senses and had taken a good look at his other qualities and soon found there wasn't much to build on. And then, he didn't want any children. Lyn thought he felt this way because he would have had to share her attentions with another human being. She would have loved a child, but as her biological clock was unwinding, she began to feel it was too late. After the divorce became final, he went his way grumbling and she, having been stripped of all confidence, went hers.

She liked her job at the Hamlet Community Arts

Center; she worked with great people. But nighttime was the worst because these negative reels played in her head. Would she ever be free of Roger? Painfully, slowly, she was re-learning how to think for herself and how to live. Roger had never been content just to live his own life; he had seized control over hers as well. And, ten years of being put down were going to take a lot of recovery time. How much, she didn't know.

"Damn! I can't sleep and I know why; it's Mom's comment about the 'tall, handsome, and intelligent man' coming into my life." Instead of counting sheep, Lyn started counting the word *NO*, and though still unconvinced, she soon drifted off to sleep.

# Amelia

"Say, Ms. MacInnes, where do you want these donations?"

"Oh, Tom, how about on the folding tables by the window; we'll need to check for expiration dates and enter everything into the database."

"I'll do whatever you need, Ms. MacInnes. I thought I could save you some lifting; these boxes with canned goods are heavy." Tom was a new volunteer and a star athlete. The high school required its juniors and seniors to get involved in a community volunteering project. Mel was happy to have the kids and often had as many as six, as well as local adults, helping her at the Hamlet Food Pantry, though not everyone came in at the same time.

"Tom, please put sorted food items into the dry storage cabinets."

"Sure, Ms. MacInnes."

"Hi, Amelia. What do you want me to do?" asked Jennifer, an older woman with grown children who helped occasionally.

"We've received several cartons of canned and boxed food donations, and there's data entry to do. A voicemail message was left from a Mrs. Clark, an elderly lady across town, who's moving to Hamlet Nursing Home, and she wanted to donate all the unopened food items in her house. Some of those donations may have passed expiration dates; you never know. Here's my cell phone number in case you need me. I'll be back in a bit."

"Okay, Ms. MacInnes. We'll hold the fort."

Mel got into her SUV and headed toward the address left on the voicemail. She noticed stiffness in her neck and shoulders and wondered if it was from all the paperwork she'd been doing, as well as being scrunched up over the computer. She'd been meaning to walk the woodland trails at the conservation area but never felt comfortable doing so by herself, and everybody she had asked always seemed to be too busy. Perhaps Lyn would be her walking partner. As she drove past the new health club, she thought about joining a yoga or Pilates class. Besides exercise, she would meet new people. Maybe she should post in the *Hamlet Weekly* that she's looking for someone to walk with.

As she approached Mrs. Clark's house, Mel suddenly remembered Selden Clark. Selden had been a quarterback and star athlete on Hamlet High's football team, the Ospreys, as well as being vice-president of his class. He had been a senior when Mel was a junior. They'd dated once, but she'd never been to his house and now wondered if Selden had been related to Mrs. Clark.

Mel noticed the house was quite run down and the yard hadn't been tended to in a long time. The faded name CLARK was barely visible on the rusty mailbox out front by the edge of the walk. Overgrown shrubbery blocked the light from entering the rooms at the front of the house, but someone could reclaim this once-cute house with money and elbow grease.

"Come in, dearie," a cheerful voice called out through the battered screen door.

"Hello, Mrs. Clark, I'm Amelia MacInnes, a volunteer from the Hamlet Food Pantry. You called?"

"Please come in and sit down. I can't get up, and I can't see."

"Oh, I'm sorry."

"Never mind, Ms. MacInnes, I was able to walk for seventy-five years, and macular degeneration didn't set in until a couple of years ago, so I've been blessed. I grew up in this little house my father built with his own hands, a lot of memories here. My brother and sister are gone, but I'm still around. What more can I ask? No one lives forever, dearie, so I will be grateful for all the blessings I've had. I will be moving to the Hamlet Nursing Home next month. My brother's daughter, Amber, will be holding a yard sale in a couple of weeks, and then the house will go on the market. Do you want to buy it?"

Taken by surprise, Mel didn't know what to say. "Ah, I don't know. I've never owned a house. I live in Hamlet Meadows; they're townhouses on the south side of town. I don't know if I'd be able to manage a house by myself."

"If I could, you certainly can. I did manage until the last few years; not being able to walk and no longer being able to see has its drawbacks. I don't know what I'd do without Amber; she checks on me every day, once before she goes to work and then again in the evening. What a treasure she is, and I have a personal care attendant from Senior Homecare who comes at midday and brings my hot lunch. You see, I'm getting along pretty well, and moving to the nursing home should make life easier on Amber, don't you think, dearie?"

"Well, you won't have to worry about a lot of details and responsibilities any longer," replied Mel. She wondered if she should mention Selden to Mrs. Clark.

"Yes, dearie, the details and responsibilities of life have

often been a lot to manage. Amber, my niece, did I say she's my niece? I forget things so often now it scares me. Well, Amber will take care of things; she's a huge blessing, so sweet, not much older than you. How old are you, Ms. MacInnes?"

"Oh, please call me Mel. I'm a third-grade teacher here at Hamlet Elementary School."

"Oh, really? Well, Amber is quite a bit older than you are. She had a son named Selden. Perhaps you knew him? I was a nurse and later became a teacher. Straight out of high school, I went to work at the New England Home for Little Wanderers, and later I attended the Salem Normal School so I could become a teacher at the Perkins School for the Blind in Watertown. It's why being blind now doesn't bother me so much. I worked quite a few years with blind people and helped them learn to be independent. I have nothing to complain about; you see, I've had my sight, but most of them never knew what it was like to be able to see. Imagine you couldn't see the sky or know what the color blue looks like? Yes, I've been blessed all my life. I want you to take a look at the two boxes on my kitchen table. Amber put things in there for the food pantry. Now, don't feel obligated; if they aren't of use to your clients, you needn't take them."

"Thank you for thinking of us, Mrs. Clark. I'll take a look."

"You can do whatever you want, dearie."

As Mel turned on the kitchen light, she tried not to look at the condition of the room but couldn't help herself. The curtains on the window over the sink were tattered with the faded hint of teapots and roses on them. One green plastic pot with a dead plant was on the worn paint of the windowsill. The insides of the twin stainless-steel sinks were filled with unwashed dishes, and the sinks hadn't been scrubbed in a very long time. As she moved closer to the boxes, she had to un-stick her feet from the linoleum floor. The toe of her right shoe kicked something under the table; she was almost afraid to look down until she noticed it was only a shriveled pickle, dropped some time ago. The two donation boxes were on top of a disorganized pile of mail, opened and unopened, as well as newspapers and junk. Mel didn't want to go through the boxes; she didn't want to take the donations because she knew, without knowing for certain, the items were most likely expired. She picked up a couple of rusted, dented cans.

"Mrs. Clark, thank you so much for thinking of the food pantry. I will take everything with me."

"Really? How lovely! You are such a dear, Ms. Mac-Innes. If you have any clients who need household items, please remember Amber will be having the yard sale in two weeks. Whatever doesn't sell will be given to charity."

"You have a generous heart, Mrs. Clark. Before I leave, can I make you a cup of tea or get you something to eat?"

"You're kind, dearie, but Amber will be coming soon. It's been hard since I lost my grandnephew, Selden. Amber was devastated and has never been the same. He was her only child. She's my lifeline now, my connection to the outside world. From my experiences, dearie, I've learned God always places someone in your path when you most need help. It's been pretty miraculous, actually."

"Mrs. Clark, I went to school with Selden. I remember his playing football. The coach always put him in when his ability to make a touchdown was most needed; he could always count on Selden. I remember him as a quiet, shy kind of guy. In fact, Mrs. Clark, Selden and I went on a date once."

"Is that right, dearie? Well, Selden didn't date much in high school. He was a homebody, and when he wasn't playing ball, he didn't want to be in the limelight. Amber always worked to make ends meet, so Selden often came after school. Over the years, he and I spent lots of time together; we grew close. I feel as if he's my son instead of my grandnephew. Did he tell you that his father ran off when he was just a little tot? Oh, perhaps not. If it weren't for that one night when Selden went to a house party here in Hamlet ..." Mrs. Clark couldn't continue.

"I heard what happened, Mrs. Clark. He came home from college on semester break—that house, that party, lots of alcohol and drugs—I'll bet he had no idea what he was walking into."

"I still can't understand why Selden wanted to be accepted as part of *that* crowd. It was supposed to be a celebration. Selden's college team had won an important game. I heard him come in late that night. Next morning, we couldn't wake him. The police came. The ambulance came. Tough to talk about it; let's just end this sad conversation by my saying he never came to. He was our greatest joy! Losing my eyesight and being in a wheelchair are insignificant compared to—Amber's and my greatest pain."

"I'm so sorry, Mrs. Clark." Mel put her hand gently on Mrs. Clark's shoulder, hoping to comfort her. "I'll go now and put your boxes in my car. I wish you well in your new home. Please, if you or Amber need help, have her call me; I have volunteers who can assist you. I'll leave a business card right here next to your phone."

"Bye, dearie. Come anytime."

Mel drove to the transfer station and disposed of the contents of the boxes. On her way back to the pantry, she thought about Selden and how good and bad choices can—instantly—influence our lives. "I wonder, if I were Mrs. Clark's age and had faced the hardships she's endured, would my outlook on life be as positive?"

# Matilda

It was after nine o'clock, and Bertie had gone to bed. Tilli sat at the desk in the den. Several years ago, she'd bought her first spiral-bound journal, entitled A Year in Your Garden: Month by Month, in which she'd kept up-to-date recordings of her garden plants and their care. Each year, she'd drawn a layout of her vegetable garden to show where she'd planted what and had kept a three-year crop rotation. Their friend Woody had built a compost bin with three compartments. As each was filled, she'd put organic matter into the next one. By the time the third one was started, the first would be emptied of its contents of black gold, which was put on the vegetable and flower gardens as organic fertilizer.

As the years went by, Tilli continued to keep yearly gardening journals, and they now filled an entire shelf. At the back of the journals were sufficiently blank, lined pages for notations. For example, sometimes plants were winter-killed, or hungry animals—chipmunks most likely—unearthed bulbs, and then she'd either replace plants or add something new to fill the gaps in her borders. She recorded rainfall, temperatures, and the first frost in the fall.

One year, Tilli began entering information about herself, and the journals naturally evolved into personal diaries where she wrote thoughts closest to her heart.

Just to be safe, she kept the journals hidden in plain

view, surrounded by other gardening books in this floor-to-ceiling bookcase in the den. Bertie had never read a gardening book in his life, so she considered it the perfect place to keep these entries private. Sometimes, early in the morning while he was still asleep, she would read over old entries or feel the need to add something new.

With pencil in hand—she liked pencil because it allowed her to make changes as needed—she now turned to a fresh, blank page. Then changed her mind and decided to read over passages from earlier times.

**February 15, 1999,** *Dear Diary, I visited Bertie's mother, who we've had to put into Hamlet Nursing Home because of her many health problems. For two years, we cared for her at home, and it got complicated. At the nursing home, she fights the staff instead of me, falls out of bed in the middle of the night, refuses to take baths. She's not cooperating! She says terrible things to me like, 'Love is the closest emotion to hate, and you and Delbert must really hate me to put me in a place like this!' I try to reason with her, but she won't listen. On another visit, she pushed her food table over, spilled milk and pudding all over the floor; and screamed, 'How would you like to eat rubbery carrots every day?' I know the nursing home wouldn't serve the same thing every day. Today she said, 'Leave me alone on top of a mountain. Go away!' Oh, Diary, how would I survive without you for my sounding board?*

Tilli frowned as she pondered those days. Bertie's mother hadn't been easy to get along with when she was healthy! And, after several strokes, she'd become angry and resentful of all the attention she needed from others—

everyone—who never carried out her wishes in a manner quite good enough to suit her standards of perfection.

"Only God will ever know how hard I tried to please her," Tilli said softly before turning to another entry.

**May 24, 2000,** *Dear Diary, If I don't write about my greatest wish in this journal, I fear my heart will burst! I've maxed out on how long I can hold this in. You are my only sounding board!*

*Before I met Bertie—oh, he's been such a good husband—I had a passionate affair with a man who shall forever remain nameless. I was obsessed! Every moment with him was ecstasy.*

*He was a young naval officer who left me to fight in the Vietnam War. Though I never saw him again, we wrote letters back and forth, and I told him I was pregnant. He wrote that we would marry as soon as he got back; then abruptly, his letters stopped coming, though mine were never returned. I was afraid he'd been killed. I was scared and, at nineteen, faced being a single parent.*

*I was able to finish secretarial school in Boston before it was obvious that I was pregnant. At the time, I was living in an apartment with three single women; we all had shared expenses equally. My roommates had seen how much he and I were in love, so it was no surprise when I told them about my situation.*

*Soon after graduation, I had to decide what to do. I would never have risked an abortion. My parents were very strict, and I thought they'd disown me if they knew. I was alone, afraid, and ashamed to involve my family. My roommates said they'd provide for me until such*

*time as I could have the baby, give it up, and find an-*
*other job. 'Don't worry about payback,' they said.*
*'Someone may need your help one day, and you can pay*
*it forward.' Wise words from such young women. As the*
*months elapsed, I felt new life inside me. I imagined my*
*baby was a boy and named him Jonathan. I dreamed of*
*keeping him and finding a solution.*

Tilli paused to consider how many times she'd re-read this entry, only to become overwhelmed with emotions again. She repeatedly blinked as tears fell on the page. "I'll always wonder if he got my letters.

"Oh, drat! I promised I wouldn't shed another tear over that man. He broke my heart! Two questions I'll never be able to answer: did he die in the war, or was I deserted?" Tilli continued reading this entry, her longest.

*I decided to enter a program at the New England*
*Home for Little Wanderers, where they paid all mater-*
*nity costs if I turned my newborn over for adoption. I*
*gave birth to a healthy son who was given to a married*
*couple that couldn't have a child of their own. But I,*
*Matilda Eiser MacInnes, will never forget my Jonathan!*
    *I believe God punished me with miscarriages after*
*Bertie and I got married. I worried I'd never be able to*
*have another child. And not keeping Jonathan has*
*haunted me every day.*

Tilli paused. Enough! Each time she re-read what she had written years ago, this deep wound was scratched open and pain poured out fresh and raw. Despite this anguish, she would finish reading it now and vowed to finally let it rest.

*A year after I gave up Jonathan, I met Bertie. My parents lived in Connecticut and never learned about my son, and I certainly never breathed a word about it to Bertie. What does my son look like? Where is he living? What is he doing? These unanswered questions nearly drive me nuts! I've dreamed of finding him—disclosing the truth—but I don't think Bertie or the girls would understand. I feel some relief now that I've written my biggest secret in this diary.*

Tilli started to tear the page out of the journal. "I've been blessed with a good husband and two beautiful daughters. I need to stop revisiting this chapter of my life." With reading glasses fogged up, she blew her nose but left the pages intact. Having given up her precious son, Jonathan, was a rupture she knew would never heal, and re-reading this entry was cathartic.

**October 9, 2002,** *Dear Diary, I've had certain dreams for years. I wish they could be real. Only you know how important they are. Fear has kept my feet firmly planted in Hamlet; I need a kick in the pants to get me moving and following my dreams!*

**June 11, 2003,** *Dear Diary, So much time has elapsed since I wrote about not realizing my five wishes, and I still haven't done any of them. Last night I dreamed of gentle movements through the summer air, the country-side gliding beneath me, and white puffy clouds playing peek-a-boo with my hot-air balloon. If Bertie weren't so afraid of heights, I'd go up in a heartbeat.*

She remembered the reason why Bertie was so afraid of heights. When he was ten years old, he'd taken a dare from some older boys: a challenge to climb onto the roof of a one-story shed that held sports equipment for the Hamlet playground. If he jumped off, they'd catch him and pay him a nickel. Gullible and trusting, Bertie got boosted onto that roof, and after several tense minutes, with those children calling him a sissy, he jumped. No one caught him; they ran away, and no nickel! But he got a sprained ankle, scraped knees, and damaged pride for trusting them.

"And because of that silly nonsense, I have a husband whose feet won't leave the ground." Tilli looked at the Seth Thomas clock on the shelf; it was getting late. Shaking her head, she decided to read a bit more.

**April 26, 2004,** *Dear Diary, your pages are fast running out. Just realized another year has gone since I mentioned my dreams. Don't know how much longer I'll be able to climb into a hot-air balloon basket. If I can't do that, how can I do the other things that take stamina and courage? I thought writing would help, but I'm wondering if I shouldn't stop this teenage activity. I've been living in dreamland. What am I afraid of?*

*I've never flown in an airplane. Where would I go? Perhaps Scotland to visit the MacInnes castle Bertie's been talking about for decades!*

*National Geographic magazine has written about Peru a couple of times. At my age, I suppose I can forget about climbing Machu Picchu, what with arthritis from years of gardening—pulling weeds season after season for forty years—and my high blood pressure from burying my deepest desires. I know Bertie would laugh about going to Peru!*

*I dream of taking one of those long walks, the kind where people wear out several pairs of shoes. Spain, California, or the Appalachian Trail from Georgia to Mt. Katahdin. Maybe scary things would happen along the way, but people write about gaining courage and strength. They learn new things about themselves and life. I could never hike alone through the forest; there are bears! But, maybe with the help of a motivational counselor, I could conquer my fears and get out of my comfort zone?*

*I don't mind heights like Bertie does, but being on a high ladder and flying in an airplane are quite different. My list of five wishes has been amended—several times—I can no longer learn scuba diving, nor do I want to skydive. So, here is my revised list of five wishes, but number one will always be on top:*

*1. Find Jonathan!*

*2. Go up in a hot-air balloon.*

*3. Visit a national park.*

*4. See the Great Pyramids in Egypt and visit the Holy Land.*

*5. Go to Scotland and visit the MacInnes castle.*

**April 10, 2005,** *Dear Diary, how will I ever be reunited with Jonathan? I must* STOP *these diary entries! They remind me that I am stuck! No excitement! No adrenaline rushes. I'm living, but I'm not alive!*

Tilli wiped her nose, then slid the journal back into the bookcase. "Tomorrow morning, I'm going to AAA to book that bus trip. If I don't unstick myself, my life will never change. I'm done writing in journals!"

# Evangeline

Funny how our past can come up and surprise us when least expected, Bertie thought as he was walking home from Peach of a Sole. He had just crossed Maple Street when a slender young woman with long brown hair, wearing a peach-colored sheath dress, hurried past him, going in the opposite direction. "Her stride and smile: Evangeline!" Bertie's heart was aflutter as he whispered her name softly, then looked about to be sure no one had heard. Gosh! That young woman could have been her twin, except it had been fifty years since Evangeline was that young and fresh. He paused and bent down to tie his left shoe.

As he passed the familiar yard of a long-time Hamlet resident who was mowing his lawn, Bertie waved a greeting. He continued down the sidewalk and thought about tomorrow's new adventure to New Hampshire and Vermont and his impending hot-air-balloon ride. "I'll not fret about any of it. Tilli wants to do this, and I think it's way past time for me to get over my silly fear of flying. I owe it to both of us." He realized he'd again spoken aloud and nervously looked about; people might think he had bugs in his head.

Bertie's thoughts returned to Evangeline. He and she had had the hots for each other while in high school, though nothing serious had happened between them. Oh, yes, there had been one time—it had been so spontaneous—when she grabbed his shoulders and kissed him square on the mouth. One act that had stirred him all the way to the lower part of his anatomy. Even now, just thinking about it caused goose bumps. But then she had latched onto and run off with a good-for-nothing, son-of-a ... "Oh, what's the use," Bertie said under his breath. "Evangeline, what I wouldn't give to reset the clock. How foolish I was then, too young and unschooled to keep you from running off with a bum. I did the best I could, my dear, but I never felt my efforts were good enough.

"Even after that creep left you high and dry, you still loved him. It must have taken great courage for you to put aside your pride and write to me for help. You knew I would *never* turn you down. So, for years I was able to send you money without my own family suffering any consequences. I helped you with your bills because I loved you then, Evangeline, just as I still do. Otherwise, why would some unknown, young, look-alike woman raise up strong emotions in me even after I've grown into an old man?"

# The Bus Trip

It was before five o'clock in the morning on Father's Day when Tilli and Bertie's tour bus left the Lincoln Inn in Woodstock to drive the short distance to the field in Quechee, where the hot-air balloonists were to meet up with their pilot. At first, the bus traveled past open fields and farmhouses with cows grazing peacefully, then past white wooden fences surrounding horse pastures; mares swished their tails while colts and fillies gamboled close by. Soon the open land gave way to the many red brick homes of downtown Woodstock, with neat plantings and manicured walkways leading to freshly painted front doors. The town green was surrounded by stately, well-maintained trees and shrubs.

Tilli saw a wrought iron bench along the curved path in the park and squirmed in her seat, wanting to jump off the bus.

"Isn't it a pretty town?" she remarked, her eyes never leaving the window.

"Glad I came," Bertie smiled and reached for Tilli's hand.

Minutes later, they were out of town and on a stretch of road with gentle hills on both sides and the Ottauquechee River to their left. Next, the bus took them over an ancient bridge in Quechee by the old mill, which now has shops and restaurants, and in the distance, Tilli and Bertie could see a few colorful hot-air balloons already aloft.

"Oh, Bertie, this is going to be such fun! Especially since Mel and Lyn are coming."

Bertie turned his head towards the sky where Tilli was pointing, and he tried to look enthused. "I wonder how high we'll go. I don't like the way one balloon is already disappearing into those low clouds. How will they know where they're going? Oh, I do wish the weather were better, Tilli."

She patted his arm. "Bertie, I'm sure they wouldn't be taking us up if it were dangerous."

Of course, not all of the forty bus passengers would be going aloft. Some only wanted to watch, others couldn't wait to head for the nearby shops, and a third group had opted to go up in balloons that would remain tethered several feet above the open field.

All too soon, Bertie and Tilli learned they had to help the balloon pilot and crew inflate their balloon. Most of the professional pilots were waiting for the clouds to lift, but the stubborn drizzle simply refused to stop. As the mist and low clouds prevailed, the balloonists sipped coffee and ate doughnuts provided by the crew. Some milled about talking with others and speculating about what was going to happen. Bertie walked over to one of the Johnny-on-the-spots and secretly hoped the balloon ride would be canceled and they could just continue their trip looking at the bucolic New England countryside.

"Hi, Mom!" Lyn was walking across the damp field towards Tilli.

"Where's Mel?"

"She's parking the SUV. Don't worry; we're both here. Tough to get up so early, but the drive from Hamlet was a breeze. We're so looking forward to this. Where's Daddy?"

"Oh, here they both come. Too bad about the weather. I hope we can go up." Tilli frowned as she adjusted the hood on her jacket.

By six-thirty, the clouds had lifted, the mist had stopped, and the low hills surrounding the grassy field became visible. More balloons had taken off, and others were in the process of letting go of the lines holding them to the ground; their balloon was the last one ready for boarding.

"Let's go folks!" announced their pilot. "Who's going up with me?"

Tilli raised her hand and grabbed Bertie's as they walked towards the basket, which was still tethered to its stake.

Bertie eyed the tiny basket. "We're all going to fit in *that*?"

Bob smiled. "Yup!" He was already helping Tilli get from the portable steps over the high side and into the basket.

Bertie felt ridiculous, at his age, having to lift his short legs over those high sides just to go up into the sky and float about like a boat in the air, but he didn't want to make waves and upset Tilli, so he pasted on a smile and clambered in.

Mel and Lyn were right behind them. It would be four passengers with Bob, their pilot.

Bob explained about the basket, the fuel tanks, and the ballast while the crew untied their line. With a whoosh, they lifted gently upward.

A photographer was running about the field, calling

up to them to look out over the basket as she was going to take some pictures. "Bob, don't forget to have them come and see me when you get back," she hollered.

Up and over the grassy field, they rose as the river and the mill with its shops became tinier. They went higher and traveled effortlessly on the gentle air. Bertie even un-peeled his fingers from the edge of the basket to look out—but, heavens, not down—at the beautiful country-side and all the other colorful balloons in the distance.

"Tilli, why was I reluctant to go up in a hot-air bal-loon?" His broad smile beamed happiness to his eyes.

"Happy Father's Day, Bertie." She kissed his cheek.

"Yes, happy Father's Day, Daddy. This is a wonderful way to celebrate." Mel and Lyn were having the time of their lives. Blue sky poked out between the white puffy clouds; the sun peeked through, and there was the tiniest breeze: a perfect June day.

Tilli wished they hadn't waited so long and considered all of the missed opportunities, while at the same time, she thought about the possibilities of other fun things they might still do together. It was definitely a milestone; they'd turned over a new leaf, a fresh chapter. She noticed Bob had taken them low over the Ottauquechee River, and the bottom of their basket skimmed the top of gently lap-ping waves. She noticed the river rocks in the clear, shal-low water, glinting in the sun, and imagined fish darting below. They laughed as their balloon lifted once more to travel towards the treetops surrounding houses along the shore. Mel waved at a couple having breakfast on their patio. At an apartment building, a family, still dressed in pajamas, looked up and waved from their balcony. Soon, everywhere they looked below, people were pointing and waving as the balloon floated overhead.

"How perfect to be here in this moment," Tilli managed to say with a lump in her throat.

# Delbert and Woody

"Hi Ho, Hi Ho, it's off to work I go." Delbert chuckled as he hummed a little tune on this beautiful June morning. He was thinking about his and Tilli's hot-air-balloon trip. "I should be kicking myself for waiting so long to do it, but I will try to be satisfied with the fact we actually went and everything was pleasant."

He rounded the final corner to Peach of a Sole, and— wouldn't you know—a customer was waiting on his stoop.

"Top o' the mornin' to ya, MacInnes," shouted Woody, a former firefighter and long-time friend. Woody was known as the best carpenter in Hamlet.

"Morn, Woody. What's up? You're bright and early."

"Well, it's like this, MacInnes. It's me leather work apron; stitchin's come undone."

"I suppose an old Irishman would expect an old Scot to fix it pronto?"

"Yup! You got that right."

"All righty, come on in."

Woody made himself at home on the old oak railroad chair behind the counter while Bertie turned on lights in front and in his workshop. Woody heard Bertie moving about, turning on switches, and warming up equipment. The last thing turned on out back was Delbert's television, which was now loudly broadcasting the morning's news.

"Hand me your apron, Woody. The stitching machine's ready."

Delbert disappeared through the opening into his workshop. Everywhere were bits of trimmings: on the floor, in the trashcan, on the counters! Near the ceiling, on a shelf, was Delbert's nineteen-inch Zenith television, which came in handy when times were slow or when Bertie wanted to find out what was happening outside his world.

Several lasts were on stands; these were where Delbert placed a shoe when he worked on it. The purpose of a last was to hold the shoe steady so he could nail on new heels or do other tasks to the shoe. Each shoe repair job was a custom piece of work. People had no idea how involved it was to make repairs to shoes or how long it took to do these repairs. Shoes were like people: each one was different.

Several heavy-duty machines, such as those made by Landis of St. Louis, Missouri, were in his shop. He had a soling machine by Auto Soler and a heeling machine, a three-sided contraption where he placed shoes under heat lamps to re-activate the glue on a pair of shoes before the new heels and soles were put on. Several buffing and trimming machines stood ready for duty. In addition, Delbert used a grooving tool to prepare a leather sole before it was sewn on by his rugged sewing machine. Nearby was a small oilcan for when he needed to lubricate these old machines.

Everything Delbert used was heavy duty, even the smelly glue that was now imported from Germany. The soles were made by Cat's Paw and Neolite. Many supply items now came from China and were no longer manufactured in America. There were two metal cans containing permanent shoe dye, one with brown and one with black, to put around the new heels and soles so replacements matched the shoes.

On his workbench was a disorderly array of hand tools: various pliers, nippers, clippers, hammers, die sets, insoles, heel pads, brushes, and bits and pieces of the business of shoe repair work. A wooden rack stood ready to receive the finished repairs.

In the past, Delbert MacInnes even sharpened skates. He was a man of action! And now, he was stitching his friend Woody's leather carpentry apron on the stitching machine used to repair baseball gloves.

"Here you go, Woody, good as new." Delbert handed the repaired apron over to his friend. "How about a cuppa before you head off to your first job of the day?"

"Don't mind if I do, MacInnes."

Delbert took the tin of Irish breakfast tea out of a cupboard, poured water into the electric kettle, grabbed two heavy-duty Honey Bun mugs, and while the water came to a boil, the old friends had a chat.

"You've been to Ireland how many times, Woody?"

"Two or three, maybe. The wife and I fly to Shannon and visit the relatives in Ballinasloe, County Galway. They're old now, same as us." He stirred sugar into his tea.

"Tilli and I have never been on a plane, but we just came back from a hot-air balloon ride in Vermont. Mel and Lyn drove up on Father's Day and joined us in Quechee, the place on my calendar." Bertie pointed to the wall behind him. They sipped their tea while Bertie waited for his words to sink into Woody's head.

"Yer joshin' me? I'd never a thought yer legs'd be

leavin' the ground, MacInnes. How'd you like it?"

"Well, Woody, I must say it was very pleasant, very gentle movements, nice views, and Tilli absolutely loved it. The bus trip with overnights wasn't too shabby either. Of course, I was glad to be back in my own bed when we got home. Next trip, I'll remember to take my bed pillow with me. I might have slept better in those inns!

"Did I ever tell you, Woody, that I've thought of going over to Scotland? Mentioned it to Tilli more than once, but I'm not sure she'd want to go."

Bertie pointed to the picture of the MacInnes castle on his wall. "That's where my great-great-grandfather lived. For years, I've wanted to see where my roots began, but my ears would probably bother me on the plane, and those airports are so huge that I'd probably get lost and the plane would take off without me. The hot-air balloon got me off the ground, and my ears were just fine. I know Tilli's going to come up with another trip idea before too long; I don't think it will include an airplane trip. But, since we're chatting about traveling, how do you get around when you go to Ireland, Woody?"

"A family member comes and fetches us. Once, we rented a car. Jeez! Those narrow, curvy, hedgerow-edged roadways are somethin' else. If we ever go again, I think we'll have to be picked up. You take your life in yer hands, MacInnes. It's nothin' like here." He set down his cup. "Gotta go, MacInnes. How much I owe ya?"

"'Tis nothing, Woody. I'm owing you for not charging me enough for building the pergola for Tilli. It's still holding up the wisteria. Go and have a good day."

Woody turned around at the door. "I heard the shop's for sale, MacInnes. What are we goin' to do in Hamlet without you? Jeez! Well, I'll say a prayer to St. Patrick that a lot of shamrocks will have pushed up through the soil before it ever gets sold. We need you, MacInnes. Who's goin' to take care of our shoes, bridles, leather aprons, and such? Besides, what's a man like you goin' to do in retirement? It's a dirty word to me. I'm plannin' on workin' 'til I drop dead on a job. It will be a hammer in one hand and a nail in the other. Toodle-oo, MacInnes. Thankee."

The buzzer rang loudly as Mr. Buxton opened the shop door and stepped onto the welcome mat. The lights were on, the radio volume was turned up, and he imagined Mac-Innes was out back, firing up his equipment for the day.

Mr. Buxton called out in a loud voice: "Delbert! I'm leaving my wife's handbag for re-sewing! The stitching's come undone. I'll be back at six when the train gets in." And, quickly glancing at his wristwatch, he hurried out.

At about five after six in the evening, Mr. Buxton walked across the railroad tracks and headed up the street to the brightly lit shoe repair shop to pick up his wife's handbag. The buzzer under the doormat rang loudly as he entered the front of the shop. The radio was blaring, so he imagined MacInnes was still working out back. His wife's brown handbag was no longer on the counter where he'd left it early in the morning; that was a good sign, he thought.

Mr. Buxton called, "Delbert!" followed by, "Hello there!" in an even louder tone. "Strange," Mr. Buxton thought, "there's no response." He was annoyed; all he wanted was to retrieve that handbag and hurry home to his dinner.

"I wish Delbert would invest in a hearing aid," he announced to the four walls.

Though the lights were on in the workshop out back, Mr. Buxton didn't hear machinery noises. "Gee! I know I shouldn't do this, but how will I get Delbert's attention?" With great reluctance, Mr. Buxton walked behind the cash register, poked his head through the open doorway clearly marked *OFF LIMITS*, and entered forbidden territory.

Sure enough, Delbert was there all right. His head rested on the workbench, one arm stretched out straight ahead, and the other hung towards the floor. A tool was clutched in his fingers. He wore his denim apron, and the item he was repairing lay at his feet: Stacie's brown handbag! Mr. Buxton paused to take it all in before rushing out of the shop. The doormat buzzer echoed loudly as he hurried away. The Hamlet Police Station was just around the corner. Thoughts of Stacie's handbag, as well as his dinner, evaporated. He guessed Delbert had died some hours ago.

# 5 Cedar Street
# Caitlyn and Amelia

"When the policeman came to my apartment after work today, I couldn't imagine what I'd done wrong. I wasn't prepared for this horrible news," cried Lyn.

"Officer Peters knocked on my door this evening, shortly after I'd returned from shopping. He must have watched me park my car, then enter the building. He was obviously waiting for me," said Mel.

"What a shock!" they both said together.

"I still can't believe this happened. I keep thinking the police made a mistake, came to the wrong family, that Daddy will walk in here and set things right," Mel wept.

"Why did Daddy have to die so soon? I hoped one day, a long time from now, he'd go quietly in his sleep. Actually, I never really thought about him dying at all." Mel grabbed another tissue from the box.

"It's awful how sudden it was and that he was *alone*. He was just the best father!" Lyn pressed her moist tissue to swollen eyes.

"We don't even know his final wishes. Did Daddy ever talk to you about those kinds of things, Mel?

"No."

"I guess we'll have to use our best judgment. Mom's a basket case, so I'm sleeping here, in my old room, tonight. Funny to think I'll be in the *guest* room. I wonder if a guest has actually slept there. Anyway, tomorrow morning we can try to talk with Mom. I'm so glad Dr. Franklin gave her a sedative to knock her out. I hope she sleeps for twenty-four hours. I was frightened when she passed out from hearing the news!" For once, Lyn wished she wouldn't have to take the lead.

"I'll sleep on the sofa in the den," replied Mel. "I want to be here with you and Mom tomorrow morning."

"You're right, Mel. I don't know how much sleep we'll get; it's past midnight. Let's turn in, though I'll probably toss all night. Maybe in the morning, we'll know better what to do."

Tilli told the girls she didn't think their father had prepared any final directives. In the den, they searched through the old MacInnes desk, where Bertie kept some papers. It was the most likely place he could have put a health care proxy, durable power of attorney, his will, or life insurance policies, but they found nothing.

After much discussion, they agreed to have Bertie's remains cremated and his ashes buried at the South Hamlet Cemetery, where his parents and grandparents had been laid to rest.

On the day of the funeral, Tilli was held together by the anti-anxiety pills Dr. Franklin had prescribed. Lyn and Mel had taken on all the immediate responsibilities because she couldn't.

After the graveside ceremony, Mel and Lyn had to physically support her 'til they got to Mel's waiting SUV for the ride back to 5 Cedar Street. Along the way, Tilli stared out the window at the cloudless sky and the bare branches of trees and shrubs: a beautiful November day. How was it possible that the sun was shining and the world bustled with activity when her life had fallen apart and Bertie was gone? She couldn't think about tomorrow; today was already too much. She sensed Mel and Lyn close by, but her head was filled with a dense fog, and her surroundings were dreamlike. Would life ever be normal? Bertie would come home and . . .

"No!" Tilli suddenly cried out.

Lyn moved closer in the back seat and put her arm around her mother's shoulder and pulled her close; Mel glanced in the rear-view mirror at the two of them.

After they arrived back at the house, Lyn prepared to meet the many people arriving downstairs; Mel helped Tilli upstairs to her bedroom.

"Go and leave me be; I'll be all right. Just need a little rest."

And, as soon as Mel had taken off her mother's coat, hat, and shoes, Tilli lay down on the bed, motionless. Mel covered her mother with the down comforter and headed downstairs. The house was overflowing, and everywhere she turned, someone took her hand, gave her hugs, or kissed her cheek. She didn't even know some of them.

"Thank you, Woody, for coming. You were Daddy's best friend," said Mel.

"Your father set aside what're he was doin' to help me," replied Woody.

"Mr. and Mrs. Brewster, and John. We really appreciate your support," said Lyn.

"Your daddy and I graduated from Hamlet High together, and he won the technical award, a handsome medallion. They only give it to one student each year, you know."

"Mr. Brewster, my daddy never wanted to be in the limelight. I didn't know about the award; thank you for telling me. I'll bet that medallion is somewhere in this house, hidden away with other keepsakes we don't know about," replied Lyn.

Many other Peach of a Sole customers—even Mr. Buxton and his wife, Stacie—came to offer their support, as well as Hamlet firefighters; members of the local American Legion; Garden Club members; library-goers; school children with their parents; Hamlet Community Arts Center people; food pantry staff, volunteers, and patrons; and the MacInnes' long-time neighbors.

"Oh, my goodness, Mark! I never expected *you* to come, but I'm so glad you did." Mel reached out to shake hands with her former boyfriend.

Mark wasn't happy with a handshake; he reached for Mel and hugged her for a long minute. "I read about what happened to your father, Mel, and just couldn't stay away. If there's anything—anything at all—I can do to help you or your family, I hope you'll call me."

"But, Mark, I haven't heard from you in such a long time. I don't want you to feel obligated."

"Obligated? Mel, I want to help. You're absolutely right; it's been way too long. I do hope we can fix that."

"Well, when I never heard from you again, Mark, I thought you weren't interested. What was I supposed to think?"

"I've never stopped thinking about you. Perhaps—after a little time, when you feel more like yourself—we could have coffee together."

"I'd really like that, Mark; please call me because I

don't have your number. Oh, I see some friends are getting ready to leave, and I want to say goodbye to them. I'm very glad you came. I appreciate your kindness."

Mark held both of her hands in his and said, "I care about you, Mel."

"There's lots of food and a fresh pot of coffee." Mel pointed towards the dining table. "Please help yourself, and don't rush off; I'll be back."

Though the sisters had ordered food and beverages for the reception, many people also brought food, and every available surface overflowed. Three women from town were at the kitchen sink washing dishes, scrubbing empty casseroles, and wiping down the counters, getting ready for people to take their empties home.

The show of love and caring from the people of Hamlet was beyond anything Mel and Lyn could have imagined. After some hours, the house gradually quieted down as, one by one, everyone went home.

It had grown dark outside, and peace had settled over the house when Mel and Lyn took a tray upstairs to their mother's room.

"I'm exhausted!" Lyn kicked off her shoes, yawned, and settled on the bed next to her groggy mother.

Mel did the same, then gently massaged her mother's shoulder. "Mom, come on now; everyone's gone. You need to eat. Lyn and I brought you something."

Tilli opened her eyes and looked at her daughters. Slowly she sat up. "Off and on throughout the day, I'd awaken and hear the commotion downstairs. How could so many people fit into this house? Your daddy would have been pleased, though he wasn't one to entertain guests. Family was all. What are we going to do now?"

Lyn and Mel decided to be with their mother as much as possible for the rest of the year. Their employers were understanding of the time the sisters needed for grieving after such a sudden loss. Lyn made arrangements with her co-worker to run weekend events at the Hamlet Community Arts Center, and Joanna was happy to earn time and a half. Lyn came in early on the morning of these events to be sure everything was in order, but then she'd go to the house at 5 Cedar Street. Unfortunately, Mel wouldn't have a school break until Christmas. She asked if the school could arrange for a substitute so she could have additional leave time.

In the beginning, the sisters spent these weekends cooking and baking together. They were reconnecting with one another after living on their own. These weekends brought them closer to each other, as well as to their mother.

One page after another was torn from the wall calendar in the kitchen to reveal a new month. Mel and Lyn tried to carry on as before, but there were times throughout each day when something triggered thoughts of their father, and they'd pause to reflect. He'd been such a quiet strength in their lives; he'd never let his family down. How long would their grieving last? How long until their mother would be able to function without their constant help?

It was the first Sunday in June, when the three of them sat down to a delicious meal, that Lyn made a proposal: "Mom, what do you think if Mel and I took you on a little trip this summer?"

Tilli had lost quite a bit of weight since last November and hadn't had a good night's sleep in months. She'd just sliced a piece of her chicken piccata and was about to put it into her mouth when she welled up with emotions. Putting her fork down, she tried to speak past the tightness in her throat. "I'd have to ponder what I'd do and where I'd go if I could do anything I wanted. Don't you think it's a bit too soon to be talking about a trip when your father has been gone such a short time? You know, Lyn, I still feel like I'm moving through fog. I look at that doorway and imagine your father walking towards me. No, please don't let's talk about trips right now; maybe next year."

"Well, it's been seven months," replied Lyn as she ate some of her wild rice.

"I'm not ready for fun and excitement, Lyn. I don't want to jump into anything," Tilli said with unintended vehemence in her voice.

"So, I'm hearing exactly what Daddy would have said to you. He couldn't leave his customers, I'll bet. He was so concerned about his customers. Who's taking care of them now? The shop's closed. The lights are out. And Daddy could never find anyone willing to buy the real estate. No one wants to fix people's shoes today. Would it have hurt him and you if he'd closed for a week or two each year just to have more time together? It's too late for him, but not for the three of us, Mom. We have to keep on living!"

"You're not hearing me, Lyn; I didn't say I *wouldn't* go with you. I need more time." She pushed her chair back from the table and began walking away from her half-empty plate. She couldn't listen to this now. She was grieving—so were they—but it was her *husband* who died. She realized then that grieving was going to take time—

lots of it—and she was not about to be rushed!

Mel got up and went into the kitchen. "Mom, you didn't finish your dinner. Can I get you some more rice? Anything while out here?"

Tilli didn't answer; she simply kept placing one heavy foot in front of the other up the stairs leading to the sanctuary of her bedroom. She realized her grief wasn't only because of Bertie's dying so suddenly. The grief she felt was like a seed germinating from the core of her body. Bertie's death had been intermingled with the loss of that tiny child so long ago. She realized that by giving up Jonathan at birth, his loss was as permanent as that of her husband. "Oh, just let me be," she whispered.

As she closed her bedroom door, she could hear Lyn calling out to Mel in the kitchen, "Please bring in the white wine; I'll have another glass."

"I've put my townhouse up for sale, Lyn; I'm moving back here to Cedar Street. No sense paying taxes on two properties." Mel was rinsing dishes and putting them into the dishwasher.

"That may be fine for you, Mel, but I really like my apartment and my independence now that I've gotten used to having it again. I think I'll hold on to my place and keep visiting here. This arrangement has worked fine for me since Daddy's passing."

"He's been gone ten months now. Hard to believe, isn't it? Oh, Lyn, I forgot to tell you Hamlet Realty called today, saying there's been an offer on Daddy's building. I guess someone wants to put a restaurant in there and live on the second floor. They'll have their work cut out for them because it was never finished off. We'll have to find out what to do with all of Daddy's equipment; everything's still in there as he left it, dirty tea mugs and all. Have you set foot in there? The shop out back is full of old stuff. I don't think Daddy ever threw anything away. Who do you think would buy that machinery and tools, or should we call the scrap man? Mom seems content to leave everything to us. When I told her an offer had been made on Peach of a Sole, she gave me a blank stare and didn't say one word." Mel untied the blue apron and hung it on the hook.

"Mom is owned by her grief. I'm worried about her. You're right; she doesn't want to be bothered about anything; she's given up caring. I remember reading somewhere one shouldn't make any major decisions in the first year after a major loss; Daddy's death has impacted her deeply. We can think clearly about the day-to-day running of things, but with Mom, it's like she's stuck on day one. Look at her: she's getting thinner by the day and goes around in circles muttering to herself. I think we could ask Woody, who has a good head on his shoulders; he'd know what to do with all the equipment at Peach of a Sole."

Lyn and Mel took their lemon lift tea and a plate of oatmeal raisin cookies into the living room. As Mel went to flick on the switch of the gas fireplace, the framed picture of the four of them taken by the photographer at the Quechee Balloon Festival caught her eye. Their mother had put it on the mantle for all to see. She couldn't help smiling. "Look how happy Daddy was last year on Father's Day! Wasn't it the most perfect day?"

Mel settled into the comfortable sofa with Lyn at her side.

"I've been thinking, Mel, and wondering if we could persuade Mom to go with us to Pittsburgh for a few days. I've heard they have an exciting modern art museum there, and an excellent symphony, too. We could fly and then rent a car. I know we'd enjoy visiting Fallingwater—the house cantilevered over a waterfall—the one designed by Frank Lloyd Wright. It's not far to drive there from Pittsburgh. I'm thinking three or four days; it might be just enough to get Mom moving forward. You've got some time off in October. What are your thoughts, Mel?"

"I have school break around Columbus Day. Haven't made any plans. Maybe a trip to Pittsburgh with Mom would be good."

"We've *got* to do something, Mel."

"All right, Lyn. If *we* can't get through to her, who can?"

They went upstairs to introduce the Pittsburgh trip while they had the courage. After all, when Lyn had suggested going on a trip, their mother had been pretty upset at the dinner table and hadn't finished eating.

"Mom, may we talk with you for a minute?" Mel asked after knocking on her mother's closed bedroom door.

"Come in," Tilli said in a muffled tone without enthusiasm.

Mel and Lyn found their mother in bed with the covers pulled over her head. As the sisters waited for her to sit up, their eyes met. They were ready to hear all of the reasons why their mother wasn't going anywhere.

"Pittsburgh, I thought that city was the armpit of America."

This wasn't what they'd expected to hear, and Lyn started to laugh. Mel threw her sister a sinister look, indicating she should stifle herself.

Lyn was not put off by Mel's look. "Mom, that's absurd! I've done some research, and Pittsburgh, whatever you think it might have been, is a lively city with a world-class modern art museum. You love the symphony; we could attend a concert. Come on, Mom, you'll like visiting Fallingwater. Mel and I insist!"

Mel couldn't believe how pushy Lyn was being.

Tilli let out a long sigh. She looked from one expectant face to the other. How could she disappoint them: these two young women—her daughters—whom she loved with all her heart?

"All right, I'll go, but just for a few days. Then will you leave me alone?"

"You bet, Mom! This will be so good for all of us." Mel smiled.

# Six Months Later

Lyn decided it was time to talk with Mel about a trip to the southwest before bringing their mother on board.

"So, Mel, guess what I've been doing?"

"I think I know what's coming, Lyn."

"Okay, I'm going to get right down to business." She smiled. "You and I know how much Mom enjoyed the trip to Pittsburgh. She was all bubbly and happy; for a few days, she was herself. It was good to see that, wasn't it, Mel?"

"Of course, Lyn. I'm glad you insisted Mom go. It was fun."

"Now, I've been doing some plotting, or shall I say planning, again. Here's what I've been thinking. As soon as your summer break begins, we take off. I know you and Mom are going to want to tend to the gardens around the house, so maybe we go away for two weeks, still leaving plenty of time to play in the dirt together before school reopens. One of the high school students who volunteers at the Hamlet Community Arts Center does lawns, and I've already asked him to take care of ours while we're away. I've put a bug in my employer's ear, and he's indicated there'd be no problem in going on vacation because I've rarely taken time off during my twelve years working there. Joanna has been chomping at the bit to take on more of a leadership role; I have full confidence in her to run things in my absence."

"Okay, Lyn. I'm ready to talk this over. Where are we going?"

"I've got a fresh pad of lined paper and a pen. Let's start. Oh, and I just so happen to have picked up some guidebooks from the Hamlet Library and have been studying them over the past weeks, as well as maps. Mom said she enjoyed her balloon trip with us so much that I thought maybe we could go for a hot-air balloon ride somewhere in the Southwest, which is an area of the country she's indicated she wanted to visit, so I've planned our next vacation around these two."

"Excuse me, Lyn, but do you think another balloon ride is a good idea? She'll be comparing it to Quechee the whole time. It will stir up old memories for her."

"Listen, Mel, we're bringing up memories all the time, so I don't think raising good memories is a bad thing. Sure, she'll be thinking of Daddy. We all will, but she will enjoy this trip just the same."

"Okay, Lyn, I didn't mean to interrupt. Go ahead."

"I've got lots of notes, Mel, but will give you some options without going into detail. We could go to the four corners area: Colorado, Utah, Arizona, and New Mexico. There are so many possibilities in this region."

Mel kicked off her shoes, put her feet on the hassock, and took her teacup in her hands. She nestled into the sofa cushions, ready to imagine her sister's descriptions.

"So, as I said, I've put together a list of options. Just hear me out; I'm not suggesting we do all of what I'm about to say. Option one: we could fly to Las Vegas and see the lights and take in one of those glitzy shows."

"Well, somehow, I don't think Las Vegas would be first on my list of places to visit. I'm not a gambler, Lyn, and I think I know what Mom would say." Mel frowned.

"No, no. We don't go there for gambling; we go for the bright lights—one night only—stay right on the Strip in the middle of everything in a nice hotel, and we take in one spectacular show. Then we rent a car and drive up to Utah and visit five national parks! Imagine, in southern Utah, there are actually five of them? We'll visit from west to east: Zion, Bryce, Capitol Reef, Arches, and Canyonlands. The interplay between the angle of the sun and the colors of sandstone and the landscape sculpted by erosion are endlessly fascinating. For sure, we'll need to buy a new digital camera to replace Daddy's old thirty-five-millimeter Agfa.

"Let's see; so many possibilities, great scenery, such fun. Here's another idea: we could go to Bluff, Utah, and take a rafting trip on the San Juan River through a section called the Goosenecks. You've probably seen pictures on wall calendars and didn't know where the Goosenecks were. After the river trip, we could continue west, through Valley of the Gods—the reddest sandstone you'll see anywhere—into Mexican Hat and south into Arizona. In Monument Valley, we could go on a trail ride, or an off-road jeep trip into the hinterlands, away from the crowds and tour buses.

"After Monument Valley, it's off to Canyon de Chelly. Both of these places are beautiful, but each is different from the other. Whatever we didn't do at Monument Valley, we could do here: hike a trail, ride horses, and take off-road trips into the wilderness with a Navajo guide. So many possibilities! I'm getting goosebumps thinking about these wide-open spaces, Mel! These areas are where Mom always talked about going when we were kids."

"Take a breather, Lyn. I see problems already. I can't picture Mom getting on a horse, but bumping across the desert in a Jeep, she'd probably go for that. I have some questions. Do you want me to ask now or wait until you've finished?"

"No, go ahead. I want your input, Mel. This is our trip and should reflect what all three of us want to do—Mom's desires are most important."

"You know I love to swim, Lyn, so when you plan lodging places, be sure to find ones with pools."

"Absolutely, Mel. I think many places have pools, so I'll be sure to make it a priority. Also, there are many natural hot springs in the Southwest, especially New Mexico; it might be quite a nice experience to soak in one of those." Lyn took the notepad and started a list of must-haves. "Okay, where was I?"

"You got us to Canyon de Chelly, I think."

"Oh, right. After Canyon de Chelly, we head east to Gallup, New Mexico, an interesting stop along Route 66 with Old West memorabilia; it has over one hundred trading posts. It would be fun to stay at the El Rancho, which is on the National Register of Historic Places. This is where dozens of movie stars stayed whenever Westerns were filmed. Oh, and yes, there's an outdoor pool at the El Rancho. Hmm, let's see, from Gallup, we'd head east until we get to Albuquerque, and then we could fly home from there."

Lyn spread out a four-state map, with the routes highlighted, on the coffee table in front of them. "I want to know what you think, Mel."

"Wow! You've been busy, Lyn. I'm impressed by your thoroughness and had no idea you'd already done so much planning. I think you've found your calling; you should be designing custom vacations. All of this sounds amazing. You could stop right now, but I know you've got more to share, so go ahead. I can't imagine what else we could do in the Southwest. I wonder what Mom will make of all this?"

Lyn was happy to hear Mel's excitement. "Okay, here goes. We could fly to Santa Fe, New Mexico, and spend a few days there. There are several museums, over a hundred art galleries, a four-culture environment, and a summertime open-air world-class opera house.

"From Santa Fe, we could head north to Taos and visit the Taos Pueblo, which is a Native American community with one hundred and fifty artists who live there without running water or electricity. There's Abiquiu, the location of Ghost Ranch, an area Georgia O'Keefe made famous by her paintings. The colorful strata of the sandstone are like none anywhere else. Again, we could go horseback riding or take a float trip on the Rio Chama to experience this incredible landscape. If we hiked, we'd probably find ancient pottery sherds and arrowheads or maybe see dinosaur footprints in the sandstone! And, Mel, we wouldn't want to miss Ojo Caliente, which means 'hot eye,' where all of us could spend a day in the natural mineral baths and choose a relaxing massage, followed by a healthy meal in their restaurant. We'd probably want to spend the night in their historic lodge—we wouldn't want to rush the Ojo experience.

"Any one of these trips is more than enough for a two-week vacation. In the future, if we decided to return to Santa Fe, we could go back to the Abiquiu area and continue on our way to Chaco Canyon National Historical

Park. I've always been interested in archaeology, as you know, and Chaco is the largest ancient Native American site in North America, with ruins dating back to before 1250AD, when the site was abandoned. It's located down a washboard dirt road, but well worth the visit. And, since it's so remote, there's no light pollution, which means they have a dark-sky evening astronomy program.

"From Chaco, we'd head north into southwestern Colorado to Mesa Verde, which means Green Table. We'd need a minimum of three nights here because there are several cliff dwellings and trails for day hikes. Wooden ladders reach into a couple of the cliff dwellings, so as long as we don't look down, we'll be fine. Mesa Verde sounds wonderful, Mel. And I've read online that Mesa Verde has one cliff dwelling accessible to people in wheelchairs, so I think this is certainly doable for Mom."

"I can see you've done a lot of research, Lyn, and I don't mean to interrupt you, but the place I thought you'd be making plans for is the Grand Canyon. Everything you've been describing sounds wonderful, but would it be too much to try and work up an itinerary for the Grand Canyon?"

"Of course, that would be fabulous! And, if you wanted to go to the Grand Canyon, we could make that our option for this year and put the rest of these suggestions aside for future vacations. I've read that most tourists spend only three hours at the Grand Canyon, and they see it only from the rim.

"At the Canyon, we could go hiking and visit various outlook points along the South Rim and go on a float trip on the Colorado River through Marble Canyon, which departs from the base of the Glen Canyon Dam at Page.

Don't worry, it's not a whitewater trip by any means; the rafting trip ends just before the rapids start. Mom will love the float trip; it'll be relaxing."

Mel had never seen her sister this excited. As Lyn continued talking about vacation ideas, Mel became caught up by her sister's energy, and they agreed that any one of these had to pull their mother out of despair.

"Oh, and there's a day trip or overnight trip on the mules." Lyn read from her notes, saying, "The overnight mule ride goes down one mile to the bottom of the canyon, on four-foot wide switchbacks, dating back to the earliest people who lived there. We'd spend the night at Phantom Ranch. I know you have some hesitation about Mom riding a horse or mule, but if I remember correctly from stories Mom used to tell us when we were little, she took up horseback riding when she was quite young. There was a mare named Diamond that she loved to ride at an equestrian center somewhere in Connecticut. She told us she learned to ride English, so sitting on a big comfy Western saddle should feel like a BarcaLounger in comparison!

"To go to the South Rim of the Grand Canyon, we'd fly to Phoenix, rent a car, and drive north through Sedona. If we wanted to spend a couple of days in Phoenix, there are a couple of places we wouldn't want to miss, even though it will be hot during the summer. For example, there's Frank Lloyd Wright's Taliesin West in nearby Scottsdale. He designed his school of architecture to fit into the surrounding desert landscape, which was pretty much deserted when he built it.

"There's also the Heard Museum, a real gem according to the guidebook, and of course Arcosanti, a school started by an Italian artist, for students interested in casting bronze bells. We can watch them pour the bronze into the molds; the finished bells hang outdoors, where we can ring them to see which one we'd like to buy to bring back to hang in the garden."

"You're right, Lyn, we want to enjoy every minute of our trip. Now I'm excited but also a bit overwhelmed by all of these possibilities. I had no idea there was so much in the Southwest. Great job, Lyn!"

"Wait, Mel, I'm not done," Lyn paused because Mel had taken their mugs away and was out of earshot.

"Don't move, Lyn; I'm coming right back." Mel soon returned from the kitchen carrying another plate of oatmeal cookies, which she held out to her sister. "Can I ask a couple of questions now?"

"Sure, Sis, whatever; I hope I have the answers." Lyn popped half a cookie into her mouth.

"Lyn, I like everything you've talked about. My only concern is there'll be a lot of driving. Just one of those four states you mentioned is larger than all of New England combined. I like to drive, and I know you keep your license up to date even though you gave up your car, so we'd have to share the driving of a rental car. Have you calculated the mileage on any of this?"

"Well, not exactly. I'll do it after we decide where we're going. I didn't know how you'd feel about these itineraries, so I've held off."

"Lyn, I agree two weeks away from home is long enough for now—at least for Mom. You said yourself there's so much to see and do in the Southwest, we'd have to return a few times."

"All right, Mel, I'll work on the itinerary to allow for more relaxation and less driving, but before I do, I need to hear from you and Mom about where we should go."

"I think Mom might want to visit the Grand Canyon first."

"Let's go upstairs and ask her; no better time than now, Sis!"

They found their mother sitting in their grandfather's wing chair, sewing up a split seam on her gardening pants. "You want to hear my thoughts?" Tilli continued sewing without looking up.

"Of course, Mom. This is about the three of us, not just what Mel and I want."

"You know I enjoyed our trip to Pittsburgh, and I'm glad you encouraged me. That getaway did improve my energy and give me a lift, but we shouldn't make plans for a bigger trip yet. We're going to need time to get your daddy's affairs in order, and we need time to form a travel plan. You're talking about going away for two weeks. After taking that bus trip through Vermont and New Hampshire, I can tell you I wouldn't like to go on a tour with a lot of people. That business of being in the lobby at eight am with your suitcase packed was not relaxing." Tilli kept sewing. She wasn't in the mood right now to talk about this; maybe her daughters would get the message.

Lyn didn't want to wait; she knew her mother had no idea how much time she'd spent on planning.

"All right, Mom. Keep in mind, though, it's April now, and I'm talking about going away this summer. We need to make reservations ahead of time because we don't want to go to the Southwest and find ourselves without a decent place to stay or then learn that the day trips are sold out! How am I ever going to meet my tall, handsome, intelligent man if I don't go exploring? I'll never meet him in Hamlet! Besides, planning is something I do every workday; I'm good at it, and I like to plan and organize. Mom, listen to me. I have already put a trip together for us."

Mel laughed. "Oh, Lyn, you're not going to leave Mom's prediction alone."

"I mean it, Mel, the guy's out there. Instead of finding romance, I'm sitting here twiddling my thumbs." It had been a long time since Lyn had heard Mel laugh.

"Mom, I think Lyn and I understand you need more time. I'm trying to be realistic, considering the only place I've ever been is to the British West Indies."

"And I've barely left New England," Lyn chimed in.

"We know you've always wanted to visit a national park, Mom. The longer we wait, the more effort will be needed to get ourselves up onto those horses!" Mel continued.

"I guess maybe I've grown content to stay in one place, like your father. Oh, sure, I'll go on a trip with you, but I'm not ready to commit—yet."

"Okay, I hear you." Lyn knew she couldn't force the issue. "How about we revisit this topic in a couple of weeks? I'll put my notes aside for today." Lyn shuffled her papers into a neat pile. "But, Mom, don't expect me to give up!"

It was a good day to clean, and it was time to investigate Bertie's closet and chest of drawers. Just getting started had been difficult for Tilli. All this time, and what had she accomplished? In fact, time had taken on its own meaning since Bertie died. Days had become weeks, and weeks had become seventeen months. When would the numbness go away? How was she to move on with life? She reminded herself that Bertie would want her to find her way. This April was especially rainy and cold, and the dreary weather matched her somber mood. She sat down on the bed and looked around the room.

Everything reminded her of Bertie. His notes were still piled on his night table—neatly now because she had gathered them into one place—his pocketknife, pill organizer, wristwatch, and tape measure lay as she had placed them when she had last dusted. Just like her life, the room was in a state of suspension. If he walked in that door, he'd wonder why she was loafing.

A voice in her head prodded: *Get moving, Tilli!* But her heavy limbs, combined with the weariness she felt, had permeated her very bones. She moved over to his chest of drawers. Happy smiles greeted her from the framed photos of Lyn and Mel, as well as the faded and crackled wedding photo of her with Bertie. His tortoiseshell comb and brush sat neatly next to a shallow pottery dish. The dish, which held loose change and old keys, had been given to him long ago by the local Girl Scout troop for services he had provided. Why had he saved old keys that didn't fit any locks? Funny, he could be such a neatnik and then be a packrat with other stuff. For all their years together, there was so much about Bertie she could never understand. For example, his early morning greeting had changed at some point from "Good morning, my dear Tilli" to simply "Morn, Tilli." How did that happen? After she married him, he had become a man of few words, and with the passage of time, conversation had been reduced to a minimum, just enough to make his desires known. She realized it was her fault; she had anticipated his every need. Well, she wouldn't be finishing his sentences anymore.

Her eyes welled up, and from out of nowhere, she could hear him laughing. That was enough to break Tilli's reverie. "I hope I'm not losing my mind!"

Opening the topmost drawer, she began putting things into bags: some for charity, perhaps that shirt for Woody. Some stuff she set aside for the rubbish; not much in this category, though, as Bertie was very thrifty—a true Yankee at heart. Even when something was worn out, and before discarding it, Bertie would consider other possible uses, so it would get a second life. There was always the rag pile!

As the bags on the floor began to fill, she continued opening and emptying his drawers. Here was the argyle sweater his mother had knitted for him over forty years ago! It never fit him right; the sleeves were long enough for a gorilla, so he never wore it, and his mother saw him in it only once. What's this at the bottom of his underwear drawer? Tillie sat down on the bed again and opened the packet of papers she had discovered. She felt strange—now that he was gone, going through his things—like a snoop. But he wasn't here to stop her, and someone had to do the job of cleaning out. She recalled her own secrets, like the diary inside her gardening book. How would *she* feel if another family member—most likely Lyn or Mel—went through her personal belongings? "After this job, I will definitely tear up my journals," she said.

But he was dead—gone on to who knows where—

and she was faced with this task. The packet was securely tied with an old piece of string. Yes, it looked like it hadn't been opened for a very long time. Perhaps she should have waited for Lyn and Mel to help her with this difficult job, but they were both at work, and she had felt confident and wanted to move on.

"Dear Del," she read as she unfolded the first of what appeared to be several hand-written letters. The handwriting was definitely feminine—lovely writing style—the Ts neatly crossed, the words spread across the lineless pages evenly, and the letters close together. Tilli envisioned a woman of delicate stature writing these words. Who was she?

Tilli skipped to the end of the first letter and read the signature, "Yours always, Evie." Tilli counted at least a dozen letters, all signed by Evie, and all had been mailed to Bertie's Peach of a Sole address, which explained why Tilli had never seen them. The envelopes bore no return address, and the postmark was a general one, not traceable. The letters began a few years after she and Bertie had married, and the last postmark was from about five years ago. Five years ago, Bertie was writing to this woman! What was the tie that bound them? She read the contents of one letter—there were too many to read all at once—and immediately assumed Bertie had been involved in a romantic relationship.

"Damn!" said Tilli. "That bow-legged old coot was cheating on me! The devil! And I cooked for him, washed his dirty clothes, cleaned up after him—all the while, he was cheating on me!" Tilli was ripped! She wept out loud, and the pain she felt made her start throwing things. His wristwatch hit the wall; his tape measure was next.

Somehow, it felt good to throw his stuff against the walls. She grabbed the pottery dish that held the keys and change and flung it as hard as she could; the pieces flew everywhere. Next was the lamp on his night table; it hit the floor with a crash. The bulb splintered and the lampshade tore. Her grief had mixed with anger at her discovery. All these years, she'd respected his privacy— never went through his belongings, never took money out of his wallet like some wives might have done. How could he have betrayed her?

"That weasel! Everybody, including me, thought he was such a great guy, such an honest businessman, such a charitable person, such a great family man, and now I find out he had another side to him. If he hadn't died, would I ever have learned about Evie?"

The destruction of his belongings somehow brought on a sense of relief as she continued to read through her tears: "Dear Del, I need to pay the rent next week, and the oil tank is low."

Tilli was sickened. This was so unfair! Bertie was dead, and she couldn't scream at him. She wished she could punch him! She thought back to all those years together when she'd never yelled at him or thrown a fit—like some wives—it was always, "Yes, Bertie; of course, Bertie; absolutely, Bertie." She never looked for arguments with him, and even when he sometimes got angry, which wasn't often, she would walk away rather than fight. She'd held a lot in. Now this: Del—her beloved Bertie—had paid for Evie's household expenses, even as he supported his own family.

"Hello, Mom?" Tilli heard Mel hollering up the stairs. "Hi, Mom, it's us; Lyn and I've come to help." Tilli looked at the alarm clock on her nightstand and realized it was after five o'clock; the girls were coming home from work.

"I'm upstairs in my bedroom," Tilli called out in a choked voice.

"Oh, Mom! What happened?" Alarm was clearly written on Mel's face as she took in the destruction around the room.

"Are you okay?" Lyn had sat down on the bed and put her arm around her mother's shoulders.

Tilli tried to shrug Lyn's arm away and stared straight ahead; she couldn't look at either of them.

"Come on, Mom, you shouldn't have tried to clean out Daddy's things without our help. It's too much for you. We're here to help. But why's the room such a mess?" She and Lyn looked at each other. They'd never seen their mother in such a state.

"Let's go downstairs. I need to fix dinner now."

"Oh, no you don't, Mom; Lyn and I can send out for something. You're in no state to cook. We want to know what's going on. Why you're upset. This room looks like a hurricane hit it!"

"Okay, you want to know? Really want to know? Want an explanation for why I went berserk? Why I lost it? I'll tell you why. Your beloved daddy was a bastard!"

Mel and Lyn were stunned as they searched one another's faces for meaning and shrugged.

"Here, take a look and tell me what *you* think." Tilli pressed the letters into Mel's hands.

Lyn and Mel each read one of Evie's letters. They were equally astounded to learn their father had led a double life. How could they and their mother not have known? Why did the letters stop five years ago? Had Daddy broken off his relationship with Evie? Perhaps she'd died. Certainly, there had to be some logical explanation other than romance; it was a puzzle.

"Come on, Mom, let's put all this on hold. I'll phone Hamlet Pizzeria, and one of us will go and pick up our order." Mel tried to get her mother to move off the bed.

"You're right, Mel; he's gone, and whatever happened between him and this Evie woman can wait. Let's go downstairs." Tilli raised herself from the bed and realized how stiff she was from sitting.

In the kitchen, Tilli opened the refrigerator and took out a bottle of Corona. "It'll go great with pizza. There's some for you girls, and limes are there, too. I think mourning your Daddy's loss has gone on long enough. Lyn, I hope you and Mel have that vacation planned 'cause we certainly could use one now. I'm ready!"

# Here We Go

"Five in the morning? Why so early?" Mel wished she could have slept longer.

"I guess it's 'cause there's no wind at that hour," Lyn replied, shivering.

"There's also no sun. Brrrr! It's cold out here in the desert." Tilli hugged herself, trying to stay warm.

Under a cloudless sky, Oak Creek Canyon lay in deep shadows, and the red rocks surrounding Sedona, Arizona, were dark silhouettes as Tilli, Mel, and Lyn arrived at the launch site for their hot-air balloon ride.

"Oh my god, where's the balloon?" Lyn asked Ned, the operator.

"Hello, ladies, is this your first time up?" asked the friendly man dressed in jeans, a snap-front red plaid shirt, cowboy boots, a bolo tie, and a broad-brimmed hat.

"Not quite, Ned. We've been up once before in Vermont," replied Lyn as she rubbed the goosebumps on her arms.

"'Cause we need to get the balloon ready for lift-off, ladies."

"Oh, no, not *we*," said Mel.

"Oh, don't you girls remember that part?" Tilli asked.

"Yup. I need your help. Now, it's not hard, but it takes all of us workin' together to git it ready. So, here's what we gotta do. We spread out the nylon fabric of the balloon, nice and flat on the ground, like so." Ned proceeded to unfold the enormous red, yellow, and orange layers of fabric, and Lyn and Mel took their cues from him. Tilli was happy just to stand aside out of their way.

"Next, gals, I'll need your help with the flame torch to fill the balloon with air. It'll take a bit, so we can't hurry it none. Mel, you and Lyn go on either side of the balloon, like this, to help lift up and separate the fabric, so when I turn on the heat and wave it back and forth along the opening of the balloon, we all help things along. Mrs. MacInnes, come on over here; you can help, too. It's not heavy; I just need another person to separate the nylon so the balloon will fill quicker. You got it. Great job!"

Minute by minute, for a seemingly long time, the balloon slowly began to puff up with warmed air until it no longer lay flat on the ground. As it filled, the sisters and their mother began to see the colorful zigzag pattern of the fabric.

"Great! Now, we're ready to attach the ties to the basket over here." Ned had two of his own helpers for this part of the preparation, and Lyn, Mel, and Tilli stood aside while the balloon was attached to the basket.

"How many people fit in there?" Tilli asked Ned.

"Four."

"This one's tinier than the one in Quechee," remarked Mel.

"Now, gals, as soon as I give the signal, you climb in; there's a step stool so you don't need to strain yourselves." Ned was already inside the basket, and his assistants held onto its sides. The enormous balloon dwarfed the tiny basket, which was still tethered to its spikes.

"Okay, gals, up-itty up now," Ned called out to them.

"Oh, my legs just don't want to go over this high side,"

said Tilli.

"Oh, come on, Mom, you've done this before. Think how far we've come today. Think of the fun!"

To show her mother how easy it was going to be, Lyn stepped on the stool and flung her right leg over the side. She was in the basket and motioning to Tilli and Mel to do the same.

As Mel joined them in the basket, Ned said, "Okay, now, before we go anywhere, I'll go over the rules. Mel, as you can see, the basket is a rectangle; you stand in one corner. Mrs. MacInnes, you will stand in the opposite corner. Lyn, you have a spot over there, and where I'm standing is my corner; the gas canisters are right here next to me so I can switch them from one to the other as each one runs out. Let me know if you want to come out of your corner; don't make sudden movements. See how high the sides are? You can't fall out! At times, we'll want to go up, and you'll see me turn up the gas canister we're using at the time; when we want to come down, you'll see me letting off gas. When you hear the sound of the flame entering into the balloon, heating the air, we'll go up. And, conversely, when you hear—*whoosh!*—the sound of air escaping, I'll be wanting us to go lower. Understand? The movements will be gradual, so don't worry about anything quick happening. Gals, this is no fighter jet! But I do have a commercial pilot's license and have been operating hot-air balloons for over twenty years. Any questions?"

"Will we land on this same spot?" asked Tilli.

"No, prob'ly not. I will have radio contact with my ground crew. They'll be tracking our course and will follow our path from their vehicle on the road. We have several landing spots the crew knows about, and the plan is to go to one of those locations, depending on wind direction. Any other questions?"

"How high will we go?" asked Lyn.

"Well, we want to clear that mountain over there, and we'll probably go about five hundred feet over the top of it, so I guess we'll be up, above the ground, about fifteen hundred feet or so. Not to worry, we won't head into the stratosphere today. Okay? Ready? All right, guys, untether us. Gals, we are airborne!"

Up and away, the balloon lifted from the launch site. The ancient junipers and century plants on the red ground beneath them receded, and as the sun rose, shadows fell onto the canyon walls. The air warmed quickly with the arrival of the sun, and the sky was a deep, cloudless blue. No wind. As the balloon rose higher and higher, Tilli and her daughters let any fears or worries float away and focused on the beauty of their surroundings. How sad Bertie couldn't be here with them; he had enjoyed the Quechee balloon trip so much. Amazingly, Tilli wasn't a bit afraid of being aloft, floating about like a downy thistle. She put thoughts of Bertie behind her and relaxed. The only sound was the whooshing of the gas-fed, bright flame entering into the center of the balloon high above their heads. It was so peaceful right here, right now. If only she could wrap her arms around this magical moment and keep it forever.

The silence was broken by Ned pointing out sights. "See the antelope on that outcropping of the canyon wall below? I'm always amazed when I see that; I wonder how they get onto those seemingly impossible-to-reach ledges. Or how about the bald eagle soaring in the distance? Look closely; there are two: one is the mother, she's larger and is flying higher but near to her offspring, watching and teaching the youngster how to hunt prey. Can you spot those openings under the overhang just below us? It's where ancient peoples lived and stored their food. They used natural fissures or chiseled toe holds into the rock face, and that's how they climbed down from their garden on top of the mesa." Ned's eyes were tuned into the landscape's nuances and the movements of animals.

"Ned, do you know why we wanted to go up in a hot-air balloon?"

"You gals wanted to get an elevated perspective of Arizona?"

"Nope; we're here today because of our mother. You see, our daddy died rather suddenly almost two years ago; it was only months after we had gone with him on a hot-air balloon ride in Quechee, Vermont. It was the first vacation my parents had taken since they'd married about forty years ago. For a long time, he had wall calendars hanging in his shoe repair shop, ones with hot-air balloons on them; he loved the colors of the balloons. Even though he was afraid of heights, he finally agreed to go up. Mom's wanted to travel for a long time, so Lyn and I decided to go on this trip and include a hot-air balloon ride in honor of our father. Mom's always wanted to go to the Southwest, and we have her to thank for this incredibly beautiful experience, Ned."

Tilli was beaming as she listened to Mel. Yes, this day was one she would never forget.

"I'm really sorry to hear about your father, but it sounds like y'all listened to your inner spirits."

"What do you mean by inner spirits, Ned?" asked Tilli.

"Well, Mrs. MacInnes, the Native people believe a lot

in spirits. Whereas we lean more toward the concrete and what we can see—our outer selves—the Native people are taught as children to listen to their inner selves—their spiritual side. If you end up doing things you've never done, things out of the ordinary for you, they would say you have allowed your dreams to whisper what is important to your outer self, and your spirit got you to act. You've had a yearning, a desire to strike out into unknown territory, to chase dreams. The inner voice is a siren, a shapeshifter, and a seductress. It's why you're here. Your outer life has been about working, cleaning, sleeping, and eating, but your inner life is much deeper. You're experiencing the evolution of your soul." The sudden release of hot air into the balloon broke Ned's mesmerizing monologue, and the sisters gazed at their surroundings with a fresh awareness.

"Wow, that's pretty deep!" said Mel.

"Have you read any books on Native American thought?" asked Ned.

"No, but it sounds like we need to do that," replied Lyn.

"The Native people believe everything in nature—rocks, water, sun, sky, earth, humans, animals, birds, fish, and plants—has a spirit and is connected to the whole of creation. Whenever we harm any part of nature, we harm the spirit of that individual part as well as harming the Great Spirit. Mankind's role is to respect, appreciate, and be a guardian of nature. We are not better than any part of nature, but we are connected to this integral whole. Of course, there's lots more, but this gives you an introduction to Native American thought," said Ned.

"I've been gardening and tending plants most of my adult life," said Tilli, "and it must have been my inner spirit that encouraged me to connect in this way with nature."

"We all have a purpose for our existence, Mrs. Mac-Innes, and each of us needs to connect with our inner selves to find that purpose. And, when we do, we need to listen and act."

About an hour later, Mel said, "I can see a town down there, Ned."

"That's Clarkdale; we'll be coming down shortly."

As the balloon floated lower and lower, Lyn, Mel, and Tilli could see they were headed for someone's house. "Ned, are you planning on landing here?"

"Yup! Sometimes the balloon has a mind of its own; it'll be wanting to come down right smack in this front yard."

Lyn, Mel, and Tilli saw the road crew approach and pull into the dirt driveway. After the balloon touched down, two young guys grabbed it and held on tight while Ned ran up to the front door and knocked. "Hi, there!" he said to the woman opening the door. "Mind if we land our balloon in your front yard?"

The wife, husband, and three kids came outside. The balloon's energy source had been shut off, and it was flattening out on the sandy dirt, as lifeless as when they first saw it in the early morning twilight. Ned and the guys set up a folding table in the front yard, complete with biscuits and tortillas, fresh fruit, local cheeses, orange juice, and pumpkin muffins.

"Come on—everybody—let's have some breakfast." Ned stood away as he popped the cork on a cold bottle of champagne, which the road crew had brought along in a cooler. The guys were able to quickly gather up the balloon and stuff it into the now-empty basket. The canisters were stowed away just as quickly. Then they hefted the basket into the back of the double-cab pickup truck. With everything put away, Ned called out: "We're celebrating the realization of dreams with these two sisters and their mom from New England. Come and share some bubbly. Cheers to everyone!"

Tilli held up her glass and reflected on the tiny rising bubbles. She took in the scene around her. This was one of life's perfect moments, except that one very important person—Jonathan—was missing. She saw Mel and Lyn giggling with the young children. Sunlight and shadow drifted across the red sandstone hills in the distance. The air was so gentle; the temperature comfortably warm. One cicada chirred in the Rabbit Brush nearby. Would she ever look into Jonathan's face, hold his hand, hear his voice? Tilli sighed as she thought about her five wishes. She hoped one day—someday, somehow—he would be in her life. Only *then* could she fully celebrate a joyous moment like this.

# Robert Redford

"Gosh, Mom and Lyn, that mule skinner's breakfast at the El Tovar Hotel was huge, but delicious. I feel sorry for the mule I'll be riding on to Phantom Ranch today."

Laughing and twirling, Tilli spread her arms wide. "Not to worry, Mel. It may be hours before we get dinner, and who knows what we'll get. I've prepared myself for a simple meal and primitive lodging, but the experience of fulfilling this dream will be worth it. I could be riding the lawn mower at 5 Cedar Street right now, and you could be pulling weeds in the garden. I'm not going to think about altitude or clinging to a mule's back; this will be an amazing experience, and I'm having the time of my life. I feel like a girl again, though I'll probably suffer from saddle sores tonight. Can you believe it? We're at the Grand Canyon!"

Mel and Lyn chuckled to see their mother so happy. "Wasn't yesterday's walk along the South Rim amazing?" Lyn hooked her arm into Mel's as they chatted and walked the short distance to the corral, where riders were being matched up with their mules.

"As I looked over the vastness of this canyon and stared into the depths, I couldn't believe it was real." Mel continued, "it was as if I were looking at a canvas painted in pastels." She stopped to adjust her wide-brimmed hat against the glare of the sun.

"Look, Mom! A little girl is sitting on that low wall

with a sheer drop into the canyon right behind her! She can't be more than four. Can you believe her parents put her there? If she fell backwards, she'd disappear into the abyss." Mel shook her head.

"Amazing what people will do to get the perfect photograph."

Lyn pointed in the direction of the mules. "It looks like we'll be a small group."

"That's okay with me," replied Mel. "I don't much care for crowds. And, you know, I've had my doubts about doing this in the first place. Have you *really looked down* the Bright Angel Trail into that Canyon? Oh my god! The Colorado River is just a shiny silver ribbon, and to think we're going—on mules!"

Lyn was the first to get into a saddle. The cowhand adjusted her stirrups and tied the small waterproof bag, filled with her overnight stuff, behind the saddle. Next, he slung a leather bota bag filled with drinking water onto her pommel.

"Ya got sunblock on, young lady?" asked the tobacco-chewing cowhand as he checked to be sure she was wearing a wide-brimmed hat, a shirt with long sleeves, jeans, and sturdy footwear.

"Yessir," replied Lyn.

"Okay, young lady. Next!" The cowhand indicated to Mel he was about to give her a ten-finger boost into the saddle. Before she could think about anything, she was astride and being prepped for the ride.

"Oh my god, Lyn, I've been on a horse twice in my life but never on a mule. What happens once it moves?"

"Just hang on to the pommel, relax in the saddle, and look at the scenery as we go down the trail. Remember what Ned told us. We're part of the Great Spirit, and we're listening to the voice of our inner selves. We're realizing dreams. That's all we need to think about. Enjoy yourself, Sis; it's what I plan to do."

Tilli was last to get up on her mule. After so many years of not being on a four-legged animal, the distance to the mule's back seemed very far from the ground. How was she ever going to get up there? Would riding the mule be like riding a bicycle: once having learned it, never forgetting how? Just as doubts began to creep in, the mule approached the mounting platform, where the guide indicated Tilli should follow. She went up the two steps to the platform, inserted her left foot into the roomy stirrup, and flung her right leg over—just as she'd done getting into the basket of the hot-air balloon. She was in the saddle and smiled at Mel and Lyn, who smiled back. How she was going to get off again was a thought she didn't want to entertain.

"All right, everybody; listen up! My name's Bill Brodie, and I'll be your wrangler for this here ride to Phantom Ranch." Bill indicated he and eight riders were going down together.

"You," he said as he pointed to Lyn, "are to ride directly behind me. You are riding on Vacation; it's the name of your mule; remember it." He peered from under his wide-brimmed hat and scanned the riders.

"You," he addressed Mel, "ride behind Vacation. You're on Robert Redford; remember that." As Mel laughed, he continued peering and pointing until all eight riders knew their positions in the line-up and the names of their mules. Tilli's mule was positioned directly behind Mel's. When Tilli learned the name of her mule was

Gorgeous, she smiled and patted the smooth brown neck and scratched behind Gorgeous's antenna-like ears. The last guy in the line-up was on Dolly Parton, and he ended up wearing a happy grin for most of the trail ride.

"All right; listen up!" Bill Brodie said again. "You're astride animals that have been up and down these here trails, into and out of this here canyon, hundreds of times. Make no mistake: they know the way. They are more sure-footed than if you were hiking down this trail on your own two feet. Remember, they've got four! I caution all of you not—I repeat not—to allow your mule to eat the vegetation growing along the sides of the trail. If you do let them eat this vegetation, they will get their noses to the inside of the trail—which is only four foot wide—and their tail ends will be on the outside of the trail. Guess what happens when they do that?" Bill Brodie waited to be sure everyone was listening. "The mule and you will slip over the side of this here trail, and it's bye-bye to you and the mule. You're prob'ly thinkin' you've never heard about mules and riders goin' over the side of the trail on the nightly news. Well, it's simply 'cause we don't broadcast bad publicity. It's not good for business, but make no mistake, accidents can and do happen, and we don't want any accidents. Do y'all understand?"

And with these words, Bill Brodie and his entourage began the descent down the topmost part of the Bright Angel trail. At the first sharp fork, he stopped his mule, turned around in the saddle, and, peering at the riders, said, "Anybody who wants to turn around now will get seventy-five percent of their money back." He waited until he was certain no one wanted to turn back.

The group continued on their downward trek until

they'd reached the next switchback in the trail. The canyon began to open up before them, and they had a peek at its vastness. "Okay; listen up! Anyone who wants to turn back now gets a fifty percent refund."

"Oh, jeez, Lyn and Mel! Maybe I should turn around now while I still have the chance." This was the first glimpse Tilli had of the narrow trail winding down in front of them. What had she been thinking? At 64 years of age, wasn't it too late to be gallivanting down the Grand Canyon on top of this mule? She bit her lip.

Lyn looked at her mother's face and said, "Mom, if you turn back now, Mel and I will never speak to you again."

Seeing no one wanted to turn around, Bill Brodie said. "All right; that's it. No more refunds! We're all going down together." At these words, everyone laughed a bit nervously. "Just kidding, folks. We've got a perfect day for the trail, and you're all on top of the world's finest." Bill led the way to the next switchback, and everyone followed close behind. The mules didn't have a prayer at taking a nibble; the riders made sure of that.

# Indian Garden

Into the canyon, the mule riders followed the switchback trail, which hugged the rugged cliff sides and could be seen zigzagging ahead and far below them. Every now and again, the riders could see what looked like ants, but were actually other groups of mules far in the distance navigating the Bright Angel trail. As they rode, the layers and colors of the rock strata—thousands of years old— began to tower up around and above them with shades of red sandstone, green shale, and white limestone.

Whenever they looked up towards the South Rim, it grew farther and farther away; gradually, the previously unseen side canyons with jagged pinnacles, spires, mesa rock formations, scrubby plants, and cacti were revealed. The canvas changed with every switch in the trail and with the movement of sun, clouds, and shadows across the landscape painted by the hand of God. It was impossible to chat with Lyn and Mel as they rode. Tilli concentrated on keeping Gorgeous facing forward, and she was completely taken in by the views.

"Oh, my goodness, this is a dreamscape," Tilli said to her surroundings, which were presently painted in soft pastels: blues, pinks, tans and browns, shades of red and gray. It didn't take long before the mule riders met their first hikers, who navigated the same narrow trail. Tilli wondered how the riders would be able to pass the hikers and soon learned about protocol.

Bill Brodie stopped in the lead, and all the mules stopped, too. "Watch your mules—no eating—remember what'll happen if they do!" The small group of hikers, dressed inappropriately in flip-flops and shorts, and carrying no apparent water containers, flattened themselves as much as possible by pressing up against the wall of the trail. Unfortunately, now that the mules had come to a complete stop, they had something else on their minds besides eating scrub.

"Sorry, folks!" said Bill as his mule, Mae West, released a torrent of urine onto the dirt trail directly next to the sunburned and weary hikers, who had no choice but to stand still and wait until all the mules passed by.

After Mae West finished, it was not the end of the pit stop! Each mule, as it came to the spot where Mae West had urinated, contributed its own torrent until there was a huge puddle on what had been a dry and dusty trail.

Lyn laughed as Vacation's turn came; Mel laughed, too. Even though the riders felt compassion for the hikers, the pit stop would be something they'd never forget.

The South Rim had disappeared from view completely, and a flat plateau stretched out before them. Here grew cottonwood trees and grass.

"All right, y'all, listen up!" Bill Brodie waited for the riders to approach. "This here is Indian Garden. We will dismount and let the mules rest and drink."

Everyone was relieved to get out of the saddle except Tilli, whose immediate thought was about how she would get back on again when it was time to leave.

"Okay, ma'am," drawled Bill Brodie as he walked over to her and reached for her mule's bridle. He led the animal over to a mounting platform located off to one side. "I'll hold Gorgeous while you take your time gettin' off. We don't want any accidents here."

Getting off was not a problem, but when she discovered the lack of feeling in her legs, standing up was another matter. While Bill Brodie took Gorgeous over to the water trough, Tilli wobbled to the nearest cottonwood tree for shade and a chance to refill her now-empty bota bag.

"Oh, Lyn, am I ever stiff. My legs feel like rubber bands. I can hardly stand up."

"Mom, isn't the ride just great, though?" Lyn started to laugh as she thought of the hikers up on the trail. In fact, she laughed so hard that she couldn't stop.

"Lyn, it wasn't that funny. I really felt bad for those people; they got drenched. People up top must have smelled them coming before they saw them. Oh, oh! Stop that! Stop it, I say!" Tilli cried out. "Why did you stick that hose with icy cold water down the back of my shirt, Bill? I'm soaked right into my boots!"

"Listen up, ma'am," said Bill Brodie with a chuckle. "'Cause it'll be gittin' hotter as we go down this here trail. You'll be thankin' me in about ten minutes when you're bone dry again. Listen up, everybody! Wet yourselves down good before we git back on our mules; we're in for a hot ride from here."

Everyone was grateful for the box lunches they found inside a cooler placed in the shade of the cottonwood trees. These had been dropped off by pack mules, the ones they'd seen earlier far ahead in the distance.

"All trash goes into the cooler when you're done eatin'," said Bill. "Other pack mules will come up the trail later today, and the trash will be hauled away to the top.

Everything that goes down must go back up. Everything! We leave no trash behind."

"Sure enough, Lyn," said Mel after finishing her lunch. "I wouldn't have believed it, but I'm dry all over."

Lyn, Mel, and Tilli took the hose, which was draped over the mule trough and still flowing with cold water, and poured water down each other's backs, right into their pants and boots, then refilled their bota bags. Everyone laughed and squealed as the icy water poured into their clothes.

"Uh, oh!" said Lyn.

"What? What's 'Uh, oh'?" cried Tilli.

"It's your white shirt, Mom; now that it's drenched, it's transparent!"

"Oh, my god, Lyn, everyone can see my bra and skin."

"I think Bill Brodie knew that when he got you wet."

"Well, that guy's a sleazy good-for-nothing. Wait 'til I nail him." And Tilli took the hose and drenched Bill Brodie as he had his back to her and was talking to another rider.

"Yikes!" he hollered. "Who's doin' that?"

"I just wanted to give a man a taste of his own medicine," said Tilli, laughing.

# Phantom Ranch

Hours more elapsed before the mule riders reached the bottom of the canyon. By now, the walls towered all around and above them. As far as they could see, the South Rim no longer existed. A hot sun pressed down as they saw the Colorado River up close for the first time. No longer a distant ribbon, the river was a raging torrent with back-flipping waves and muddy waters. The power of the rushing river made it nearly impossible to hear anything else.

Bill yelled, "Now, listen up! See that dark hole in the rock ahead of us?"

Everyone in the group looked for the hole and then nodded in Bill's direction.

"You will follow me into and through that hole in the rock. Understand? Do not let your mule stop inside that tunnel. If your mule stops, all the mules will stop, and guess what happens then?"

Lyn yelled, "There'll be a bottleneck inside that dark tunnel."

"You got that right, young lady! So, what are we going to do now?"

Everyone indicated they understood the mules must be kept moving or else there would be chaos. These animals had been through this dark tunnel hundreds of times, and yet, Bill's mule, Mae West, was excited. She jerked her head up and down. She snorted loudly. She pranced a little dance. And before anyone could give it another thought, Bill and Mae West shot into the rock opening.

"Oh, my god," said Lyn as Vacation made a dash for it.

"Oh, my god," repeated Mel as Robert Redford bolted forward.

"Oh, shit!" Tilli said as Gorgeous leaped forward into the black hole.

As all the mules followed, the riders kicked them in the ribs to keep them moving. Inside the tunnel, it was like being in a dark cave. A pinprick of light was ahead, and they moved towards it, but that wasn't all. Bill Brodie hadn't told them what would happen *after* they emerged on the other side.

Lyn, Mel, Tilli, and surely every other rider were momentarily blinded by the blackness inside the rock, but when the animals shot out into the bright sunshine on the other side of this tunnel, immediately ahead was a narrow metal bridge, the bottom of which was covered with sturdy wooden planks. The mules moved quickly over this bridge with inches to spare on either side of their bodies. And, the entire way, the roiling waters of the Colorado River raged deafeningly just a few feet below them.

As Lyn looked ahead, the other side of the river came up suddenly. The mules and riders touched land once more. It was much cooler this close to the river, and it was a relief for everybody.

Bill Brodie had stopped Mae West and waited for everybody to make it across the bridge. "How's everybody doin'?" he asked with a big grin on his face.

Lyn was first to ask, "You told us about the tunnel, but how come you didn't tell us about the bridge?"

"Well, young lady. Why'd I need to? Ya knew you'd

have to cross over, didn't ya?"

Before Lyn could respond, one of the other guys yelled out, "Hell no! I had no idea Phantom Ranch would be on the other side of the Colorado. Nobody told me that."

"Well, my job is to tell you what I think you need to know. The tunnel was enough of a surprise. If I'd told y'all about that bridge, you might not have crossed it. Right?"

Tilli said thoughtfully, "I guess so, Bill; the tunnel was about all I could handle. I can't believe I just did what I did."

"We never know what we're capable of most of the time, ma'am. We don't challenge ourselves enough. Come on, everybody, we're not at Phantom Ranch yet." Bill reined in Mae West and gave her a little kick in the ribs. Everyone followed him along the trail.

"Hi, there!" Someone waved and called out to them. "Soon as you can, come and join us; the water's great!" Riding behind Bill Brodie, Lyn was first to see the small group of people soaking, up to their necks, in a shallow pool nestled in the rocks. The Colorado River raged close by but posed no danger to these bathers.

Mel saw the cold beers they were holding. "Boy, I sure could use one of them!"

Around the bend, Phantom Ranch came into view. The buildings were brown and weather-beaten and looked as if they'd grown out of the canyon soil. The largest building had an enormous chimney built of natural boulders, like those seen along the trail. Smoke was wafting towards a clear blue sky. Next to this building was a corral where other mules were already munching hay. A few lifted their heads and brayed as Bill's group approached. Near the cluster of individual cabins with porches stood a bathroom building that housed cold-water showers.

Bill led them to the corral. "End of the line, folks," he said as he dismounted from Mae West. "Everybody, get off your mules now. Tie your animals to the hitching post; the crew will take care of your animals while you untie your belongings and head to the main lodge with the chimney. You'll be directed from there. Great job riding down today; you've earned a rest. See y'all later at dinner." Bill Brodie proceeded to take care of his mule while young workers hired for the summer came and took care of everyone else's. One young person helped Tilli dismount and told her that she could use the mounting platform in the morning, when they would ride up and out of the canyon.

"I don't think I will be able to stand up straight ever again," Mel rubbed her legs.

"I stink and need a shower," Lyn groaned.

"I was thinking of putting on my swimsuit and joining that group down by the river," Mel nodded in the direction from which they'd come.

"Boy, a beer would go down easy right about now, Mel." Tilli continued, "I can't believe I actually accomplished this ride today. I could cry when I stop to think of all I've missed because of procrastination and fear!"

"Oh, Mom." Lyn and Mel put their arms around her. They stopped on the spot, and their eyes filled with tears as they felt how tired, sweaty, and hungry they were, but most of all, they were happy about this extraordinary day.

And so the conversation went as they entered the lodge. Much to their surprise, it was not primitive at all! Three large illuminated wagon-wheel chandeliers hung from the hand-hewn beams on the ceiling. Preserved wild animal heads hung above the fireplace, which took up one entire end wall. Chairs made from branches and twigs and with leather seats surrounded thick plank tables, which were set for dinner, and the aromas from the adjoining kitchen wafted into this room.

"Forget the swim and beers; I am ravenous, Lyn."

Lyn laughed. "You just want it all, don't you, Sis?"

Listening to the joyous banter between her two daughters, Tilli was so overcome with emotions so that she couldn't speak. The beauty of everything they'd experienced today made her think of Jonathan—he should be here, too!—and Tilli considered telling the girls about him. How much longer was she going to keep Jonathan to herself?

As they continued walking towards their cabin, the girls were chatting and laughing while Tilli quietly pondered her secret. This trip would be perfect if only Jonathan was here with them. She wanted to tell Lyn and Mel. Why couldn't she just let it *out?*

"Mom, we need the key!" Mel called from the cabin door. Tilli put her thoughts aside and returned to reality. She remembered the shiny key fob in her hand and stepped onto the covered porch, which had a glider on it. She unlocked the door. Again, they were surprised by the interior. First, they saw the three freshly made twin beds, then the small round table with three wooden chairs, and on the far wall hung pegs for their clothes. A colorful braided rug lay on the floor. At the picture window hung red-and-white plaid curtains, which could be pulled closed for privacy. Everything coordinated with the woven red and tan wool blankets. A couple of framed prints with western motifs decorated another wall. As if a signal had been given, the three travelers flopped down in unison on the comfortable beds and stretched out.

"I could just go to sleep, Lyn."

"Me, too, Sis, but don't we want to soak in that pool by the river?"

Tilli sighed contentedly. "Let's get cold beers to take with us, but not until we've spent five minutes relaxing."

It wasn't long before, swimsuits on and beers in hand, the three of them walked down to the pool. Some people were leaving, and others had just arrived. They soaked and sipped with the canyon walls towering over them. The river snarled and growled nearby, reminding everyone of its wildness, but in the pool, all was serene. People chatted and exchanged names and talked about where they came from and where they still planned to travel. One couple announced they were seventy years old and were riding down the Grand Canyon for the second time in their lives. The first time had been fifty years before, when they'd come to Arizona from Japan on their honeymoon. Everyone enjoyed a wonderful time before the dinner bell rang in the distance.

"I don't want to say I could eat a horse." Lyn patted her growling stomach.

Mel laughed softly. "I don't know what I am: more tired or more hungry."

"Don't mind saying I could eat a side of beef and sleep like a lamb," added Tilli.

The surprises just kept coming. Dinner included juicy grilled steaks, baked potatoes, garden salads, homemade rolls made on-site, and slow-cooked beans with bacon; delicious chocolate cake was for dessert. The hungry mule riders devoured it all!

"It gits dark early down here," announced Bill Brodie. "Y'all better head for your cabins soon, or y'all be stumbling around in the dark. We only have a generator down here, and it gits shut off soon after dark. Bell will ring at six thirty in the mornin' to git y'all up for breakfast. Mules will be saddled and ready to hit the trail at eight. Good night, everybody." Bill headed out the door.

"Jeez! Lyn and Mel, I'm stuffed and can't even think about breakfast."

"I hope I have enough energy to walk to our cabin!" Mel groaned.

# Kaibab Trail

The next day they awoke to the sounds of the triangle being rung next to the lodge. "Morning," said Lyn as she stretched leisurely, testing for sore muscles; she uttered a sigh. "Did you hear the thunder last night?"

"You know, at first, I wasn't sure what it was. The sounds kept booming and echoing all around these rocks and cliffs; it was the most dramatic display of thunder I've heard in my life. We're down one mile in this canyon, and there are so many surfaces for thunder to bounce off," Mel replied.

"Well, from the light coming around the curtain at the window, it looks like it'll be another sunny day in paradise," said Tilli.

"I'm putting on my jeans and heading to the bath house; nature's calling." Mel was already on her feet.

"I'll be right behind you, Sis. I thought I'd wake up stiff and sore, but amazingly I feel refreshed. I wonder what's for breakfast."

Tilli said, "You know, girls, I'm getting hungry, too, and I'd sure like a cup of coffee. Yesterday was beyond anything I could have dreamed. I wonder what new experiences we'll have today. You two go ahead; I'm going to just lie here and stare at the ceiling and stretch my leg muscles before I get up."

After a hearty breakfast, they got their things together and headed out to the corral, where the mules were saddled up and waiting.

"Mornin', y'all. Everybody got water? Sunblock on? How y'all feeling this morning?" Bill Brodie asked each person individually while he personally checked saddle cinches and gear.

Tilli didn't think much about the slight headache she woke up with, so she didn't mention it; she told herself it was nothing. And, she was thinking, perhaps she shouldn't have had the second mug of coffee, but that thought was fleeting, too.

"Now, listen up, everybody!" Bill yelled and made sure he got their attention. "Yesterday we rode down on the Bright Angel trail; today, we go up the Kaibab, it's an old Injun trail, steep but shorter, and we'll be up at the South Rim by one o'clock. Along the way, there'll be no Indian Garden where we or the animals can refresh and rest up, so make sure y'all filled your bota bags to the brim. Everybody's got a granola bar and an apple: that's all you'll need for this ride. Ready for the bridge and tunnel? Then, let's move on out!" Bill reined in Mae West, gave her a little nudge, and the riders followed in the same order in which they'd come down.

The bridge of yesterday was no problem this morning. The hole in the rock and totally black tunnel were now second nature, but next, they all turned in another direction from yesterday's, and the climb began immediately.

"I don't know how many times I've told those cowhands at Phantom Ranch not to feed baked beans to the mules," said Bill Brodie after several mules had let off large amounts of gas. The riders were laughing at these emissions.

"Well, no wonder they're passing gas; look how steep this trail is," said Lyn.

Steep wasn't the word for it; for one thing, this trail was wide open to the sun, and there wasn't anything with leaves on it anywhere in sight. The footing alternated among being gravelly, rocky, or sandy and was never friendly. The sure-footed mules strained to make progress while at the same time carrying their human burdens. And it got hot!

"I feel dizzy," Tilli imagined herself rolling off Gorgeous.

"Bill, stop a minute; my mother doesn't feel well!" shouted Lyn.

"What's up?"

"She's dizzy, Bill."

"There's a slight overhang up ahead and a large cactus that's casting a shadow; we'll stop there." Bill led them just off the trail to a spot suggesting a sliver of relief from the merciless sun.

"I had a little headache before we left, Bill, but I didn't think much about it."

"Well, ya shoulda told me! That's why I ask how's everybody doin'. It wasn't a nicety, ma'am; I ask 'cause I want to know everybody's feeling okay." Tilli wanted to get off Gorgeous, but she was afraid she wouldn't be able to get back on—no mounting steps up here.

As Bill assisted her dismount, he said, "Don't you worry about gittin' back on this here mule. If we have to, we'll toss you on broadside and haul you up like a sack of grain." He helped her sit with her back against the rocky outcropping next to the tall skinny cactus, and then waved his broad-brimmed hat back and forth in front of her. He even stood so his body cast a shadow across her face. Then he removed her hat and poured water over her head, and went so far as to soak her bandana, which he wrapped around her neck. "Feelin' better now, ma'am?"

"Yes, thanks; I guess I shouldn't have had those two mugs of coffee."

"Yup! Coffee'll do it every time. I don't know why they serve it to folks when they know they'll get dehydrated on this here ride up the canyon." Bill looked around at the other riders and asked if they were all right. Everyone was hot, but fine otherwise.

"Okay, ma'am, here's some water. Don't gulp, though. Ya hear?" After ten minutes of remaining stationary in the intense sunshine, everybody, including the mules, was eager to get up the Kaibab to the top.

Tilli was too embarrassed to make a fuss about getting back onto her mule. Bill gave her ten fingers, a big upward shove, and somehow, by sheer willpower, Tilli miraculously got back on. The riders pretty much rode along in silence as their mules concentrated on their footing

Once back at the South Rim, the only things the mule skinners wanted to do were dismount, find shade, and get a cold drink. "Listen up; hold on!" Bill Brodie hollered at a couple of riders who were already walking away. "Ya forgot your re-wards; git back here!" Bill handed each rider a scrolled piece of paper tied with a red ribbon.

Once back in their room at the El Tovar Hotel, the sisters unrolled their scrolls.

"It's an Official Mule Skinner's Certificate," Mel read aloud.

"I'm going to frame mine and hang it on the wall," replied Tilli. "We sure earned these, girls! Now, I'm drawing a bath and have no idea when you'll see me next. I ache all over."

"We're taking naps, Mom; wake us in time for dinner."

# Marble Canyon

The massive concrete wall of the Glen Canyon Dam in Page, Arizona, which holds back the waters of Lake Powell, rose over them as the rafters boarded the three pontoon boats. Each khaki-colored craft carried six people, who sat perched on the wide, rounded rims. A rope ran through loops attached to the top of this rubber seating area so rafters could hold on to something. Each craft had a rugged oarsman, who was seated on a wooden plank stretched across from side to side. His job was to man the heavy, ten-foot-long wooden oars. These boats had been built for river navigation by American troops in Vietnam; they were not built for speed.

"I wonder what Mother Nature has in store for us today," queried Tilli.

Lyn assured her, "It's supposed to be a milquetoast river-running trip, Mom."

"Well, after our mule ride two days ago, I'm ready for anything at this point," Tilli smiled.

Marble Canyon's walls rose as smooth, sheer cliffs. At the narrowest point in the canyon, the builders had constructed the dam; but after the pontoon boats had glided through the glassy waters and around a bend, the canyon opened up, and more sunlight filtered onto them. A tiny breeze fluttered. With no motor noise and only the dipping of the oars, the riders spoke in whispers.

"My name's Garth," their oarsman boomed in a loud

voice, which reverberated all around them as it echoed from the towering cliffs.

The peace of their surroundings had put Mel into a trance; she was unaware she'd been meditating. When Garth spoke to Mel, it seemed blasphemous for anything loud to interrupt the cathedral-like peace of their surroundings, but after Garth introduced himself, the riders' tongues loosened, and others began to chat. Time elapsed as gently as the waters in the river.

Mel exclaimed, "Oh, there's a waterfall up ahead."

"Well, let's row on over there," replied Garth. "Who wants to take a shower?"

Several people were wearing bathing suits, and even those who had on shorts and t-shirts didn't mind getting wet. Garth rowed over to the skinny waterfall that was coming out of a fissure in the rock face and got the stern end of the pontoon boat just so it was under the waterfall.

"Oh, Garth, why didn't you tell us it would be cold?" squealed a woman.

Her remark didn't keep others from wanting to get under the waterfall, so they were there for a while until everyone who wanted a shower got one. Other waterfalls cascaded throughout the canyon, but Garth and the other pontoon rowers steered by them.

The sun rose higher as noontime approached, and the shadows, which had provided shade earlier in the day, were now gone; it was still pleasant because the cold water of the Colorado River provided relief from the heat.

"Time for lunch," announced Garth.

The other two pontoon boats had pulled up on a sandy bank of the river, and that's where Garth headed.

"We'll be here about an hour, and if anyone wants to

take a dip in the river, this is as good a place as any." From the cooler stored in the bottom of his pontoon boat, Garth took out lunches and passed them around.

"Lyn, this is my cup of tea. Sunny, but not too sunny. Breezy, but not too breezy. Calm waters, serene surroundings. It couldn't be more perfect!" Mel had untied her sneakers and was wiggling her bare feet into the soft beach sand; she was lying on her back with her head cradled in her arms. "I could just fall asleep here."

"It is lovely, isn't it, girls? The water is as calm as a mill pond." Tilli was happy.

After lunch, Garth called out to get their attention, "Okay, everybody, before we leave the beach, who's discovered the petroglyphs and pictographs?"

Several people had been walking around the edges of the beach, where it met the desert varnish on the sheer cliffs of red sandstone.

"Oh, look, Mom. Wonder what these squiggles mean?" Mel pointed at circular lines on the rock face.

They also saw what clearly represented a herd of antelope scratched into the blackened coating on the smooth rock. Was it a hunting scene?

"Lyn, here's one that looks like someone drew a maze. And how about these stick-like people?"

Garth overheard and hollered out to Lyn, "Those stick-like *people* are called anthropomorphic figures. Rock-art people have been trying to interpret images like these for many years."

Some of the glyphs defied interpretation, as they'd been drawn low on the cliff wall and were partly covered by the beach sand, while other drawings, higher up on the rock face, were now in shadow.

"How did the ancient people reach those higher places on the rock; who were they, and where did they go?" Tilli questioned no one in particular.

Tilli had only seen pictographs in books. She looked around in all directions and tried to gather up the entire scene and store it in her mind for future retrieval—for those days when she would be back in Hamlet, and life would have returned to normal. The sheerness of the canyon walls, the ripples in the river, the soft sand underfoot, and the intense pleasure of being out in this wilderness with her daughters brought tears to her eyes.

"How sad your father isn't here to experience this with us, girls."

Lyn had stepped away from the rock to get a better look. "Look up there, Mom, more drawings: there's a sun, some handprints, and more animals. One looks like a big snake. Maybe the ancient people were on a hunt here, and these symbols represent the animals they killed. Interesting to think we're here today on the very spot where Native people hunted, perhaps a thousand or more years ago. I've read that there are also cliff dwellings in the Grand Canyon, but their access is restricted. I think only Native Americans and archaeologists are allowed to go near those sites." Lyn had her arm around her mother's shoulders and gave her a comforting squeeze.

By four o'clock, the pontoon boats had reached the spot where Marble Canyon opened into the Grand Canyon. Ahead of them bobbed flotation devices strung across the river from one canyon wall to the other to indicate the end of their trip.

Garth spoke, "Before we disembark, I'd like everyone to look down into the river and tell me what you see."

"There's a large dark shape down there. What is it?" Mel asked.

Garth answered. "This is the spot where a steam locomotive sank into the river. There used to be a railroad track running along this side of Marble Canyon, and one day, about a hundred years ago, the river raged and undermined the tracks. The engine was never retrieved. The dams along this river now control its flow, so events like that will never happen again. If we went around another bend or two, you would see a very different river from what you've experienced today.

"Folks, the gravel parking lot is off to your left, and your bus is waiting to take you back to the South Rim, where we started from this morning. Hope y'all had a good time today. Thanks for choosing Marble Canyon Outfitters."

As Mel, Lyn, and Tilli walked the short distance to their bus, they thought about that different river, where they had crossed the narrow bridge to Phantom Ranch on the backs of mules over the raging torrents of the Colorado. Even though they knew there were courageous river runners looking for heart-stopping excitement, battling those untamed waters gladly, the milquetoast float trip on Marble Canyon had been perfect for them.

# 5 Cedar Street

"Another cup of coffee, Lyn?"

"Sure, Mom, don't mind if I do. It's nice not to have to rush back to work. I'm happy to have another week off, and you, Mel, have three more weeks to play in the garden with Mom. You're so lucky!"

"Well, you should take up teaching school."

"Umm. No, thank you! I like my job just fine. I don't know how you do it, Mel. Don't those little rug rats ever get to you?"

"Now, now! I would never refer to all my children that way. Sure, sometimes a few can and do get out of control. For the most part, teaching third graders is very rewarding; otherwise, I wouldn't have been doing it for fifteen years." Mel took another bite of her Weetabix with sliced bananas and sipped her coffee. "But frequent school breaks do help. Funny, when I was a child, I always thought kids had school vacation because they needed a break; it never occurred to me then that teachers needed the R and R every bit as much, except most of them didn't get a break, what with required professional development and summer jobs needed to pay their bills."

"Yes, Mel, I guess our perspectives change with time. Wonder how you'll feel once the children you've had in your classroom come back for parent-teacher conferences with their own children."

"I think, Lyn, you've asked me that very question more

than once!"

"I seem to remember your saying it would be time to retire when that happens. So, what do we do now that we've come back from our first vacation? Wasn't it just great? Mom, what did you think about the hot-air balloon ride in Sedona, the mule trip to Phantom Ranch, and our Marble Canyon float trip?"

"I've looked at our pictures several times already," Tilli said, "and can't wait to see more of the Southwest the next time we travel. So glad you decided to get a digital camera before we left. Do you girls realize we took over two hundred pictures? Oh, I've been reading the book I bought at the Sedona Bookman, *Earth Medicine*, by Jamie Sams. Here's something from the Navajo that spoke to me. I'd like to share it with you. Now, where's that page? Oh, here; here it is:

*May my house be in harmony*
*From my head, may it be happy*
*To my feet, may it be happy*
*Where I lie, may it be happy*
*All above me, may it be happy*
*All around me, may it be happy.*

"Navajo thoughts are about walking one's path in the beauty way and being content with whatever life brings. Jamie Sams also wrote about the Navajo way of sharing whatever food the hunt brought in. When there was plenty, everyone partook of that, and when times were harsh and food was scarce, everyone went hungry to-gether. No one was left out of the tribal circle. By sharing, the circle was strengthened. It made me think of Mel's volunteering at the food pantry and how people contribute to its shelves, so there's always something for those in need. Lyn, you planned our vacation like a pro. I am so proud of you!"

Lyn said, "Well, during Mel's October break from school, we could take a drive on the Blue Ridge Parkway and go to Asheville, North Carolina, and back. Think about it, Mom. Anyway, I'm heading to the mall to look for a new pair of shoes. Anybody want to come?"

"No, Lyn, that's fine," Tilli replied. "You go ahead. I want to walk to the grocery store to get a few items, and I need some fresh air." Tilli headed out the front door, and they could hear it closing softly.

Mel stood up. "I'm planning on pruning one of the shrubs in the side yard; it's overgrown and ungainly, but I'll have to look in one of Mom's gardening books for instructions so I don't hurt the poor thing."

Lyn asked, "Do you need me to bring back anything from the mall? There are all kinds of sales mentioned in this flyer from the *Hamlet Weekly*. Oh, and how about we go to the Tally Ho Club for burgers tonight? We're out of practice from not having to cook for all those days."

"Mom, don't forget the milk and maybe some bananas." Lyn hollered to Tilli, then realized her mother had already left. "Okay, I like the Tally Ho, Mel. Let's do it! I can't imagine Mom saying she wouldn't want to go with us, but there won't be any green chili cheeseburgers around here!"

Mel put the breakfast dishes in the dishwasher and wiped the kitchen counters. She'd always liked her grandparents' house, which had become her parents' house, and which now belonged to the three of them together. It had a great layout and was just spacious enough without the rooms feeling crowded. Plus, it was close to everything, including the commuter rail into Boston, for those times she might want to go into the city.

Since their father died, they'd donated some of the contents of this house to the local thrift shop connected with one of the churches, and they'd given a few pieces of outdated furniture from her grandparents to the Salvation Army. Clearing out those items had made room for belongings Mel had brought back after she'd sold her townhouse. She hadn't regretted selling it while Lyn had decided to remain in her condo. Since the death of their father, she and Lyn had become a good support system for their mother. This house was plenty big enough if Lyn should decide to move back in.

Mel was just about to take the first gardening book off the shelf when the telephone rang in the den. Her mother had only two hard-wired phones in the house: a wall phone in the kitchen and this portable one on a small table in the den.

"Hello?"

"Mel?"

"Yes, who's this?" She wasn't certain of the man's voice on the other end.

"It's Mark. Did I get you at a bad time? I can call again."

"No. No, Mark. This is a good time. How are you?"

"I was about to ask you the same question, Mel. I've been thinking about you since the repast after your father's funeral. And I've tried calling a few times, but your phone number was disconnected. So, I looked up this number. Glad I reached you."

"Well, Mark, I decided to sell my townhouse some

months ago and moved back home. Lyn and I were away on vacation with our mother, and we just got back. I still haven't set up an answering machine at this number. My parents never believed in gadgets, as they called an answering machine."

Mark chuckled. "I know what you mean; my folks never moved into the twenty-first century either."

"Since my father died, I've taken on the responsibility of helping my mother with the gardens while Lyn cuts the grass. Lyn kept her condominium but comes over here almost every day. I was trying to simplify my life and couldn't think of any reason not to come back home to live."

"What about meeting me for that cup of coffee we talked about?"

"I'd like that, Mark; I was wondering when you might call. Want to meet at the Honey Bun some morning?"

"How about breakfast there tomorrow, say, around eight?"

"That's perfect, Mark; I'll look forward to it."

After Mel hung up, she just sat there. All sorts of thoughts about Mark began to run through her head. Somehow, the pruning of the shrub had lost its importance. "Oh, I can do it any time," she said aloud to the four walls.

It wasn't too long before Lyn returned from shopping. Mel knew immediately it was Lyn because of the way she stomped around downstairs. Well, to be fair, Lyn didn't actually stomp, but it was the sound of her footfalls and the manner in which she closed the front door.

"Hi, I'm up here in the den."

"Be right up, Sis." Lyn carried a shopping bag. "I found

a nice pair, and they were on sale, my favorite brand." Lyn pointed to her feet.

"Oh, you've got them on already!"

"Yup! My old pair is in the bag. These are so comfortable, Mel; try them."

"Your foot is larger than mine, Lyn; they're way too big."

"Well, pardon me. Take them off right away; I don't want them stretched out."

Mel laughed, "Lyn, I can't stretch them out if they're too big, silly."

"I know, I just said that because you don't like them."

"Now, you're really being goofy, Lyn. I never said that. I do like them; they're nice. They suit you perfectly, so never mind what I think anyway. Mark called."

"Oh, ho! That's why you're so uppity."

"No, I'm not; I'm just happy. After all these months, I didn't think I'd hear from him again." Mel said.

"So, when are you two getting married?"

"Lyn!" Mel laughed again. "You're too much! We're having breakfast at the Honey Bun at eight tomorrow morning."

"Oh, can I come, Sis?"

"No! Of course not."

"I'm joking, Mel. I don't want to come, that is, unless he's tall, handsome, and intelligent. Then he was probably meant for me, according to Mom."

"No, he's not particularly tall. Five feet eight or so, I think, if I remember correctly. He's got sandy blond hair, and yes, I think he's intelligent. Wait! Didn't you meet him at Daddy's memorial visitation?"

"No, he came and went before I could size him up."

Mel smiled. "Lyn, you're just too much."

"So, what did you learn from the gardening book about pruning the shrub?"

"Oh, the shrub, I never got to it."

"Well, I bought something else at the mall." Lyn pulled a narrow, two-foot-long wooden sign out of the bag and held it up. It was engraved and painted in gold letters and attributed to Eleanor Roosevelt: *You must do the thing you think you cannot do!* "I couldn't resist it, Mel; it so reminded me of our vacation to the Southwest. Now we just need to hang it up in the right spot."

"After all the clutter we've cleaned out of this house, you couldn't resist bringing that thing home," said Mel.

"I bought it for Mom."

# Matilda's Walk

"What was I thinking when I said I was walking to the grocery store and back?" Tilli thought to herself as she returned a wave to people that she knew across the street and stopped to chat with friendly folks from the village. It was taking her a long time to get a bottle of milk. And, then along came her gardening friend, Margaret Flannery, who Tilli hadn't seen since the gathering at her house after Bertie's funeral.

"Hi there, Tilli. How nice to see you out walking."

"Well, we needed a few things, and the weather's nice today, not so hot and humid as last week. How are you, Margaret?"

"Tilli, I haven't stopped thinking about you since Bertie died. I want to know how you and the girls are getting on?"

"Oh, we're managing. For months, I was a wreck—we all were! But we just came back from a wonderful trip to the Southwest, somewhere I've always wanted to go. Bertie never wanted to fly, although he did go up with me in a hot-air balloon once. The airplane flight was marvelous; I had a window seat and never stopped being amazed at all those clouds. When the sky cleared, I could see circles and squares on the ground, over thirty thousand feet below! It was my second time flying, Margaret; can you imagine that?"

Margaret laughed as she patted Tilli's arm. "You've

become a jetsetter, Tilli!"

"Well, I wouldn't go so far as to say that, Margaret, but it did feel good to get out of Hamlet for a while. Good to see you. Stop over for a cup of tea sometime. I'm home now until Lyn plans another get-away for the three of us, maybe the Blue Ridge Parkway to Asheville in the fall. Mel sold her townhouse and is living with me now while Lyn kept her condo. She's over a lot, though, and certainly, it is nice not to be alone."

"You're so fortunate to have them, Tilli. I will stop by soon."

As Tilli continued on her way, her thoughts turned to Jonathan. How fortunate she'd be when he would be in her life, too. Now that Bertie was no longer at her side making all the decisions, she could do anything she wanted. Funny how the freedom to choose filled her with fear. Fortunately, she didn't have to worry about how to manage the finances; she'd taken care of all that since she married Bertie, and even though the income from his shoe repair shop had dwindled considerably over time, their thrifty living had left enough so she didn't have to worry. It would be a fine day when the sale of Peach of a Sole was finalized. The process of selling a piece of commercial real estate was taking longer and was far more complicated than she could have imagined.

As Tilli walked past the old church on the green, she thought to herself, "Perhaps I'll call that new pastor and make an appointment to talk with him. He seemed like a nice enough young man when he took care of Bertie's graveside service." She remembered what Ned, the balloon operator in Arizona, had said about the importance of helping others; there must be volunteer opportunities here. Once, years ago, this church had been their second home, as Lyn had said when she was a little girl. The Mac-Innes family had been pillars here for decades, but after Lyn and Mel had grown up and moved out of the house, she and Bertie gradually stopped attending.

She continued her walk past the annex of the local community college, where Spanish conversation lessons were currently posted on the marquee. "If I keep visiting the Southwest, I might need to learn a bit of Spanish," she thought.

She walked and continued to ponder life's possibilities. Out of the blue, Bertie's voice cut in: "Now, why would you want to do such silly things? You're too old to start in new directions, Tilli; stick with the familiar. I don't think you'll like studying. Remember the adage about teaching an old dog new tricks? Remember doing home-work? Now, Tilli, listen to me; I know best."

Tilli paused on the sidewalk and realized her footsteps had somehow led her to the AAA office. A colorful sign promoting an upcoming safari in Africa was in the window. A second poster showed a woman riding a camel in Egypt. Attractive and interesting pictures of river cruises and European tours were lined up against the window-pane. Though she and the girls had enjoyed their vacation immensely, she realized the places she would want to visit might not appeal to them, but, unlike Bertie, they would never stand in the way of her realizing her dreams. Oh, and then, of course, there was Jonathan! Finding him re-mained number one on her list. She wondered how diffi-cult it would be. Once again, she considered that it might be the right time to share Jonathan with Lyn and Mel.

# Take Five

"Ooh, there's a jazz concert playing Saturday night at Scullers in Boston." Lyn said. " Want to go, Mel?"

"Mark and I have plans to go out for dinner, Lyn; otherwise, I'd love to. Who else could you ask to go?"

"Well, there's Tom, Dick, and Harry."

"Lyn, come on."

"Don't think about it for a minute; I'll be fine. Have a great dinner with Mark. I mean it, Sis. Go, go, go!"

Lyn was not about to miss this concert. She knew jazz wasn't her mother's favorite music, so she decided to go alone. After all, she was an independent woman, mature, and of such an age that most men probably wouldn't even give her a second glance, so she'd be safe in Boston without a bodyguard.

As Lyn walked through the well-lit parking garage next to the hotel that housed Scullers Jazz Club, she felt good to be in the city again. She hadn't worn her black crepe dress in a long time and was happy she'd bought the new high heels.

The escalator to the second floor was inside a soaring atrium that rose ten stories to the roof. With her head tilted back, she looked all the way up to the skylight and smiled because nothing had stood in the way of her going out alone. "Who cares!" she said aloud when she saw there wasn't anyone within earshot.

Tonight's musicians included Elmira Jordan, a young

Asian-American woman who played the saxophone as if it were an extension of her own body. Also, Joe and Pete Marvin would be playing with their terrific jazz band. After fifty years on the scene, the Marvins were considered "Boston's Jazz Band." As Lyn entered the intimate nightclub, she saw the scullers out on the Charles, most likely from Harvard's boat house across the river. They were practicing for the Head of the Charles, a yearly race event, which was a popular tradition. The setting sun was casting lengthening shadows along the river, and the city's lights were coming on—a lovely sight.

Lyn zigzagged her way among the maze of impossibly small round tables and bentwood chairs, which were almost all occupied, 'til she found one empty seat. A waitress came almost immediately to ask what she wanted. Everyone was chatting, waiting for the program to start, and Lyn had to raise her voice to be heard by the waitress.

"I'll have Dewar's with ginger ale and a splash of soda, please," said Lyn.

The man immediately at her left elbow, whom she hadn't paid any attention to when she sat down, voiced his opinion, "Why pollute good Scotch?"

"I beg your pardon?" Lyn hadn't expected a stranger to get familiar.

"Dewar's: why add ginger ale to it?" he replied in a snooty tone.

She wanted to tell him to mind his own business. Right away, she was reminded of Roger, and that certainly wasn't a good beginning—if there was to be any sort of a beginning—to sharing an evening with a total stranger. She noticed the intimacy of this jazz club; its tiny tables with chairs almost touching were now the reason his knees were rubbing against her left leg. She shifted in her seat while looking around the room for another seat. Not a chance; the place was packed.

"I suppose I could make negative comments about your drink, but I'm too polite."

"Ha, ha!" He chuckled good-naturedly. "I didn't mean to act out of order. I'll admit it was a poor conversation opener. Please don't be offended. My name's Paul."

She told herself to relax, "Hi, Paul; I'm Lyn."

"The program's so good this evening that I had to come into town."

"Oh, where do you live?" Lyn's drink had arrived, and they clinked glasses. All was okay now that she saw he really wasn't like Roger.

"Marblehead. I've been there for about ten years now, and every once in a great while, I make my way into the big city just to get connected to someplace other than the countryside and suburbs. I'm content in Marblehead. Do you like to sail? Again, don't misunderstand me, Lyn; I'm only making conversation."

"I've never been sailing. I live in Hamlet, which is inland; the focus there is more on horses and riding, not that I'm much into riding. I just came back from the Southwest, though, and my sister and I, along with our mother, rode mules down to Phantom Ranch at the bottom of the Grand Canyon. Ever done that?"

The band was tuning up, and their first set was about to begin. The crowd was settling in for the evening, and conversations were more muted with anticipation.

"No, Lyn. That's something I've never even considered. It must have been special."

The Marvins' first number was a favorite of Lyn's, but

with her leg rubbing against Paul's knees, she still thought of fleeing. Too many people, too close together. Why was she so skittish? Again, thoughts of Roger, but just as quickly, they flew away. The band was great. The Marvins played for about forty-five minutes, and then it was time for a short break. Waitresses seized this opportunity to squeeze themselves among the tables, clear away dirty glasses, and take new drink orders. Some people went to the powder rooms.

As Paul stood up, Lyn noticed his dark, wavy hair, kind smile, and good quality clothes—maybe Brooks Brothers.

It felt good to stretch. Lyn saw that he was tall, slim, physically fit, and either her age or a bit older. Good looking, she thought.

"I'm just going to the lobby for some air; it's a bit close in here, don't you think? Want to join me, Lyn?"

"You're right, Paul. It's because the club is packed."

People milled about in the lobby, where someone had set up a table with CDs, so fans could buy copies of music pre-recorded by tonight's jazz musicians.

"Do you come to Sculler's often?" he asked.

"No, actually, I haven't been into Boston in more than two years. My former husband and I used to come in occasionally, whenever I could persuade him, that is. He didn't like jazz; he was more into elevator music."

"That's funny, Lyn. My former girlfriend also didn't like jazz, so I came in alone a few times, but I haven't been to Scullers in quite a while. Something urged me to come tonight."

"Are you married, Paul?"

"No, never been caught."

"I thought it was the other way around—you know—guy catches girl." Lyn realized she'd been bold to ask him if he were married, but she'd heard of men taking off their wedding bands and then hitting on single women. She wasn't about to have that happen! Well, he was just a guy at her table, and why should she care? After all, she'd certainly never see him again after this evening's program.

The lights dimmed a couple of times, indicating the next set was about to begin. People headed back into the clubroom; Paul and Lyn followed and re-took their seats. Knees and legs rubbed. Lyn felt comfortable with him. He wouldn't be interested in pursuing anything after this evening. She hadn't gotten his last name, and she hadn't given hers. She forgot about everything but enjoying her favorite music. Lyn had never experienced any musician who got as intimate with an instrument as when twenty-year-old Elmira Jordan played on her saxophone. All too soon, she was given a standing ovation.

After the applause died down, the final musical group of the evening took to the tiny stage. After a couple of numbers, the lead player asked, "Anyone have anything they'd like to hear before we close our set this evening?"

"How about 'Take Five' by Dave Brubeck, please?" Paul requested. He leaned over to Lyn and whispered in her ear, "It's my favorite."

She felt his breath on her neck, and goosebumps shimmied all the way down her shoulders to her fingertips.

Afterward, when the lights came up, couples gathered up their belongings, and people jostled one another, heading towards the escalator.

Lyn recalled his warm breath and the touch of his lips on her ear as she walked through the lobby—quickly—

heading towards the escalator. She didn't want to give Paul another opportunity to say something to her; she sensed him keeping up—a very determined guy. She had enjoyed this evening, but her one thought now was getting to her car and driving home. His familiarity had raised emotions she hadn't felt for some time, and she was afraid of starting something. Here was the revolving door leading to the parking garage. A few steps more, and she'd avoid any complications.

"Will I see you again, Lyn?" Paul asked.

"No!" was her first thought. "Why spoil a perfect evening?" was her second thought.

But she replied, "I'd like that, Paul."

# Gardening 101

The next Saturday morning, Mel was in the den looking through the gardening books in her mother's collection, with the purpose of finally learning how to prune the overgrown shrub in the side garden. Her mother had decided to walk over to the church on the green to talk to the pastor about possible ways she could volunteer and help others.

Identifying the shrub had been easy, as her mother had everything labeled, either with small metal signs placed near the bases of flowers and plants or, in this case, a wired-on metal tag affixed to one of the branches. She had determined it was a *Syringa vulgaris*, or common lilac. Her mother had a large collection of books on herbs, organic vegetables, fruits for the home garden, perennials, houseplants, interior flower arranging, trees, wildflowers, garden design and layout, the color wheel and a garden, and finally, a book on pruning and training techniques.

Her mother had wedged the many volumes tightly into the cases, and Mel had to wiggle the pruning techniques book away from *A Year in Your Garden: Month by Month*, which appeared to be a monthly gardening calendar.

Since Lyn was at the Hamlet Community Arts Center preparing for the opening of a new show this Saturday morning, Mel thought it was the perfect time to get the pruning job done. Mel planned to have the brush picked up by the time Lyn came over, so her sister could mow the lawn.

As so often happens in libraries, Mel became curious. She found herself thumbing through one gardening book with lots of colorful pictures and thinking about which flowers she had never seen before and which might look nice in their garden. She turned to the zone map at the front of this particular book and noticed some of these beautiful flowers, such as gardenias and camellias, would not grow outdoors in their region. She picked up the next book and looked at the color wheel. She always thought of a color wheel as having to do with painting or decorating and hadn't thought about how the same principles applied to designing a garden. She hadn't considered her mother to be an artist, but now Mel saw Tilli was exactly that.

"No wonder everything out there looks harmonious and as if it belongs there," Mel said aloud.

The longer Mel read about gardening, the more interested she became. Now she had three or four books on the coffee table, and she'd put little scraps of paper into them to mark certain pages she planned to revisit. She'd found out how to prune lilacs and learned it was too late to do it this year. So, she took *A Year in Your Garden: Month by Month* down from its shelf, thinking she would put the pruning of the lilac into next spring's calendar after it had bloomed.

"What a treasure chest of helpful garden information. I had no idea Mom kept such an accurate calendar of things to do in the garden, month by month, as well as a log of what vegetables she planted and where. This will be a big help to me as I learn how to help Mom take care of her plants," Mel voiced her thoughts.

Mel left the gardening calendar book open on the coffee table and went to the kitchen to make a cup of tea. While she was waiting for the kettle to come to a boil, she looked out the kitchen window into the south side of the garden. Now she understood why her mother had chosen day lilies and other sun-loving plants for this side of the house. The kettle whistled, and Mel poured water over the little mesh bob filled with loose English breakfast tea leaves. She set the stove timer for five minutes and went back upstairs to the den.

Turning to the next page, which was blank, she almost closed the book, thinking she had read her mother's final entry, when she noticed her mother had written more after several blank pages.

"Why would Mom have skipped pages?" Mel wondered aloud.

Mel was surprised to see her mom had made notations all the way to the very last page. The kitchen timer rang and rang.

"Oh, the tea!" Mel went downstairs and shut off the timer, took out the tea bob, and brought her cup back to the den. She sat on the sofa and sipped. She picked up the gardening calendar book again and turned to read the first page after the blank one.

"Oh, Mom, you're the last person I would have thought would keep a diary." Mel gave out a soft whistle.

Downstairs, the front door opened and closed, and then footsteps. "It's me: Lyn."

"I'm in the den, Lyn. The kettle is still hot if you want to pour tea."

"Great. I'll be up in a jiff, Sis. Wait 'til you hear some great news."

"It can't be any greater than the news I have for you."

Mel and Lyn sat in the den for a long time. Together, they read the entry about Jonathan several times; how sad that their mother had held this in for decades. There were questions to ask and conversations they could share if she were willing to talk. Of course, learning about Jonathan, their brother, was wonderful news! Since the diary was found by accident, their mother shouldn't be angry.

# A Discovery

"Spanish, that's what I need to learn if I'm going to be traveling to the Southwest. I've signed up for classes at the community college starting in September. I have to say I feel comfortable going back to school. My class will be on Monday evenings from five to seven o'clock." Tilli was beaming at the breakfast table as she shared this news with Lyn and Mel.

"Of course, I'm in full agreement about going to school at any age, Mom," responded Mel. "You'll have fun, and I've read somewhere it's good to challenge our brains by learning something unfamiliar; it creates new connectors, which helps to keep our memory sharp."

"You'll meet new people, too, and who knows, a tall, dark, and handsome widower might just be sitting next to you." Sipping her coffee, Lyn couldn't resist bringing that topic up.

"Okay, enough! If you girls think I'm looking to hitch myself up to another man in this lifetime, you are way off target. I loved your father, but one husband was quite enough! Besides, now's the time for me to live *my* life."

"Bravo, Mom!" cheered Mel. "You go, girl!"

"Anyway, the reason I'm bringing up my Spanish class this morning is that I know Lyn probably wants to plan another trip for us in October during Mel's break from school. Columbus' birthday week, I think? Although I know I won't need Spanish on that particular road trip, it's still good to get started, so I'm ready the next time we head to Utah or New Mexico." Tilli took a bite of her toast.

"Yes, Mom," said Lyn, "I've been looking at a road trip on the Blue Ridge Parkway down to Asheville, North Carolina. It's a pleasant drive, no truck traffic, and there are two nice park lodges along the way where we can spend the nights without having to drive off the ridge into distant towns. What do you think, Mel? We could share the driving."

Mel had risen from the table to refill her mug. "Sure, Lyn, if Mom wants to go there, it's absolutely okay with me. Anyway, she'll have that week off, too, as the community college will be closed. By the way, Mom, how was your talk with the minister at the church in town?"

"Yes, I did go into Hamlet, but rather than visit the minister at the church on the green, I had a talk with the new priest, Father Thomas, at St. Francis Church. Father Thomas was very kind; we had a great first meeting. He's already working hard to find opportunities for parishioners to volunteer in the greater community—outside the church—because he knows there are people in need who may not have any religious affiliation.

"I told him I'd been a Catholic before I met your father and all about how your father wouldn't take up the Catholic faith since he was a Protestant. I explained how his family had been long-time members of the local parish church, but now that he was gone, I wanted to see if I could rejoin the faith I'd been raised in.

"Long story short, after he shared with me all of the volunteer opportunities, I told him I'd like to try visiting elders in Hamlet Nursing Home. Next week, I'll be meeting with the director to see what I can do to help. I've really given this some hard thought, as I don't have the best memories of visiting your grandmother in that home. It will be a test of strength to see if I can overcome my hard feelings about grandma. Your father's mother was miserable there; every chance she had, she let me know it!

"In the meantime, Father Thomas is planning a pilgrimage to the Holy Land for next January. I've always wanted to visit that part of the world. Now, there's someplace I wouldn't want to visit without being part of a group."

"Mom, you are amazing! I'm so proud of you for reaching out to find ways to make positive impacts in the community, and a pilgrimage—Wow!"

Mel and Lyn made eye contact across the table, waiting for a pause in the conversation. At last, Mel had a chance to bring up the topic of Jonathan. She'd waited a couple of weeks since finding the diaries, until all three of them could be together, and she didn't want to lose this opportunity.

"Mom," she said, followed by a pause as Mel tried to get her mother's full attention. "Lyn and I have had something on our minds for a couple of weeks now, and this seems as good a time as any to bring up the topic."

"Yes?" asked Tilli. She had started reading clues to fill in the blanks on the crossword puzzle in the *Hamlet Weekly*, which she liked to work on at the breakfast table. She couldn't imagine what else Mel and Lyn had to discuss.

"You know your gardening diary in the den? Well, I was looking for how to prune the old lilac when I turned to the back of that book." Mel watched her mother's eyes lift from the crossword puzzle and her questioning look turn to abrupt knowing.

"Oh" was all Tilli could think of to say.

Lyn squirmed in her seat. "Mom, Mel and I would love to talk with you about finding our brother, Jonathan. We weren't snooping; Mel just came upon your personal diary, and when I came over after shopping, she shared it with me. We love you, Mom, and we're with you a hundred percent; whatever you want or don't want to do, we will support your decision."

Tilli was shaking as she fought back tears. Jonathan had been her secret forever. She had considered telling her daughters about him so many times! But reconsidered— let things lie—they'd learn about him after she'd gone. Well, too late now. How should she respond? Jonathan's existence was kept from Bertie for decades. Damn that Evie woman!

Tilli had become more emotional since Bertie ... How would she—they—find Jonathan? Where to begin? Her greatest wish had been safe while on paper, but now that it was out in the open, she felt overwhelmed, exhausted, really, as emotions long held in flooded out. She looked across the table at their expectant faces, waiting for her to speak.

She sighed. "Of course, I want to find my son—your brother—but I'm afraid." She couldn't stop the flow of tears. Grief was a strange thing; it grabbed hold of you from out of nowhere. Certainly, she grieved the loss of Bertie, but she had missed her son every single day of her adult life. With an involuntary sigh of relief, Tilli buried her head in her hands and wept openly.

"Mom, we're with you no matter where this search

leads." Mel and Lyn went to their mother to offer support.

They strained to listen to what their mother was mumbling into her hands. "I'm so relieved my long-held-in secret is out, but I'm afraid we'll never find him."

# Home for Little Wanderers

Instead of driving to Asheville on the Blue Ridge Parkway that October, they agreed time would be better spent in starting the search for Jonathan. Lyn arranged for her assistant, Joanna, to cover for her, and once again, Joanna was thrilled for the opportunity; Lyn had no worries about things running smoothly at the Hamlet Community Arts Center.

"Well, we're lucky that the New England Home for Little Wanderers is right here in our state; at least we don't have to travel a great distance," said Mel as she raked leaves into the large canvas bag her mother was holding steady for her.

"It's a good thing I called the Home three weeks ago. Who would have thought it would take that long to get an appointment with the post-adoption director?" Tilli continued raking leaves into a pile while Mel and Lyn gathered up theirs.

Lyn said, "I wonder how long it will take us to find Jonathan. Most likely, whoever adopted him named him something completely different. Then there's the question of whether or not he's still living; we're assuming he is, but we don't know that. I almost don't want to bring this up, but since we're talking about it, I will. What if he doesn't want to connect with us? We have to be ready for disappointment, too."

"Mom, I'm getting goose bumps about meeting with

the Home's director tomorrow morning," Mel said.

"It's been forty-three years since I had to give him up. I wonder what he looks like: his hair color, eyes, and height. Will he look like me or his birth father, or a combination of both? Will it be like finding a needle in the proverbial haystack to locate him? There is no end to the questions I have."

"Mom, we have your maiden name, 'Eiser,' to go on, which is what you gave the Home when you turned your son over to them, and we know the exact date he was born. So, actually, we have a lot of information: location of orphanage, birth date, and mother's name."

"You're right, Mel. We could be looking for a needle, but we have three solid pieces of information." Tilli picked up one end of the filled leaf bag, and together she and Mel dumped the contents into one of the three compost bins on the far side of the back yard. One leaf still clung to her hair.

Mel reached up to pull away the leaf and tossed it into the bin. "Amazing how much better the yard looks after the leaves are cleaned up. I think we deserve a nice cold drink. What about you, Mom?"

"Sure, Mel; I'm parched. Good thing we haven't put the outdoor furniture away yet. Let's sit on the patio; it's too nice to go inside."

The sunken patio had been one of Tilli's ideas, and Bertie had readily agreed to have it built after she'd shown him a picture in a gardening magazine she'd subscribed to. On one side of the patio was the house, and on two sides—L-shaped—with one short side and the other longer, were low fieldstone walls. Into the crevices of the stones, Tilli had planted hens and chickens and other sedums, as well as creeping thyme. This stonewall had been back-filled with good garden soil, and into this soil, she had planted spring blooming bulbs, sun-loving perennials, and her beloved day lilies, and during the growing season, whenever plants were at rest and no longer in bloom, she'd interspersed annuals to add color. Now, purple fall asters and pink chrysanthemums were in bloom. The surface of the patio was laid in random rectangular and square bluestone pavers. A section had shade provided by the wisteria-covered pergola. On the fourth side of the patio was a bluestone walkway leading to the corner of the house, then turning and continuing out of sight along the side of the garage. The patio saw use from May through October, and over the years, it had become the focal point of the garden behind the house.

"Ever since we found your diary, Mom, I haven't been able to stop thinking about how difficult it must have been for you to have lost the man you were absolutely crazy about, then to have his baby all alone, and finally having to give up this precious child for adoption. Even worse, all these years, you've kept silent about it, thinking you'd never see your son again. It must have been agony! In your diary, you wrote that you considered your life a tragedy, even though you'd had a good life with Daddy, and you had us. Weren't we a consolation to you?" Mel took a sip of her iced tea.

"What do you mean?" asked Tilli, squeezing her lemon slice.

Mel responded, "I mean, as in Daddy wasn't your first choice because the man you loved was killed in Vietnam, and you had to give up his child. If this man had lived, then you, Lyn, and I wouldn't be sitting here sipping iced tea, and your life would have run a different course: your whole life changed direction. Think how many times over the course of human history, events have happened causing the direction of people's lives to change—another road taken from anything initially planned or dreamed about."

Tilli breathed deeply. "If you or Lyn loved a man so much that you'd risk your reputations, and then he got killed in a war and didn't come back, and you remained—giving birth to his child alone—you would never forget him or the child. Even though Jonathan and I were apart, our lives evolved; certainly, it wasn't what I'd hoped for or wanted. I was only nineteen and obsessed with Jonathan's father. I was lucky my life has been good, filled with many blessings: I walked the blessing way, as the Navajo would say. I was a loving wife to your daddy and tried to be a good mom to you and Lyn. All of you have been my greatest blessings."

Mel responded, "Mom, we know life doesn't always go the way we want. We can lay plans and do our very best, and still, things happen beyond our control. I can honestly say I have never met a man who has swept me off my feet and left me feeling breathless. Take Mark, for example, since he's the only man I've ever had a relationship with, and I really like him. He's great company, and we enjoy being together, but do I want to marry him? Now that I'm thirty-seven, I tell myself, why bother? It's too late. Why complicate my life when it's good just the way it is?"

"Oh, Mel, I'm sorry you think that way about Mark. Wouldn't you like to share your life with him? I mean, even though I imagine many people marry because they want to have children and raise a family, marriage is also about joining your life with another because it's more fulfilling than living alone. Even though you're thirty-seven, you and Lyn could still get married and be loving wives. There's a sense of security and commitment when two people vow to stay together "til death do us part,' that is different from two people having a relationship that's always open-ended, the road to escape just a door away whenever things don't go quite right. When the bloom is off, the relationship and a predictable pattern of living has been established, that's when making the marriage work begins; long-standing relationships are about love, commitment, and steadfastness."

"I understand what you're saying, Mom, but take Lyn's case; she was married and got divorced after she had been with Roger for ten difficult years. She didn't run off in a hurry when times were tough. She stuck it out as long as she could until she had to leave him or be reduced to feeling totally worthless. He was not a loving man, Mom."

At this point, Lyn got restless and began pacing back and forth on the patio. At the mention of Roger, she couldn't just sit and be silent. "So, Mel, when is it too late to marry? I've read of people in nursing homes, in the last stage of their lives, getting married! Will Paul and I marry? I don't know. He hasn't asked me; it's still too soon. As you know, I've been going for counseling for the last three years because I need to work out some leftover issues from my marriage to Roger. I didn't realize how wounded I am still, and I don't want negative thoughts and feelings to influence my relationship with Paul. When Roger and I divorced, I thought I'd never want another man in my life, except Daddy. Strange as it seems, I've changed my mind and would remarry if and when the man and the time seem right. Paul is such a kind and loving person that I find myself caring for him more deeply every time I'm with him. So, please don't rule out marriage, Mel. I encourage you to keep your heart open, Sis."

# Next Morning

"I think the street must be the next one on the left." Lyn sat next to Mel as she drove to the New England Home for Little Wanderers. The low-growing foliage on the huge maple trees made it difficult to see the street signs. "There, see that street sign? That's it!"

As they got closer to the Home, Tilli became nervous. Scenes from long ago wafted through her mind, little vignettes of her coming here pregnant with her son. Labor pains followed by lusty cries, her tears and heartache. She had passed out—blessedly—and then waking up without her baby, her aching breasts filled with milk. It was the most terrible time of her life! Now, the shade trees cast shadows on the landscape, across the car windows, and onto her lap. She looked at her now-wrinkled hands from many years of gardening and hard work and thought about the contrast between now and then. Who had raised him? She pressed her handkerchief against her running nose, mopped herself up, and told herself to be brave.

"As much as I've wanted to find Jonathan, I never could have done this by myself."

"Mom, you never have to do anything alone as long as Lyn and I are around."

As the SUV turned the corner, they saw a large red brick building on the left and a small sign indicating the entry to a parking lot behind the building. Mel found an empty space, and since they weren't in a hurry, as they'd allowed more than sufficient time to get here, even with the heavy traffic, they decided to sit in the car for a few minutes.

They studied the building. The oldest section, in the middle, was from the mid-1800s, while the building to the right had been built sometime in the early 1900s, and a third, more modern wing must have been added sometime later. The sun glared on the many tall windows, giving the impression that the building was deserted.

"Mom, is this the building you came to?"

A quiet "Yes" from the back seat, followed by sniffles.

"I know; I was thinking the same thing, Mel," said Lyn.

"We might as well go in; it's time." Mel took the key out of the ignition, and they walked slowly toward the building. A sign told them deliveries only and visitors should go to the front.

"Mom, are you all right? We don't have to go inside; we can come back."

"I can do this." Tilli stretched taller.

The main entryway was in the middle section, the oldest part of the building. It had a broad set of granite steps which were worn at the front edge from many footsteps, and a curved portico, with a pair of heavy dark oak doors holding inserts of thick beveled glass. Only the right-hand door opened, and as Mel reached for the heavy brass doorknob, shiny from years of use, she thought again of her mother: Mom touched this doorknob; she stood right where we are now—young and alone.

They walked over to the visitors' desk in the lobby.

"We have a ten o'clock appointment with the post-adoption director, Mrs. Fielding," said Mel.

The receptionist made a phone call. "She'll be down in a moment. Please have a seat."

Mel and Lyn looked around the waiting area. A pair of parlor palms inside glazed pots rested on the Persian carpet; there were two comfortable sofas with several damask pillows and two burgundy leather-covered wing chairs with a lovely piecrust mahogany table in between. Several paintings with pastoral scenes hung on the freshly painted, cream-colored walls, and one old oil painting of a solemn man hung over the fireplace. Most likely, he was the benefactor and/or founder of the Home. Along one wall, brochures and information were neatly fanned out on top of an old, narrow oak table.

"Hello, I'm Dorothy Fielding. Nice to meet you."

Mel got up and shook hands.

"Hello, Ms. Fielding," said Lyn as she took the slender woman's firm handshake into her own. "Please meet our mother, Matilda MacInnes."

"Hello, Matilda, please call me Dorothy—Caitlyn and Amelia, correct? Let's go up to my office. Would you like some spring water or tea?"

Dorothy Fielding's office had several comfortable leather armchairs. Dorothy pulled her desk chair around so she could sit with them rather than behind her large mahogany desk.

"We're fortunate to have generous benefactors here at the New England Home for Little Wanderers. One of our board members is a local bank president, and when his bank was renovated last year, we were the recipients of all their desks, credenzas, and other furnishings. We couldn't possibly have afforded to buy such good things. As you may have noticed, our lobby was recently refurbished, and all the expenses were fully paid for by our donors. We are blessed."

"How old is the organization? Was it always the New England Home for Little Wanderers?" Mel didn't hesitate to ask.

Dorothy made them feel as if she had no more important business to attend to today other than to spend time with them.

"Well, the Home has a rich history of innovative programs and organizations established for the care and protection of children and families. In 1799, the Boston Female Asylum was established as an orphanage, and Abigail Adams was a founding contributor. By the time we fast-forward to the 1960s, when your mother, Matilda, came to us, there had been many mergers with childcare agencies. In 1960, Boston Children's Services was formed through the merger of the Children's Aid Association and the Boston Children's Friend Society. We became the New England Home for Little Wanderers in 1999 through a merger between the New England Home for Little Wanderers and Boston Children's Services. There have been other mergers since 1999; we've been in existence for a very long time.

"Of course, we have not always been at this location. These buildings have a history of their own and have had other uses before we came along. The original building was built in 1857, the next addition came in 1917, and finally, in 1959, the third and last addition was built."

Lyn spoke, "As we mentioned in our initial letter and then in our phone conversation, we're trying to find our brother."

"Dorothy, I gave birth to my son here when I was only

nineteen years old and before I married my husband and had my daughters Mel and Lyn. I've prepared a typewritten sheet of paper for you, detailing my situation at the time I gave up my son for adoption. And here is a copy of my birth certificate."

"We never make promises to families looking for children. Sometimes reunions happen, and other times the seeking ends in disappointment, but let's not worry. We will see what we will find," replied Dorothy. "I'll be in touch as soon as I can. Please be patient; this process can take months, or even longer."

"I've waited almost forty-five years to do this, Dorothy. Certainly, I can wait."

# Peaches

On a Friday, two weeks later, after Mel came home from teaching school, she saw on the answering machine that Dorothy Fielding had called but left no message. Since it was now after business hours and too late for her mother to call Dorothy, they would have to wait until Monday.

Mark was coming to pick her up at six o'clock; they'd planned on walking over to the new Peaches Restaurant located inside her father's former shoe repair shop.

The doorbell rang, and Mel laughed as she jumped at the sound. No one other than Lyn and she had ever rung it, and they'd done it because it annoyed their mother; it had been a joke.

"Well, don't you look lovely," Mark said as he came into the hall. She'd changed into her new baby-blue cashmere sweater and a navy pencil skirt.

Mark kissed her lightly on the cheek.

"You look nice, too. In fact, Mr. Mark, you always look nice."

"Mr. Mark?" He laughed.

"Oh, I don't know where that came from. See what happens when I get too familiar?"

"That's just what I want you to do, Ms. MacInnes: get familiar. You can get even more familiar if you'd like." He hugged her and then helped her with her coat.

"It always seems to get cold all of a sudden each year, doesn't it?" observed Mel.

"Seeing as we live in New England, you'd think we'd get used to it, but we New Englanders spend more time talking about the weather than any other topic."

"Now, how would you know that, Mark?

"Oh, don't you know? I'm the weather reporter for the Hamlet area for WBZ in Boston. I call in every morning at five and give the forecasters my readings from the weather instruments I have on the roof; I've been doing it for such a long time. I guess I just assumed you were aware of it."

The walk to Peaches was only about ten minutes, and Mark offered her his arm. "I don't want you to trip on the uneven sidewalks, Mel; besides, the lighting is poor on this street. I think the town must be trying to save money. Look, that light's out, and so's the one across the street." He pulled her closer.

As they turned the next corner, the restaurant was directly ahead of them, but now Daddy's picture window was adorned with curtains. The window glass, with letters in an attractive font, bore the name of the restaurant. They heard soft music playing as Mark opened the door for Mel. A few of the small tables, some for two and others for four, were occupied, but it didn't appear to be too busy tonight. Fresh carnations in bud vases were in the middle of each table, resting on top of peach-colored tablecloths; it was cozy.

The new owner approached. "Good evening, Mel. How do you like Peaches? It's a little bit different from the other Sole, don't you think, my dear?"

"Hello, Henri. Meet my good friend Mark. I love the décor!"

"Your table is the best in the house." Henri lifted the

tiny lampshade and lit the candle. "My wife, Justine and I are happy with the building. Sometime, you should come during the day, so you can see what we've done with the upstairs. It is perfect for us, Mel. Now come and sit, please." Henri helped Mel with her chair.

"I like that Henri and his wife named this place Peaches," said Mark. "It's quite a tribute to your father."

"I wonder if Henri has peach cobbler on the menu?"

Mark chuckled. "You'll have to ask him, but don't you want dinner first?"

They chatted and laughed, enjoying one another's company, and combined with Henri's Chateaubriand for two and a bottle of perfectly paired French Bordeaux wine, the evening couldn't have been more wonderful.

"So, what else don't I know about you, Mr. Mark? I've just learned this evening you are a weather reporter." Mel couldn't remember a time when she had felt this comfortable, what with the excellent dinner, red wine, and good companionship. Henri had dimmed the lighting in the restaurant, making the candlelight more pronounced, and the music was romantic. She found herself looking into Mark's eyes, and her heart went soft.

"Mr. Mark wants you to know he cares about you more with every passing day. In fact, Mr. Mark would like to take you into his arms—right now—and show you firsthand how much he cares."

Mel smiled.

Mark smiled back, and then the smile grew until they both laughed.

"You're naughty," Mel said.

"I'd like it if you'd be naughty, too," he replied. "Henri, please bring the check. Ms. MacInnes and I need to be going."

"Oh, yes, it is late, and you must both be thinking about having to work tomorrow morning."

Mel and Mark were the last diners to leave the restaurant, with promises they'd sample the peach cobbler à la mode the next time they came. Henri held the door open for them. "Please come back soon."

"Oh, yes, Henri got that right; work is foremost on my mind, Ms. MacInnes," said Mark as he walked her home.

A cold breeze had sprung up, which promised rain or perhaps sleet during the night. Mel hugged Mark's arm closer to her for warmth. They walked a bit faster.

Soon they were standing in front of 5 Cedar Street's little wooden gate. "I suppose you're too tired to come in for a minute?" asked Mel. She was aware Lyn had easily talked their mother into an overnight in Boston, where they were at Symphony Hall this evening for a performance of Gustav Mahler's Symphony No. 3 and would visit a special exhibition of Monet's paintings at the Museum of Fine Arts tomorrow morning. Tilli loved classical music and the colorful garden paintings of Monet, so this was a special weekend for them.

"I'm too tired to come in for a minute, Ms. MacInnes, but I think I could manage two minutes just fine," replied Mark with a grin.

"What's the weather report for tonight, Mark? It feels like rain or sleet overnight."

"Did I hear you say 'sleep overnight?' The weather outside is going to be frightful, but it could be so delightful if I stayed with you. Henri didn't realize we have tomorrow off; what say you, Ms. MacInnes?"

She hesitated for just one second before caving in. "Why don't you stay and keep me warm, Mr. Mark?

# Finding Jonathan

Mel was at lunch, on her cell phone, and sitting in the SUV out in the teachers' parking lot on Monday.

"Hello, Dorothy? This is Mel MacInnes. Just wanted to be sure my mother returned your call from Friday."

"Amelia, yes, I had left word, but I haven't heard back from her. When can she, you, and Caitlyn come again? I'd like to meet with all of you."

"Let's see, today is Monday, and on Wednesday, I have early release from school. I have to find out if Lyn can take time off that afternoon. If it works, we could be at your office by about two o'clock. I'll have my mother call you back to confirm."

"Fine, Amelia; two o'clock would work for me; I'll pencil it in until I hear back."

After school, Mel drove over to the Hamlet Community Arts Center to see Lyn.

"Hey! This is a surprise; I don't remember the last time you walked in here." Lyn had just hung up her phone and came around the desk to give Mel a hug.

"Lyn, I came right over after school because I talked with Dorothy Fielding today."

"Well, sit down, will you? How about some cranberry or apple juice; it's nice and cold? I need something to quench my thirst. Come, follow me."

They walked through the large main hall, where the walls were covered with modern art paintings, drawings, and sketches. Several sculptures stood throughout the hall on cubes, so they were visible on all sides. Small cards with descriptions about the artists and their work neatly completed each piece.

"It looks lovely in here, Lyn. By the way, how was your overnight with Mom?"

"Mel, she absolutely loved it! The Mahler symphony was perfect, and, of course, the Monet exhibit was exquisite. Great therapy for her and me, too. Let's think of other activities to get her out, Mel; I'm open to suggestions. Did you know she's seriously thinking of going on a pilgrimage with the Catholic Church to the Holy Land that also includes Cairo, Egypt? She plans on asking her gardening friend, Margaret Flannery, to go. It's not until January. For the most part, though, she couldn't stop talking about Jonathan. Sure hope we can find him!"

Lyn waved her arms to indicate the hall they were standing in. "Getting back to this place, Joanna and I just finished setting everything up. As you know, Mel, the new show opens next Saturday at noon. We're still working out some of the last-minute details. Several artists will be coming to talk about their works, and we'll have refreshments. Any chance you and Mark can come?"

"I'll see if he's free."

"I've asked Paul. As you know, we've been seeing more of each other the last couple of months. What do you think; he's nice, right?"

"Lyn, I think he's fine, and as long as the two of you are getting along, I'm so happy to see you dating. You know, Lyn, I've noticed a very positive change: you're laughing more and seem relaxed. The art show opening sounds like fun, Lyn. I'll call Mark after I leave here."

With cold beverages in hand, Mel and Lyn went back to Lyn's office to talk privately.

"So, any news about Jonathan, Sis?"

"Mom didn't return Dorothy Fielding's call. I guess she must be filled with mixed emotions right now and hesitant. Anyway, I called Dorothy myself, and she wants to know if we can come to her office Wednesday afternoon at two o'clock. She wants to talk with all of us." Mel took a sip of her juice.

"Let's see if Joanna's still here. I'll ask if she'll cover for me; just a sec."

While Lyn was gone, Mel looked around to see where her sister spent so much time. She noticed the credenza located under the window of one wall; on it were several brass cachepots that held green plants with shiny leaves. In a corner bookcase were photographs of Lyn posing with artists, donors, and well-known Hamlet people who always came out for society events. On another wall hung a lovely wooden clock with a hand-painted face and the words: *Tempus Fugit*. Behind Lyn's desk was an old map of Hamlet depicting its main roads, with dots indicating the location of shops and houses and topographical features. Mel noticed the date 1857 written in cursive in the lower right-hand corner. Lyn's desk was uncluttered, and Mel recognized three lovely pictures taken of their parents and themselves on special occasions from years ago. A modest display of award plaques from the town of Hamlet and private organizations adorned a narrow wall near the door.

"Just as I thought, Joanna said she'd be glad to cover for me."

Mel replied, "We can drive there in an hour." She finished her juice. "I've got to go, Lyn; papers to correct. What are you doing for dinner tonight? Do you think Mom would enjoy going to the Tally Ho Club?"

"It's Monday, Sis; they're closed."

"You're right, Lyn. Do you want to come over to the house for dinner? Mark and I made hunter's stew on Saturday. I found out he likes to cook. Also, there's stuff to make a tossed salad in the fridge."

"I've been so busy setting up this exhibit, it's great that I don't have to prepare dinner tonight, and stew is always more delicious the second time around. I'm happy you and Mark had a good weekend, too. I'll be there about five thirty, Sis."

Mel went home and told her mother about Dorothy Fielding's call.

"Oh, she wants us back there so soon, Mel? I hope it's good news. I haven't been sleeping well since our visit to the Home. You know I'm excited but also fearful. Please do me a favor; you call her. Tell her we're coming."

Mel patted Tilli's arm, "Just try to relax about all this, Mom."

Afterward, Mel telephoned Mark.

"How's my favorite teacher?" he responded.

"I don't know if I'll ever recover from my dinner date at Peaches."

"Well, I hope you never do. Another dose of medicine

can be arranged by Doctor Mark any time you like." He loved the sound of Mel's voice and found himself saying things to her he would never utter to anyone else. To him, she was magic, and he dropped any pretense in her company, even when on the phone.

"I'm calling to ask if you want to go with me next Saturday for the twelve o'clock opening of a new exhibit at the Hamlet Community Arts Center. I just left Lyn, and it looks interesting. She's asking her friend Paul to come, too. Maybe the four of us can do something together afterwards. If it's a nice day, we can take a walk on one of the woodland trails. What do you think, Mark?"

"Sounds good to me, Mel; shall I pick you up at eleven forty-five, and we'll walk over there together?"

"Perfect, Mark; see you then."

Wednesday came quickly, and Mel, Lyn, and Tilli found themselves once again sitting in Dorothy Fielding's office.

"I've done some research and found your file, Mrs. MacInnes. Let's see," Dorothy opened a yellowed manila folder. "Mrs. MacInnes, you came to us in June 1963 when you were four months pregnant. The Home took care of your monthly wellness visits until you checked in to have your son on November fifteenth, 1963."

"Our mother named him Jonathan," said Mel.

"She might have done that, but the Home never named babies at birth; that was up to the adoptive parents. As you may know, the maternity hospital closed a long time ago, but while your mother was with us, we still delivered babies, and your brother was born here; to us, he was 'Baby

Eiser.' "

"Does the file indicate to whom Baby Eiser went? I mean, who adopted him?"

"Of course, Lyn. I wouldn't have asked all of you to come if I didn't have something important to tell you. It's more personal to sit down with you; I would never give you this information over the phone. We know his name and have his contact information. As so often happens these days, adoptive parents move around a lot, and it becomes difficult to trace their whereabouts; but in this case, the adoptive family remained at the same address, making our search easy. Your son, however, no longer lives in Massachusetts.

"In cases like yours, it is customary to have our resident social worker write an introductory letter to your son and send it by certified mail, return receipt requested. We've been connecting families for a very long time and know what to write as an introduction. After we mail this letter to him, he is the one who has to make the next move. Privacy laws dictate that the child gets to decide whether or not s/he wants to be in contact with the birth parents."

"That's it? You've found him! Oh, my, it didn't take long." Tilli let out a deep sigh of relief, silent tears welled up, and she reached for the tissue box. "I don't know what to say."

"Well, Mrs. MacInnes, it's only the first step. Make no assumptions. If you don't get a reply immediately, rest assured he might need time to decide how to respond. On the other hand, he may get back to you right away. Or, you may never hear anything. That's the way it is: one never knows how the child will feel about connecting with the birth mother. My experience has been that children who have been raised by loving families usually respond favorably to such requests because they have no reason not to want to reconnect, and, let's face it, they're curious, even if they reply just to get to meet you and that's that. Then again, there are cases where the child has led a very happy life and wants nothing to do with the birth mother. They may see this request as an intrusion. Each child is different, and I can only urge patience, Mrs. MacInnes, and an open mind and heart." Dorothy closed the folder on her desk and stood up, signaling their meeting was at an end.

With Mel on Tilli's right and Lyn on her left, they hooked arms and walked across the parking lot as a team, amazed at how quickly Dorothy had obtained this information. Was the hard part behind them or ahead?

# Waiting

Tilli did her best to find productive ways to spend time while waiting to hear from her son. She walked, once again, to the Hamlet Library to skim the shelves for books on the Holy Land. The only way she was going to get through this period was to keep her mind and body occupied; in addition to gardening, walking and reading were her favorite activities. Since Bertie's building had sold, she now had the money to take what she considered an exotic trip. Ever since she and Bertie had attended a lecture a few years ago given by an Egyptologist at the library, she'd been intrigued by that part of the world. Even as a young girl, she'd been interested in Egyptian culture pertaining to the afterlife, as well as the treasures unearthed from the ancient tombs of kings, especially King Tut. Wouldn't it be wonderful to visit the Egyptian Museum in Cairo?

She thought back to when she was working as a secretary in Boston and how she had taken the Green Line to the Museum of Fine Arts to visit and revisit the Egyptian collection. Anyway, the Egyptologist's slide presentation at the library had included riding camels at the Great Pyramids of Giza, as well as a river trip down the Nile to Luxor and the Valley of the Kings. Tilli thought back to comments Bertie had made after the slide show, "Now, why would anyone want to go to that part of the world? Sand, sand, and more sand, and then all those tombs? How depressing!"

Every afternoon, she checked her mailbox to see if there was a letter from Jonathan, and every evening since they'd been to the New England Home for Little Wanderers, she'd been home, but her son never called. Why wasn't he responding? Either he wanted to meet her, or he didn't. That's how she saw it! "Patience, Tilli," she told herself.

After a leisurely breakfast on Saturday morning with Mel and her mother, Lyn headed over to the Hamlet Community Arts Center to attend to last-minute details for the noon opening of the exhibit. In the meantime, Mel helped her mother tidy up, put laundry in the washer, and water the houseplants.

Before Lyn left for the Center, she said, "Mom, I'm sure there's a good reason why you haven't heard from him. The waiting is getting to me, too, but I have work to do and need to get going." She gave her mother a quick hug.

After Mark arrived, he and Mel walked over to the Center and got there just as the doors opened and a hand-ful of people began entering the building.

"Oh, hi there!" Lyn called out to them.

"Mel and I have been looking forward to this," said Mark.

"Paul!" Lyn called to a dark-haired man studying one of the sculptures; he came towards them. "Paul, I want you to meet my sister Mel and her friend Mark."

They exchanged handshakes and chatted as they moved about the room, examining the artwork and reading the descriptions of the artists.

"Come and have a mimosa; we've set up refreshments down at that end," said Lyn.

"So, Mark, what do you do?" Paul asked.

"I'm an engineer," he replied as he took a stuffed mushroom from a tray of hors d'oeuvres being passed around. "And you?" Mark was uncomfortable with introductory getting-to-know-you conversations but tried to be polite. Aren't we more than what we do for work? He pondered.

"I'm a yacht broker in Marblehead. Been at it for about ten years now. Before that, I was at the Boston Yacht Club. Made a lot of contacts in the boating world, and it just led to brokering. I love what I do, too. Get to travel to Italy, France, the islands, sometimes even to Asia—wherever there are boats my clients want to buy." Paul said all this without looking at Mark. He was too busy scanning the room. Where was Lyn anyway?

Mark knew right off that Paul was a people person. No issues with making small conversations. I don't know what this guy and I have in common, he thought to himself, but he said, "I've been with General Electric in Lynn forever. Love it. Great commute; the train stops right next to the building." Mark grabbed a big shrimp from another tray passing by.

"Paul hasn't asked me what I do, but just so we're all on the same page, I'll offer it up anyway—I teach third grade here in Hamlet." Mel sipped her mimosa and met Mark's gaze.

"Oh, yes, Lyn told me you are a teacher. It must not be easy teaching kids these days. Do they listen to you, Mel?" Paul reached over to the refreshment table and selected a few red grapes.

"Most of the time, they do; I always seem to have two or three each year who try my patience, but when they realize I know pretty much all the tricks from years of experience, they soon settle down. I do have an aide to help me. I can't imagine doing anything else; I love teaching, and I love the kids." Mel put her empty glass on a nearby tray and looked bored.

"What's up, Mel?" asked Mark.

"I'm sorry, Mark, I'm not very good company today; I have other things on my mind."

Paul noticed Mel wasn't too happy, and he wondered if he'd said something wrong.

Lyn came over to them and asked, "So, how are you all enjoying the show?"

"Lyn, it's been really nice. Thanks for inviting us, but I think I'm going now," Mel said.

"So soon, Sis? Oh, come now. You just got here."

"I think I said something to upset her," said Paul.

"No, it's me, not any of you; I just have something on my mind."

"Well, tell us about it, Mel; maybe we can help," said Paul.

"I don't know you very well, Paul, and what I have on my mind is very personal; it's not something to talk about here," Mel said in a gruffer tone than she'd intended.

"I'm sorry; I didn't mean to pry."

"No, you're fine, Paul. This isn't the place to discuss it."

Lyn saw Mel was unhappy. She thought back to how Mel always felt about initial introductions between guys and gals and how she never liked the "Who am I and who are you?" portion of getting to know someone. She was sorry

Mel wanted to leave.

"Are you going to Cedar Street?" Lyn went with them to get their coats.

"No, Lyn, I think I want to get some fresh air, maybe take a walk in the woodland by the lake. Does anyone want to join me?" Mel needed some quiet time.

Mark raised his hand, "You've got my vote, Mel."

"Okay, you two go ahead; I'm heading back to the art show. I've worked hard to get everything set up and can't go now. Paul, will you stay with me?"

"You bet, Lyn."

"Mark and I cooked up a big pot of chili last night, thinking that we'd all be together today. What say we all meet at the house later this afternoon? When's the art show over, Lyn?"

"We'll be closing at three o'clock; chili sounds yummy! See you later." Lyn gave her sister a hug and smiled at Mark; then Paul took Lyn by the arm and led her back to the show.

After a refreshing walk along the lake, Mark and Mel headed back to Cedar Street and made themselves comfortable in the living room.

"I can't believe what time it is! We were out there in the woods for almost two hours, Mark. Can I get you something to drink?"

"How about something cold; anything is fine. I think the stuffed mushrooms were salty. I don't mean to sound like a know-it-all, Mel, but even after our long walk and talk, I can tell that your burden weighs heavily on your shoulders. How can I make things easier for you?"

Mel sat down next to him and kicked off her shoes. As they'd walked the trail, she'd told him about the search for her brother and how they'd been waiting for over two weeks to get either a note or a phone call but hadn't heard anything.

"It's the waiting and not knowing how Jonathan will respond that's hard. My mother needs to know that he wants her, too. And that's the tough part. Will he respond in a positive way?" She frowned. "That's why I'm being moody."

"You're not moody, Mel. I can imagine your disappointment, but Lyn was right when she said you couldn't keep sitting around waiting for his reply. Maybe he has issues we don't know about. Maybe he's trying to figure out how, or if, to get back to you. Whatever the reason, you shouldn't give up, but you have your own lives to live, and so does your mother."

Entering the living room and seeing the two of them sitting there, Tilli greeted them, "Oh, hello!"

Mark started to get up.

"No, don't move; may I refill your glass?"

"Maybe he's dealing with a life-changing event," Mel suggested.

"Maybe he's got a wife who said don't bother," responded Mark.

"Yes, there are lots of maybes." Tilli immediately saw that she'd walked into the middle of a conversation she didn't want to think about right now. "Guess I'll go and do some chores if you don't need anything."

Mel was restless. "Mark, the sun's out, and it's nice outdoors. Let's go for a walk to Hamlet Market and get a fresh baguette to go with the chili. We've got time before Lyn and Paul arrive."

They all returned to the house about the same time and hung their coats in the hall closet. Mark uncorked the burgundy wine and took glasses down from the shelf while Paul flicked the switch on for the fireplace in the living room and studied the print of the MacInnes castle hanging on the wall. "This is cool," he said. "I've never known anyone who has a castle named after them."

Mel was in the kitchen, heating the large pot of chili on the stove. Lyn joined her and turned on the oven to warm the baguette. Together, they made the salad. Tilli came in from the garden carrying purple asters and pink chrysanthemums, which she arranged in a Navajo pottery vase they'd brought back from Arizona.

Mel's spirits perked up. The brisk walk on the forest trail had been invigorating, and now the pleasant conversations and activity going on around her made her think of bygone days, when Daddy was alive and she and Lyn had friends over. Those were such good times, and it made her realize how much she'd missed by living on her own all those years. She was glad she had moved back in with Mom and that she and Lyn had found such great guys.

She looked around the kitchen and noticed how well they got along; it was as if they'd all known each other for years. "It doesn't always happen this way," she thought to herself.

After dinner, Tilli sat with them for a bit and then said, "I'm going to the den to read my book on Egypt; got to brush up on things before the pilgrimage." She was content to take her cup of orange spice herbal tea upstairs while the rest of them gathered in the living room by the fire. It was just after six o'clock, and already the sun had set.

"Christmas will be here before long. Anyone have plans for the holiday?" asked Paul.

"Gee, Paul, don't rush the seasons. It's only late October; we still have Halloween and Thanksgiving before we get to Christmas," replied Lyn.

"I think it would be nice to go somewhere warm and sunny this winter," said Mel, looking at Lyn. "Like, maybe Florida?"

"What do you think Mom would say if her daughters took a little vacation without her? After all, she'll be jet-setting to Cairo in January." Lyn looked at Mel, who seemed pleased Lyn had suggested such an idea.

"What about the boyfriends?" Mark had the look of an abandoned puppy as he gazed at Mel.

"Yeah! What about us guys?" Paul took his cue from Mark and tried to look dejected.

It didn't take long for them to realize Mel and Lyn had no intention of letting their winter get-away become a foursome. Everyone had a good laugh over this game of verbal ping-pong.

Mel smiled. "Haven't you two heard that absence makes the heart grow fonder?"

# Saint Lucia
# in the Caribbean

"Pass me the sunscreen, will you, Lyn?"

Mel and Lyn were reclining on Marigot Beach Club lounge chairs on a spit of land that jutted into the shallow bay. Every afternoon, a variety of catamarans and yachts filed in, one behind the other like ducks in a row so they wouldn't get hung up on the coral, which was under the shallow water except in the dredged areas nearest the buoys. Palm trees, bougainvillea in purple, white, and red, as well as other tropical flowering trees and plants grew along the perimeter of the bay, as well as up on the steep hillsides protecting this lush oasis.

A man, sitting in a bathtub-size container—it certainly wasn't a boat—paddled to shore and began to sell bananas to the guests.

"Banana Ben here; best fruit on the island. Taste my fruit, and you'll want it every day. For you, miss?"

"Thank you," said Mel. "I had a banana this morning."

"Oh, and you, miss?" He held a banana out to Lyn.

"We're guests of the Marigot Beach Club and get all the fruit we need." Mel wished he'd disappear. Why wasn't he selling to the yachts and catamarans at anchor? Fortunately, Banana Ben wasn't pushy; he soon went to others, who were waving at him.

"I'm glad we opted not to go to Florida, aren't you,

Mel?

"Oh, paradise: swimming, snorkeling, dining, sunbathing." She stretched her arms wide to encompass the beauty surrounding them and let out a contented sigh. "We're going to have to make adjustments when we get back home. We've had no schedules, no clocks, only sun and fun. Wonder how Mom's getting along on her Holy Land pilgrimage. I'm so happy she's finally able to realize another long-put-off wish."

"This has turned out well for all of us. Glad her schedule coincided with our vacation, so we'll get back to Hamlet at about the same time. Can't wait to hear all about it. Aren't we lucky, Mel?"

"Can you believe we have only one more day here? I'm looking forward to our sail tomorrow. It will be a nice way to wrap up our stay." Mel stretched leisurely before adjusting her broad-brimmed hat to better shield her eyes from the afternoon sun.

The next morning at nine o'clock, the sisters stood on the pier next to the Marigot Beach Club, made famous by the 1967 film Doctor Dolittle, starring Rex Harrison. They waited for the powerboat to transport them to the 45-foot sailboat moored some distance away. A rather portly woman spoke loudly to her also-portly husband, so every word could be heard across the bay.

"Is he deaf? Who else around here wants to listen to that nonsense?" Mel was getting annoyed, just thinking she would have to spend the entire day with her.

"Ha! Ha! Ha!" The woman guffawed as she bent over

laughing.

"This is too much! Maybe we can go on another boat," said Lyn.

By now, a few more guests had gathered on the pier. The powerboat was late! They looked over the waters of the bay for a sign of anything moving in their direction—none was apparent.

"Wait, wait, and wait!" the woman said, again very loudly. "I didn't come here to wait, Rick, but that's all we've done. These island people don't know heck about clocks and schedules."

"Honey, that's right. The reason we came here from Nevada was to relax. Remember?" The husband frowned while she pouted.

Mel spied a small boat with a tiny outboard putt-putting in their direction. Only about four passengers would fit; the driver would have to make two trips to get everyone to the sailboat.

"Sorry, man, we've been having engine trouble with our sailboat, the *Serendipity*, but we're good now—no problem."

" 'No problem'! That's just when I start to worry," the portly woman said loudly.

Eventually, the *Serendipity* left the bay, and because there wasn't any wind, they motored for a very long time. All the same, it was lovely to see the lush but rugged island from the sea, its shoreline deserted except for the occasional sea kayaks or a handful of people enjoying the few small beaches. One of the local men threw a line overboard, hoping for a fish.

The seven passengers spread out over the sailboat to find comfy spots: a couple clambered to the bow, one man stretched out on the portside of the vessel, and four of them ended up in the cockpit near the stern, where the shadow cast by the unfurled sail on the mast provided a little relief from the sun. Lyn and Mel didn't want to get sunburned on their last day of vacation, but this spot with the tiniest bit of shade was where the portly woman, Sheila, and her husband, Rick, had chosen to sit as well. By now, everyone onboard had exchanged names, and the good-natured Sheila and Rick had, believe it or not, grown on them. For one thing, this portly couple helped pass the hours by telling endless jokes and riddles.

"Rick, you need to put on more sun block," Sheila said in a loud voice.

If only this woman would just pipe down a little, thought Mel as she exchanged looks with Lyn.

"I'm all right, DooDoo," he said as Sheila laughed—loudly—and once again basted his legs with a spray can of SPF15. Rick was fast turning into a pink porker! And they still had all afternoon ahead of them in this tropical sunshine.

Lyn was puzzled. "Sheila, why did Rick call you Doo-Doo? That's gross!"

"Shall I tell them, Rick? Or should we just keep it our little secret?" Rick nodded to go ahead and spill the beans. "Ha Ha! That's *because* it means 'sweetie pie' or some such endearment in the local language. We learned it from one of the wait staff at Doolittle's Restaurant. He called his girlfriend DooDoo, and so we asked."

"I'll have to remember 'DooDoo' for future use," Mel said.

"I'm going to call Rick DooDoo from now on," Sheila beamed.

"Would you like some of my SPF50?" asked Mel. "You're getting very pink."

"Naw. I always get this color before it turns to a tan. Thanks anyway."

"Time to put up more sails. Who wants to help?" asked the captain.

After all the sails were raised, there was shade along one side of the boat, and because they'd finally picked up a breeze, the boat slid smoothly and steadily through the Caribbean Sea along this leeward, southern shore. The northern side of St. Lucia faced the open Atlantic, where most of the storms came from, and was considered the wilder side. Soon they rounded yet another bend, and before them were the two majestic Pitons—Gros and Petit—as well as the city of Soufriere, a name they learned meant "sulfur."

A dilapidated van picked them up at the pier. Candy-colored houses lined both sides of the narrow streets as they headed to Diamond Waterfall, which was located on the grounds of the botanical garden and up a steep mountainside. After a leisurely stroll under the mahogany, eucalyptus, and other tropical trees and amid blooming plants that their tour guide described to them, they left this quiet place for the world's only drive-in volcano, the dormant Qualibou. They couldn't actually drive into the volcano, but they did visit the sulfur springs near the crater, which continued to emit sulfurous steam and showed signs of geothermal life. It was stinky!

By the time the van brought them back to the pier, they were hungry. Boxed chicken or fish lunches, depending on what they'd pre-ordered, had been prepared by a local caterer and were waiting. On a grassy strip alongside the pier, several picnic tables were empty.

"We're late today and need to start sailing back. If you all want to stop along the way to snorkel, lunch must be eaten on board. We know a special snorkeling spot; you don't want to miss it," announced the captain.

What they didn't know until later was that the captain and his assistants had fixed the motor on the sailboat while they were sightseeing. It was the second repair of the day.

Soon they were under sail, and the wind was perfect. The forty-five-foot *Serendipity* was not crowded; there was plenty of room to find a comfortable spot to eat. About an hour after lunch, the boat headed into a cove, where the passengers could see a couple of other boats at anchor and people in the water snorkeling.

"This is the special spot," announced the captain. "Who needs flippers and a facemask? I have enough for five."

This led to some discussion as there were seven passengers. "It's okay," said one guy. "I'm not especially interested in snorkeling."

Mary said, "Tim, my husband, is the one who likes to go in the water. I'm not crazy about it."

Lyn and Mel prepared to go snorkeling along with the portly Rick and Sheila and Mary's husband, Tim.

Before they entered the water, the captain had a word of caution as he held up a colorful picture of a fish. "This is a lionfish. If you see one, do not go near it; its sting is poisonous!"

They, thankfully, didn't encounter a lionfish, but they saw many striped fish, purple fish, yellow-and-black fish, several kinds of coral, and underwater plants that waved gently with the current. The sea was clear, and the water was calm. Lyn discovered a pretty spot and motioned to Mel to swim toward her. Together, they hovered over the scene below, and because they took their time, other fish became apparent. They didn't need to swim far at all. The underwater scenery was so captivating they lost track of time. Mel motioned to Lyn that they'd better surface to get their bearings and see what was going on up top. Immediately, they saw the captain waving to get their attention. The other three snorkelers had already gone back to the sailboat.

"That was too short, Mel. I pointed out the seahorses. Did you see them? I could have stayed longer."

As they got on board, the captain said, "We need to get back. Tim isn't feeling well."

Sheila asked Mel, "Did you girls see the flying fish that jumped in the water all around you while you were snorkeling?"

Lyn and Mel had been so focused on what was swimming along the sandy bottom that they hadn't thought to look overhead.

The motor wouldn't start! After several attempts, they hoisted the sail and prayed for wind to take them to Marigot Bay. At first, there were some gentle puffs of wind, but all too soon, it became calm, and their return voyage was long. In the meantime, Rick's skin turned the color of a cooked lobster. On the other hand, the color had left Tim's face as he struggled to keep from being seasick. They realized it would be dark before they reached their destination. After they got closer to Marigot Bay, the captain used his cell phone to call for help.

Help came in the form of the small boat they'd used

that morning to get from the pier to the *Serendipity*. The little boat did its best to tow their sailboat back to the bay.

Mel said to Lyn, "I feel like we're being towed by the *Little Engine that Could*; remember that children's book by Watty Piper?"

It was a slog, but they eventually entered the bay, which by now was dotted by the cheerful lights coming from the boats at anchor, as well as from the buildings along the shore and the villas on the hillsides. A local band was playing calypso music at the Marigot Beach Club as the day sailors walked uphill through the gardens to their rooms to freshen up for dinner.

When Lyn and Mel reached the terrace by their room overlooking the bay, they stood at the railing to breathe in the balmy air and listen to the night insects chirring in the dense shrubbery. They absorbed the scene of twinkly lights and cheerful music to store it up for the wintry New England days ahead.

"I never thought we'd make it back here, Mel. What a day."

"Let's hurry and change, Lyn; I'm hungry. We were lucky the dinghy came to the rescue; otherwise, we'd still be out there."

# Some News

Tilli hummed a happy tune as she set the table for dinner. Her homemade chicken pie baked in the oven; soon Mel would be home, and Lyn was coming, too. Tilli reminisced about her pilgrimage to the Holy Land and Cairo, Egypt. "Gosh! That was already two weeks ago," she thought aloud. She hummed and looked outside at the landscape; a dusting of snow had freshened everything up. "If I don't have to leave the house, I love the snow." While she waited, she pressed the switch on the gas fireplace in the living room and sat down on the sofa to look at pilgrimage pictures once more.

"My goodness, I can't believe Margaret and I got on those camels at the pyramids in el Giza. What fun we had galumphing over the sand! What would Bertie have thought of it all?" She sipped her oolong tea. "Wonder if it snows in Cairo?" She continued looking at her photos. "Oh, and the Nile dinner cruise with the unbelievable, half-hour non-stop twirling of that dervish: amazing! Everyone got dizzy just watching him."

She looked up and focused her eyes on the MacInnes castle picture hanging on the far wall. "Good thing Mel thought to save that picture when Peach of a Sole was being cleaned out. Poor Bertie, he always wanted to go. Why didn't he seize the moment? So many opportunities lost; now it's too late for him. Going to Scotland and visiting the MacInnes castle would be another fulfilled dream.

Wonder if Mel and Lyn would go with me? I'll have a talk with them."

She put the photos aside and picked up the new *Johnny's* seed catalog, which always arrived in January. "I don't know why they mail these out so early. I can't even think about planting until April." *Johnny's* was Tilli's favorite seed company. She always ordered organic seeds, and since the company was headquartered in Maine, she knew her seeds came from hearty stock. She'd had good luck with them over these many years. "Why try other companies?" she queried to no one in particular. The wall phone rang in the kitchen, and Tilli got up to answer it.

"Hello? ... Oh, hello, Father Thomas. ... Fine, and you? ... Of course, I'd be happy to do that. Tomorrow at two? ... I'll look forward to meeting her. ... Yes, everyone's just fine here. ... Oh, you know it. Margaret and I were so glad we went on the pilgrimage. Wasn't the young priest embarrassed about boarding the wrong bus? Margaret and I had a chuckle about that, all right. I'm sure he's recovered? ... Good. Margaret told me everything turned out all right. ... Fine, Father. ... Sure, you can count on me. Bye now."

"Mom, I'm home!" Mel walked in the door. "Something smells very good in here." She kissed her mother on the cheek, took off her coat, and hung it on the back of a kitchen chair to dry off. "It's just spitting a little snow, nothing to be concerned about. Who was on the phone?"

"Father Thomas. He asked me to go to the Hamlet Nursing Home tomorrow afternoon to visit with a resident who is also a parishioner. Apparently, one of the other volunteers is sick and can't go. I told him I'd do it." Tilli turned off the timer on the stove and reached for her potholders.

"Hi, it's me!" Lyn poked her head into the kitchen, sounding out of breath. "I can't stay because Paul is coming by shortly; we're going to the movies at the mall to see *The King's Speech.*"

"That's too bad. Oh, I mean, I thought you'd be here for dinner, and I was just about to take my chicken pie out of the oven. Why can't you and Paul have dinner here before you go to the show? Popcorn and soda don't make for a good dinner."

"Mom, we'll probably get some hamburgers on the fly. There's just enough time before the early show starts. It's a weekday, you know."

"So, it's just you and me, Mel. Have fun, Lyn."

"Mom, when was the last time we had dinner together—just the two of us—huh?"

"So, tell me about your day, Mel."

"Mom, I have some great news to share with you. I was going to tell you and Lyn, but now that she's run off, I'm too excited to wait!"

"Well, then, out with it!" Tilli felt Mel's happiness. Stay calm, she advised herself.

"Mark asked me to marry him! Isn't that wonderful? I haven't been able to think clearly all day. I was wondering why he'd asked me to meet him at the Honey Bun for breakfast on a weekday morning, but I went anyway. When I asked him to pass the sugar, he reached into his pocket and handed me a tiny blue box instead. See!"

Mel held out her left hand so Tilli could look at the gleaming diamond solitaire on her ring finger.

"Oh, it's gorgeous! What good taste he has." They hugged and kissed. "Mel, I couldn't be happier. I think you're a good match! If only your father were here."

"I think Daddy's always looking out for us. Don't you, Mom? I sense his presence often. I wish he were here to walk me down the aisle, though. No one can do that!"

"Oh, I think I know someone who would be tickled green to be asked."

"You mean Woody? You're right, Mom; he's the next perfect person. I can't imagine he'd say no. Especially since he doesn't have a daughter of his own."

"So, what do you and Mark think about a date?"

"June, Mom. We don't want to wait too long. It would be nice to have the ceremony and reception right here at the house and in the garden, maybe fifty or so friends. Mark and I agreed we want to keep it simple."

"Hold everything!" Tilli got up from the table and went into the kitchen to get a bottle of Emmet's from the cupboard and two small crystal glasses. "Sorry, no champagne for my toast. Here's to you, dear daughter, and to Mark. I wish you both many happy years together."

# Matilda and Mrs. Clark

"Oh, hello, I'm Matilda MacInnes. Father Thomas asked me to come."

"Right this way, Mrs. MacInnes; I know Mrs. Clark is waiting for you. When I told her you were coming, she seemed very pleased. I didn't know you knew each other."

"We don't; I'll be meeting her for the first time today."

"Well, here she is," the woman showed Tilli into Mrs. Clark's room and left.

Before Tilli could think of what to say, Mrs. Clark spoke. "Are you related to Amelia MacInnes?"

"Yes, she's my daughter. You know Mel?"

"She came to my house to collect canned goods for the Hamlet Food Pantry. It was before I moved into this home, oh, sometime maybe a year or more ago. How is she?"

"She's engaged, Mrs. Clark. Just yesterday, her boyfriend Mark asked her. They'll be getting married in June."

"Oh, happy day! She's a lovely young woman. You're lucky to have her for a daughter. She's kind and thoughtful. Just like my niece Amber. I don't know what I'd do without my Amber. God has blessed us, hasn't he?"

"Speaking of blessings, Mrs. Clark, would you like to see a few pictures of my recent pilgrimage to the Holy Land? For years I'd dreamed of going, and it wasn't until I reconnected with Father Thomas at the church that my dream came true."

"I've been blind for a few years now, Mrs. MacInnes, but if you describe what is in your pictures, I can imagine them. It works quite well for me."

"Oh, how thoughtless of me." Tilli was embarrassed. "Someone should have told me."

"Now, don't give it a second thought," Mrs. Clark reached in Tilli's direction to try and pat her on the hand. Mrs. Clark felt compelled to put Tilli at ease. And it worked.

Like two old friends, they sat side by side on the red velvet settee. "Oh, and here's one Margaret took of me at the Church of the Holy Sepulcher in Jerusalem. We waited in long lines everywhere we visited, but it was worth it! And, now, with these digital cameras, I took more photos than I ever would have in the past. So many amazing places to visit in Israel. Oh, listen to me prattling on. Enough! I want to hear more about you."

Mrs. Clark told Tilli about losing Selden, her grand-nephew, Amber's only child. Other people close to her were no longer here, and some of them Tilli had known also. Tilli listened intently before deciding to share Bertie's sudden passing with Mrs. Clark.

"Oh, Mrs. MacInnes, when I heard the news, I meant to send a card, and Amber would have written it on my behalf, but with my move here, the yard sale, the house, and all, we somehow never got to it."

Tilli patted Mrs. Clark's hand while, at the same time, she thought it unusual that Mrs. Clark would have wanted to send her a sympathy card. After all, they were meeting for the first time. Mel must have made quite an impression on this kindly woman.

They chatted continuously for an hour, as if they'd known each other forever. Mrs. Clark said, "I've had an interesting life so far. Of course, I'm on the sunny side of eighty, so I hope to have some time ahead of me. There are days when no one comes to visit, so I sit here and revisit my past. Where else am I going? What have I got to do? I'm not a television person. Can't see now anyway. My thoughts are full of good years. I draw on all that inventory. Did you know, Mrs. MacInnes, I once worked at the Home for Little Wanderers?"

Her ears perked up. "Home for Little Wanderers? Please, Mrs. Clark, call me Tilli."

"If I call you Tilli, then you must call me by my first name, too, or it won't be fair."

"Okay, if you like, but I don't know your first name."

"It's Evangeline, but friends call me Evie. And I consider you my new friend."

For a second, Tilli wasn't sure if she'd heard right. "Did you know my husband, Delbert?"

"Why, yes, Del and I graduated from high school together. In fact, we went through all the grades together. You're a lucky woman, Tilli. Your husband was a good man. And he was more than kind to me."

Tilli didn't know what to say. Should she ask Evangeline if she was the Evie? She cautioned herself not to jump to conclusions, but how many women named Evangeline could there be in Hamlet? It wasn't the most common first name. Come to think of it, she'd never known anyone with that name. Here, in front of her, was an elderly, sweet, blind woman in a wheelchair. Why dredge up the past and embarrass her when she had gone through so much? Tilli decided to wait and see if Evangeline raised the subject.

Tilli thought she'd better read those letters over more closely, the ones she'd found among Bertie's possessions. Had they been addressed to Del? That's what Evangeline had just referred to him as. Maybe Tilli had misconstrued the contents. She reasoned with herself to be patient.

"When did you work at the Home for Little Wanderers, Mrs. Cla—I mean Evangeline? Or Evie? And what did you do there?"

"Evie is perfect! Oh, now, let me see if I can remember. It was a very long time ago. I began working there in 1956 and left in the mid-sixties; that's it. I worked there for ten years before I went to the Perkins School for the Blind. You know, Tilli, as I've gotten older, my memory has become strange. I can tell you what happened years ago, but I can't remember what I had for dinner last night. It can be quite a nuisance."

Tilli didn't want Evangeline to get off the subject of the Home for Little Wanderers. She didn't want to appear too curious either, so she just sat for a moment, looking out the window at the cars in the parking lot. New snow had fallen since she'd come. She'd have to scrape off her windshield and get the defroster going.

"Well, since you're interested," Evie continued. "I took care of the wee babes that were left to be adopted out. My training is in nursing. They didn't have pediatric nurses, per se, in those days; I got experience and training on the job. I loved the smell of the babies—especially the newborns. The best part of my job was sitting in the rocking chair and feeding them their bottles. When I started working, I was only sixteen. I was a candy striper. Do you know what that is, Tilli?"

"Gosh, I haven't thought about candy stripers in years.

Yes, there were a few in my high school class who went to volunteer at the local hospital in Connecticut, where I grew up. I loved their pink-and-white striped uniforms and those crisp little hats, the white stockings and shoes. If I hadn't disliked the sight of blood so much, I might have been interested in being a candy striper myself.

"Do you have special memories of any of those babies? I mean, did any particular babies stand out from the others, or were they all the same, so to speak? Just asking."

"Well, since you raise the question, I do remember one occasion when all of us became ecstatic. It was just before I left. An unwed mother had given birth to a baby boy and left him with the home to be adopted out. There were so many of those cases: many young women, many baby boys and girls, but this one was different because the resident medical doctor and his wife were the childless couple who adopted this baby. We were so happy, we threw them a baby shower! We loved this doctor and his wife; she'd come and visited often, so we knew her. There was something sad about her, though, and it wasn't until later we learned she'd had several miscarriages. When this tiny baby boy went to live with them, everyone was happy."

Tilli hung on every word. Was it her Jonathan? Did he get adopted by the doctor and his wife? She wanted that doctor's name, but she kept her thoughts to herself. It was time to go home; she'd been here way longer than an hour.

"Evie, I have really enjoyed my visit with you. I know you have another volunteer from St. Vincent's Church who comes, but may I visit you again?"

"You needn't ask. Not too many people come to see me, mostly Amber. I'd be delighted. We've had a good talk, haven't we?"

Tilli replied, "Maybe the next time you can tell me about your work at the Perkins School."

"You'll have to remind me where I left off. So glad we've met, Tilli."

The next morning, after Mel left for school, Tilli went up to the Governor Winthrop desk in the den to examine the packet of letters more closely. She turned on the lamp and opened the drawer, took the packet out, and settled into the comfortable wing chair.

"Do I really want to read these? He's gone. What does it matter now?" she thought aloud.

She liked Evangeline Clark and didn't want to jump to conclusions. She told herself it didn't matter anymore what the relationship between Evie and Bertie had been. Hadn't she—Tilli—and the girls had a good life? Hadn't Bertie always been a good husband and father? And hadn't *she* kept a big secret from Bertie all these years?

"Maybe it's my age. If I'd learned about these letters years ago, my reaction might have been different. Funny, I don't remember reading this one; there's no date on this letter."

*Dear Del,*

*I couldn't have made it without your help all these years. Whenever I took in another orphan, or especially when I took in my niece Amber and her little boy, Selden, you were there to help. Remember, I told you Amber is my brother's child; he ran off and abandoned his responsi- bilities. I wasn't asking for myself, as you know; it was always for the children, and not once did you turn me down.*

*I want you to know this is my last letter. The children are grown, and I am an old lady. Amber is coming to my aid now, and I am relieved not to have to ask you for money. I knew, even when we were in high school, you were a special person, an honorable man. I have always loved and respected you, my dearest friend. Your wife and daughters are very lucky.*

*God bless you.*

*Yours always, Evie*

Tilli read a couple more letters, then retied the string, and closed the desk. Not in a hurry to get up from her chair, she reflected on the years with Bertie. Certainly, they hadn't been exciting; rather, they'd been steady-as-you-go days. You-can-always-count-on-me days. In retrospect, they'd shared a comfortable life. Their marriage had been a journey, with Bertie leading and her following along.

It hadn't always been easy to keep the peace and let him make the decisions. In the early years, she'd tried arguing with him, but his temper was such that she decided it wasn't worth the effort. In the beginning, she'd thrown dishes, slammed doors, moped, and sulked, but she'd gotten over that fast! When he was wrong, he apologized right away and got on with life as if nothing had happened while she continued to stew for days. As the years went by, it became simpler to keep her point of view to herself. She didn't think he wanted to know her thoughts anyway.

"Funny, when we first met, we had great conversations—hours of talking about everything under the sun—and then, somewhere along the way, things changed. What did I give up in order to keep peace in our house? Well, Bertie's no longer here to determine my future, and I'd like to think I still have a few good years ahead of me."

She looked up at the bookshelves lining one wall, the titles plain to see, and *A Year in Your Garden: Month by Month* caught her eye.

"I need to take care of that," she said. "Why haven't I heard from Jonathan? It's been four months since that social worker wrote the certified letter. Doesn't my son want to know me?" She reminded herself, "Jonathan doesn't owe *me* a thing!"

She telephoned the Home for Little Wanderers. "Hello, is Dorothy Fielding available? May I leave a message? Yes, I'll be here all morning. Thank you."

After she hung up, she told herself that the only response was to be patient. She did some laundry, ironed a couple of blouses, and emptied the dishwasher, but Ms. Fielding never called back. It was sunny out and not cold. She put on a light jacket and walked to the cemetery to talk to Bertie.

It struck her as strange that the South Hamlet Cemetery had originally been for Protestants only, with the Catholics buried at the newer cemetery, down the road and on the other side of the street. What would happen when her time came? Perhaps today, there was no longer such discrimination; nevertheless, Bertie was surrounded by Congregationalists, Baptists, and Presbyterians, and this cemetery was full.

The MacInnes's rough-cut and unpolished granite stone marker was visible from the street. In December, she'd put a basket filled with seasonal greens, golden pine-cones, and red berries, with a velvet bow, on the grave. Now, it was buried under the snow, with only the tips of some of the evergreen boughs poking through. She didn't like cemeteries, or funerals for that matter, and until Bertie died, she didn't need to come here because the plot included perpetual care. But ever since he had passed on, either she, Mel, or Lyn stopped by to share the weekly news with him.

Time spent reading Evie's letters had put Tilli into a reflective mood. She stood in front of the stone. "I'm sorry I misunderstood you," she whispered. "Are you there, Bertie? I know I called you some nasty names after I found Evie's letters; please forgive me. I want you to know I'm looking for my son, the baby boy I had before I met you. Such a big secret to keep—all these many years—I realize now, after meeting Evie, that if I'd told you about Jonathan, you'd probably have tried to help me find him.

"I've got good news for you, Bertie; Mel is getting married to her boyfriend, Mark. It will be a June wedding, and we're asking Woody—if it's all right with you—to walk her down the aisle. I know you'll agree, since you can't do it yourself, and he was your best friend. Well, that's all for this week, Bertie. See you next Tuesday. I love you, but then, you've always known that, haven't you?"

# Shopping for Gowns

"Mom, there's a call for you," Lyn hollered up the stairs.

"Hello? Oh, Dorothy, I knew you must have been busy when I left a message two days ago and hadn't heard back. Oh, I'm sorry; hope you're feeling better now. I've waited quite some time, and it's been hard to be patient. Has the social worker received any response to the certified letter? She has? Well, what's the next step? Oh, please don't ask me to wait longer. It's been so difficult. Okay, I understand. Thank you for anything you can do." Tilli hung up and couldn't imagine what was causing the delay.

"Come on, Mom, this is the day we set aside to go shopping for gowns for Mel's wedding. I don't know how long it will take, so Mel and I are planning to take you to Peaches for lunch." Tilli came downstairs, Lyn was in the hallway putting on her jacket, and Mel was already outside warming up her SUV.

"This is so exciting, Mom!" Mel backed out of the driveway, and they were off to Annette's Bridal Shop.

"I hope we find your bridal gown today, Mel. I've heard Annette's has beautiful dresses at more reasonable prices than Giorgio's Boutique. I wonder what kind of maid-of-honor and mother-of-the-bride dresses we'll find; some of those nylon chiffon gowns look matronly and uncomfortable," Lyn said from the back seat.

"Well, let's keep an open mind. I can't believe I'm getting married in two months. There's so much to do."

"I've told you, Sis, I have connections to caterers, musicians, photographers, and other suppliers because of the many events I've pulled together for the Hamlet Community Arts Center. I can help with anything. Just let me know, and I'll get on the horn."

"No, Lyn, all of that is under control. Mark and I've been talking about where we want to go on our honeymoon. He's got his ideas, and I've got mine; we can't seem to agree. Good thing we set our date for the last Saturday in June. With all the snow days we've had this winter, and several school cancelations, the children and I will be in the classroom until June twenty-sixth."

"It's going to seem strange when you move to Mark's house, Mel. We've been together, under one roof, for the past three years; I'm going to miss you," Tilli said.

"Jeez! Mom, I'm only moving across town, but I know what you mean. We've had a lot of fun together. That won't end. I think the three of us should plan a yearly vacation together, as long as that's something you and Lyn would want to do."

Tilli remained thoughtful in the backseat for the rest of the ride. As Mel pulled into the parking lot of Annette's Bridal Shop, she said, "I know we will always make time for each other, and a yearly trip together would be something to look forward to."

"Mom, you've been very quiet all the way over here. Is everything okay? Oh, I bet it was the phone call you got before we left the house?"

"Never mind, Lyn. It was Dorothy Fielding. Jonathan got the certified letter from the social worker, but for some reason, he still hasn't responded. Dorothy said I should be patient awhile longer, but it's been four months! Let's not talk about this now; we're here to go shopping for Mel's gown, and we should enjoy every minute."

"Thank you, Henri and Justine, for showing us your cozy upstairs apartment. I had no idea it was so roomy up there." Tilli had sat down to lunch in the new restaurant downstairs, where Bertie's shoe repair shop had been. "And this dining room! I never would have thought his shop could be delightful. I must say, Henri, it's been difficult to visit familiar places in town; Bertie's everywhere I go."

"Well, Matilda, I hope, now that you've come, you won't wait long to return."

The coq au vin with tiny roasted potatoes and fresh asparagus was delicious. They had splurged with glasses of Dubouef Morgon Jean Descombes Gamay from Beaujolais and finished with a roasted pear crème brûlée for dessert.

"What else would the mesdames like?" Henri wore a huge smile as he stood next to their table with a white linen cloth draped over his arm.

"Henri, if we eat another bite, you will have to roll us out the door," replied Tilli.

"I'm feeling more than satisfied right now," said Lyn.

"And I am happy we found my wedding gown today, and pretty quickly, I might add. And your dresses are just lovely. I like that they're both just below the knee, stylish, and appropriate for an afternoon wedding in the garden. Mesdames, I think we did well." Mel laughed as she took the leatherette holder into her hands to see the tab. This wasn't going to be an inexpensive lunch by any means, but when she opened the holder, it was empty.

"Henri, please come over." Mel waved to him as he was about to go into the kitchen. The restaurant was empty now; after all, they'd stretched lunch into the late afternoon.

"Yes, mesdames?" Henri stood alert and waited.

Mel said, "Henri, I think you forgot to put our bill into the holder."

"No, mesdames, I didn't forget anything."

"Well, this isn't acceptable, Henri. We must pay for today's lunch." At that moment, Mel thought back to the night she and Mark had dined here. Mark had told her afterward that their dinner bill had been much too affordable for what they'd eaten.

Tilli said, "Henri, if you don't charge us for lunch, we won't come again."

Lyn said, "Henri, thank you so much. This is very generous of you! It was the most scrumptious lunch I've ever eaten, and I can't wait to return with my friends, but when I do—and from now on—you must let all of us pay the full amount."

# Before the Wedding

"Hello, Evie. How are you today?" Since their initial meeting, Tilli had been coming once a week to see Evangeline at the Hamlet Nursing Home.

"Oh, fine, Tilli. You wouldn't want to hear me complain, would you?" Evangeline was always careful not to talk about aches and pains—though she had her share—because she was afraid no one would come if they felt uncomfortable.

"I brought the crossword puzzle from the *Hamlet Weekly* with me."

"Tilli, you know I can't see."

"You don't have to. I'm going to read you the clue and how many blank spaces there are, and you and I are going to put our heads together to find the right answers. I brought a sharp pencil—I always use a pencil so I can try words out—we can erase things if they're wrong."

This process worked quite well, and they laughed at some of the absurd clues. Evie seemed to enjoy the challenge, and Tilli decided, from now on, she'd bring the weekly puzzle to share.

"Next time, I'll bring a couple of books on tape with me. The Hamlet Library has classics as well as contemporary books. Oh, and they have wonderful CDs with symphony music as well as popular tunes. I see there's a CD player next to your television set. What do you think?"

"Tilli, it would be a great way to pass time. The stuff

on television is mostly garbage. Whatever happened to all the good shows, for example, the *Carol Burnett Show*, or the weekly spy or cops and robbers programs, like *Dragnet* and *The Man from U.N.C.L.E.*? They kept me on the edge of my seat without spilling blood and guts. Since I lost my eyesight, all I turn on is PBS programs, such as the weekly episodes of *Masterpiece Theater*. Thank goodness there's nothing wrong with my hearing!"

"I agree with you, Evie. I'm not much for television either, so I usually read in the evening. I'll go to the library right from here and see what's on the shelf. See you tomorrow."

"Wonderful, Tilli. You're such a good friend. Thank you."

"Hi, Evie; I brought you some goodies." Tilli brought books on tape and several CDs with her from the library.

"I can't wait to delve in—later—after our visit, that is."

"Can't stay too long this afternoon, Evie. I'll get you started on one of the books and have you touch the buttons on the cassette player, so you'll know how to run it, but then I need to get home. I want to ask you something, though. I haven't met your niece, Amber, but do you think she'd come with you to Mel's wedding? It will be in two weeks, and Mel and I really want you to come. I've brought an invitation with me, so you and Amber will have all the details."

"Why, Tilli, I'm tickled pink to be asked. Amber is coming tomorrow—it's Thursday, right? So, I can ask her then. I can't imagine her saying anything except yes! Oh, what'll I wear? I haven't gone anywhere for years! Oh, my, this is so exciting!"

"Evie, not to worry about anything; I'm sure Amber will find something appropriate in your closet."

# One Week to Go

"Mom, I'm home." Mel walked into the kitchen and put the mail on the counter next to the wall phone.

"I'm upstairs, Mel."

"What are you *doing*, Mom?" Mel couldn't believe the heaps of clothing on the bed, piles on the floor, and her mother's arms holding dresses on hangers.

"I read in a feng shui book that I borrowed from the Hamlet Library about cleaning out clutter and stuff you don't need. This is supposed to create space for new positive energy to enter into my life. Perhaps by ridding myself of all the things I never use or wear, there will be room for Jonathan to come into my life. I have nothing to lose and am at my wit's end, Mel." Tilli welled up despite her best efforts.

"Oh, Mom, come on. You won't have a thing left at the rate you're going." Mel hugged her. "Let's go downstairs, and I'll make a pot of tea. Maybe you're right about cleaning out clutter; that's good, but you don't need to deprive yourself of *everything*! This is over the top, Mom. Please stop now. What kind of tea would you like? There's afternoon delight or Darjeeling."

"I don't care, Mel; either one's fine."

"Hi, I'm home." Lyn came through the front door—heavy-footed—and opened, then closed the hall closet with her usual slam. She entered the kitchen and saw her mother and Mel sitting at the table, quietly sipping tea;

they didn't look happy.

She lifted the lid on the teapot; there was still some left. "Think I'll pour myself a cup and join the fun. What's up?"

"Mom's into feng shui."

"What's that?"

"Never mind, you two! I had to do something, so I cleaned out my bedroom closet. What's wrong with that?" Tilli took her cup into both hands and glared at them.

"This is not good, Mom. You never glare! Are you all right?" Leave it to Lyn to push buttons.

"It's the same old same old. I am tired of waiting to hear from Jonathan! There, you have it; that's my problem."

"Mom, you haven't looked at the mail." Mel smiled.

Tilli saw the mail by the phone. She looked at Mel; then she looked at Lyn. In slow motion, she sifted through the advertisements, the electric bill, and her semi-annual notice about teeth cleaning, and there, at the very bottom, was a white business-size envelope hand-addressed to her. She studied the return address: Dr. James Collen, Restful Haven, Llandeilo, SA19 6HN, Wales, United Kingdom.

She was overcome and shook so badly that she almost dropped the letter.

"Come, Mom, sit down; let me help you." Mel took her mother's arm and led her back to the table.

Tilli was immobile; it was as if she'd been struck by lightning. Mel had to slit open the envelope and hand the letter to her. Mel and Lyn waited quietly while their mother read its contents. They worried that their mother's condition was fragile and that she might not be able to deal with this letter if it brought bad news.

After some moments, Tilli looked up. "He lives in Wales! And it's a long letter."

"Do you want to tell us what it says, Mom?" Lyn asked.

"Yes, of course. I want to share it with both of you. The letter contains bad and good news, just like life. We haven't heard from him until now because his mother, his adoptive mother, was terminally ill and passed away recently. Since he got the certified letter from the social worker, he's been busy flying back and forth between Wales and Florida to make arrangements. He's not ready to meet me yet; he needs more time to settle affairs. He hopes I'll understand. That's what he writes. To think how many times, over the past four or five months, I've conjured up all sorts of reasons to explain why he wasn't responding, but this never occurred to me."

"Who could imagine such a reason, Mom?" Lyn remarked.

"How are you doing?" Mel was concerned.

Tilli took a deep breath. "I'm sad for him, of course, but it's a great relief to have received this letter. Here, girls, read it for yourselves. Now, my dream of seeing Jonathan—oh, I'll have to get used to calling him James—Dr. James Collen—is filled with hope. Knowing we will meet makes waiting bearable. But Wales! Why doesn't he live in America?"

# Amelia and Mark

After such a cool and rainy spring, Mel's wedding day was one of those perfect days in June. On the last Saturday of the month, family and guests gathered in the garden at 5 Cedar Street. Mark had asked a couple of his musician friends to play. The guests looked festive with the colorful parasols and fans they had in hand just in case the sun got too warm or the air too still.

The ceremony took place under the pergola Woody had built some years ago, which was now covered with fragrant Amethyst Falls wisteria blossoms. Here Mark waited patiently for Mel to arrive. Paul escorted Tilli down the grassy pathway to a folding chair in the front row. It had been years since she'd worn anything fancy, and the airy, green, tea-length chiffon dress suited her well.

Paul went back up the grassy path to escort Lyn, the maid of honor, to the pergola. Then he stood next to Mark as his best man. Lyn's dress was similar in style to Tilli's, but a slightly darker shade of green. Both Mark and Paul wore beige seersucker suits and had white miniature roses with baby's breath for boutonnieres.

No one had ever seen Woody dressed up, but today he wore a new tan-colored linen suit. His gray hair was neatly combed, and his beard trimmed. In addition to a huge grin, he wore a small boutonniere of white miniature roses and shamrocks. It was obvious to everyone how pleased he was to be escorting his best friend's daughter on her wedding day.

Mel wore a princess-style, tea-length, satin organza dress with beautiful lace appliqués and a cluster of fresh baby's breath in her hair. She carried a bouquet of Bridal Sunblaze miniature roses amid fragrant *Stephanotis* and baby's breath.

Tom Brewster had gone to Hamlet's town hall and taken out a one-day permit to allow him to marry Mel and Mark. In addition to being one of Bertie's best Peach of a Sole customers, Tom was a lifelong friend who had graduated from Hamlet High with Bertie. Tom came to the wedding with his wife, Mary, and their son, John, who everyone knew as the local reporter for the *Hamlet Weekly*. Tom was pleased as punch to take part in today's celebration.

Amber sat in the front row with her aunt Evangeline, Margaret Flannery, and Tilli. After Mel and Mark had exchanged their wedding vows and rings, Tom Brewster pronounced them husband and wife amid cheers and applause from everyone.

The caterer had set up a bar on the patio, and wait staff passed hors d'oeuvres among the guests. Round tables suitable for six guests each were covered in creamy white linen tablecloths. The centerpieces were small round vases filled with white and pink roses. These tables were located along the shady side of the house, under mature oak trees and amid blooming shrubs.

Tilli went over to Tom Brewster and Woody and hooked her arms through theirs. "Come along with me, you two; I think you may know someone who's here today." She escorted them to where Evangeline was sitting in her wheelchair in the shade.

"Who's that? I recognize that voice," Evangeline said when she heard Woody jabbering. "There's only one person with an Irish accent in all of Hamlet! I haven't heard your voice for years, Woody!"

Tilli left the three of them chatting away about their high school days.

"How are you doing, Mom?" Lyn was with Paul.

"Oh, I've just been wishing your father could be here today." Tilli was happy that Lyn and Paul were spending every available moment together these days. He'd become a fixture at Lyn's dinner table most evenings, and now that Mel would be living with Mark across town, perhaps Paul and Lyn would come over to join her once a week. He was quite different from Mark, but was a good match for Lyn; they both loved jazz, modern art, and traveling. Lyn was much more assertive now that she'd found her voice! Tilli thought back to the days when Bertie was alive. How might things have been different if *she'd* spoken up more often and let her wishes be known? Oh, but then again, why hadn't *he* told her about helping Evangeline all these years? "Can't change the past," she muttered.

"Who knows!" she said more loudly.

"What, Mom?" asked Lyn

"Oh, did I say something?" Tilli told herself to be careful. Lately, she'd been voicing her thoughts aloud too often; it could get embarrassing.

By early evening, Mel and Mark had changed into comfortable clothes and were ready to head off on their honeymoon.

"Mom, I want you to know you'll be seeing a lot of us after we return. This has been the most incredible day."

"Tilli, have no fear. I will take good care of Mel."

"Mark, I won't worry; she's in good hands. Just have a wonderful time in Canada."

Everyone gathered along the driveway to wave them off. It had been John Brewster's idea to tie empty soup cans to the bumper of Mark's getaway car, a blue 1969 Volkswagen Karmann Ghia convertible, and Paul and Woody had joined in this prank.

Soon after Mel and Mark drove off amid the clanking of the cans, the musicians went home. It wasn't long before most of the guests exchanged goodbye hugs and left.

"Mom," said Lyn as they kicked off their shoes and settled into comfy seats in the living room. Several long-time friends were in no hurry to go home and had joined them. "Wasn't today the best?"

"I'd have given anything if Bertie'd been here to walk his lassie to the altar." Suddenly, Woody noticed the picture of the MacInnes castle hanging on a wall in the living room, "It's the picture Bertie had hanging inside Peach of a Sole. Oh, Tilli, that castle meant so much to him. Glad you've hung it here. Wish Bertie were here to go to Scotland wit you. Did'ya know how much he cared 'bout that place?"

"Woody, I know Bertie is with us today in spirit. I could feel him smiling down on us, and maybe one day, the girls will go with me to visit his ancestral home. It's on my list of things to do, and Bertie's spirit will be with us there, too."

Tilli was tired from all the activities. She hadn't slept well last night, and she was just plain talked out. Why didn't they all go home? She couldn't say what she wanted: The party's over, folks—I want to get out of these duds!

"And lovely t'was to see Evie. We always called her Evie: me, Tom, and Bertie. Did ya know Evie and Bertie were an item in high school?"

"Yes, believe it or not, Woody, I do know that. Bertie certainly had good taste. Evie's a special woman."

"Yer not gettin' jealous or nothin', are ya?"

"No, Woody, I'm too old for that. Besides, Bertie married me! Evie and I have become good friends. I think Bertie'd be pleased."

Paul was sitting on the sofa with his arm around Lyn. She leaned into him and looked totally relaxed. Tilli wondered if they'd marry.

"Everything's packed up, Mrs. MacInnes," said the caterer. "We're off unless you want us to do anything else. All the leftovers are in your refrigerator. You won't have to cook for a week!"

"Oh, I'm so glad you said that." Tilli got up in her stocking feet and opened the refrigerator. "Everybody has to take something home. Come on! Woody? Margaret? Help us out, please." Tilli got the ball rolling.

They followed Tilli into the kitchen, where she handed them empty containers. After they'd filled them with leftovers, Tilli kissed each friend on the cheek, gave them squeezy hugs, and with a flourish, opened the kitchen door. At first, they were a bit stunned by her abrupt gesture, but then they laughed! Seeing that Tilli wasn't joking—and not offended one bit by her actions—they took the hint, gathered their leftovers, waved goodbye, and cheerfully went into the warmth of a perfect summer evening.

# Five Months Later

Everyone was gathered in the living room, the kitchen had been cleaned up, and Tilli had turned on the fireplace; they were relaxing with their cups of coffee after a sumptuous Thanksgiving dinner.

Mel had just finished telling them about their off-road pink Jeep ride in the red sandstone hills around Sedona during their vacation in Arizona two summers ago.

"Well, on the other hand," Lyn interrupted, "I really liked our quick trip to Pittsburgh. Aren't museums and symphony concerts great entertainment, too?"

Tilli said, "I'm sick of hearing about Pittsburgh!"

Mel and Mark talked about their honeymoon to Montreal and Quebec City. They all had a story to share about someplace they'd been. Paul told them about sailing and snorkeling trips he'd taken in the Cayman Islands. "It's great because the water's shallow surrounding the Caymans; the big cruise ships can't get in close, so there's less traffic, both on the water and on the smaller islands. I hope Lyn will join me next time."

This was the first time Paul had indicated taking a vacation with Lyn, and she raised her eyebrows with pleasant surprise.

"So, where do you think you girls will go with Tilli next summer? Have you given it any thought?" Paul smiled at Lyn while sipping his coffee.

Before Lyn could answer, Tilli interrupted, "It's time

to visit the MacInnes homeland on the Morvern Peninsula in Scotland. Bertie always dreamed of going there; I can't wait much longer. There! I've said my piece. Do I get my daughters' votes of approval?"

Lyn smiled. "Mom, we thought you'd never ask! I know I'm speaking for Mel, but we can't think of a place we'd rather go. Oh, and if I remember correctly, isn't visiting Scotland one of your five wishes?"

Amid all of the good-natured chatter, they almost didn't hear the ring of the wall phone in the kitchen.

"Shush!" Mel said as politely as she could. "I'll get it," she announced and ran to the phone.

"Yes, you have the right number … No, this isn't Matilda; it's her daughter Mel … Who? … Oh! So glad you called … Oh yes, I'm so very sorry. Please accept our sincere sympathy … Of course, I'll get her. Bye for now."

While Mel was on the phone, they'd quieted down and were watching the flames flickering in the fireplace. Lyn got up from the sofa and turned up a couple of the table lamps. Now that it was dark outdoors, she pulled the draperies closed. It was all busyness to keep herself occupied.

Mel returned. "Mom, it's James Collen. Are you all right, or shall I get his phone number and tell him you'll call back?"

"No! No, don't do that, Mel. Of course, I'm all right. I'm fine. How lovely he thought to call today." Tilli hurried to the kitchen.

Meanwhile, they discussed the circumstances surrounding Tilli's son and how grateful they were that he'd finally telephoned. Mel was surprised by the relief she herself felt now that James was on the phone; she welled up.

"Since Daddy died four years ago, we've kept tissues

handy." Lyn said to the guys as she held out the box to Mel.

"Thanks, Lyn. I hope we can meet him soon; this phone call is so welcome. I know how I feel right now; Mom's relief must be tremendous. It's turned out to be the best Thanksgiving ever!"

"He telephoned from Florida. Now that his mother's and the Collen family affairs have been settled, Jim will return to Wales, where he lives." Tilli sat on the edge of the old wing chair. "I told him about the MacInnes castle and that we're planning to visit Scotland next summer. He doesn't know when he'll come back to America and asked if we could come to Llandeilo, a small village near Swansea, and he said that he's got plenty of room."

Tilli's face showed mixed emotions as she settled back into the wing chair. "Oh, why does he live so *far away*! Now that I've heard his voice, I wish we didn't have to wait until next summer to see him."

"I'm afraid, Mom, if we go in the springtime, it will be rainy and cold; but, if we start planning our vacation after Christmas, the winter and spring months will fly by, and we'll be on a plane to the United Kingdom before we know it." Mel knew she couldn't go anywhere until after school let out in June.

Now that James was clearly in the picture, Lyn imagined that visiting their ancestral home had moved down a notch or two on her mother's wish list. "Since James lives in Wales, he must know his way around the U.K. Wonder what drew him there?"

Needless to say, further discussion centered on Jonathan—now James Collen—a brother Lyn and Mel had never met and a son whom Tilli hadn't seen in over forty years.

# United Kingdom

"Now I know why the British love drinking tea made with loose tea instead of tea bags: it's more flavorful." Tilli, Lyn, and Mel were sitting on the terrace, facing perfectly aligned rows of birch trees planted outside the Tate Modern museum of art on the banks of the River Thames.

"Oh, Mom, look, there's a tour boat just pulling up to the dock. Wonder where it goes?" Lyn was happy they'd agreed to spend a couple of overnights in London before heading to Wales.

"I'll bet we could catch the next one heading in the direction of the Tower of London. Did you know that the Thames is known as liquid history?" Lyn had an open brochure in her lap and was scanning it for what to see and do.

"The double decker bus tour was fun. From all the sights we buzzed by, I'll certainly remember Hatch, Match, and Dispatch: their bureau of public records." Tilli breathed in their surroundings: the Houses of Parliament directly across the river, the nearby London Eye Ferris wheel, and various boats chugging on the river below. She reflected on some of the art they'd seen inside the Tate: Rodin sculptures and Picasso paintings of contorted women. "He must have hated his mother!" Tilli blurted out.

"Excuse me?" Mel was startled.

"Picasso. He must have hated his mother. Why else

would he depict women in such grotesque images? I wonder if James ever hated me for giving him up? I've often wondered how he must have felt all these years." For a few moments, they sat quietly, each with her own thoughts, while the leaves on the birches ruffled in the breeze.

"Mom, if James ever hated you for even one moment, I don't think we'd be making this trip. Oh, look! That tour boat's back. Let's go down the Thames to the Tower of London." Mel was glad they'd already paid for their meal and could dash off.

# Train to Wales

From London, they took a train to Swansea, a city of about 250,000 people. This area on the Gower Peninsula in Wales was the United Kingdom's first designated area of outstanding beauty. At the start of their ride, they had chatted and laughed about their London adventures, but after four hours, they became drowsy from the motion of the train. Tilli leaned back and watched the countryside whiz past while Lyn dozed off.

Mel noticed her mother sitting upright, motionless, and with a far-away look in her eyes. "Mom, we need to get ready; the next stop is ours." Mel thought she hadn't heard and gently patted her mother's arm. "Are you all right?"

Tilli shook herself and stretched. "I can't believe this is the day. So many emotions! I want to remember every second when we meet. Many thoughts spinning around in my head. What does James look like? Will he like me? We're strangers—a gap of so many years—should I hug him? Kiss him? Will I cry? I don't want to fall apart."

"Mom, everything's going to be okay; just do what comes naturally."

# Swansea in Wales

The conductor helped them off the train, and they rolled their luggage into the station. It was early afternoon, not too many people milling about.

"I knew it! He's forgotten us!" Tilli was sweating and fumbled with her handkerchief, mopping her brow and wiping her nose. Anything to be doing something.

"Wonder where he is?" Lyn scanned the station's expanse. "Maybe he's stuck in traffic?"

Mel pursed her lips, quietly watching her mother. "This isn't good; he should be here," she said and sighed.

"Well, I just knew we should've booked a hotel room or someplace so we wouldn't be dependent on him. How long do you want to stand here and wait?" Lyn looked at her watch, ready to march to the information desk and ask about accommodations.

Mel reached down and unzipped a small outside pocket on her suitcase, where she'd put a slip of paper with James's phone number on it, when out of the blue, a pair of shiny brown shoes suddenly appeared in her line of vision. She straightened up to see a tall, slender man with sandy-brown hair and smiling blue eyes—her mother's eyes—standing before them.

"Hi, I'm Jim Collen. Didn't mean to keep you waiting. Sorry! Traffic's ghastly. No excuse!" He held out a bouquet of mixed garden flowers and a box of Wickedly Welsh Chocolates. "The three of you can share the sweets, but the flowers—I picked these for you." He stretched his arm in Tilli's direction.

Oh, joy! At last! Here he stood! She took the candy and bouquet from him, handed them to Lyn, and ignoring his right hand, which he'd extended to shake Tilli's, she wrapped her arms around him and pulled him close. He responded by pulling *her* closer, gently rubbing her back, and softly kissing her cheek. For some moments, they stood as if they were the only two people in the station.

Lyn and Mel watched. Would Tilli ever let go? Or maybe it was James who wasn't letting go of *her?*

Breathing in his scent, and with one last squeeze, she released him, so Mel and Lyn could exchange hugs, too. Tilli wiped away her tears and giggled.

Hearing her, James laughed. "Please don't call me James; I'm Jim. Come on; let's go! Follow me; car's not far out that door." He took two of the suitcases and, with long strides, started walking away, the three of them hurrying to keep up.

# Restful Haven

Jim, of course, navigated the busy streets of Swansea with the expertise of someone who was comfortable and familiar with driving on the left-hand side of roads. The city was soon behind them, and lovely views appeared in all directions.

They passed through seaside villages with many houses built of native gray stone. The closely planted buildings looked as if they'd sprouted from the rocky soil. The sea was at every turn, and fishing boats bobbed in harbors and next to docks. A flock of seagulls screeched and laughed, flying and diving above and around one red trawler heading into port. The road wound through open land with pebbly beaches gracing the shore.

The A483, a numbered road, turned inland and followed along the River Tywi in Carmarthenshire. Plump white sheep with black faces clipped and chewed in the undulating pastures. Contented cows, with little calves cavorting about, leisurely munched their cud. Brown pleasure horses with sleek summer coats kicked up their heels in the thick green grass. What was not to like about this corner of the world?

After passing through the village of Ffairfach, and with vast acres of National Trust land now on both sides of the road, Jim continued driving, taking them over a historic, single-arch stone bridge directly into Llandeilo, a town of about three thousand people. Here were houses, mostly stucco with dormers and steeply pitched roofs, painted in shades of red, pink, blue, and cream. Some had rusticated corners or were of the Tudor style, half-timbered with foundations of locally cut gray stone.

Along the way, Jim pointed out a few important sites: St. Teilo's Anglican Church, the distant Dinefwr Castle set on a steep rise above the northern bank of the Tywi, and the fairground where national sheep-herding trials were held each fall. Jim steered over the Tywi, once again, via another one-lane bridge, and turned onto Bethlehem Road. A quick right, followed by a left-hand hook, put them onto a gravel drive.

*Restful Haven* was painted on a modest wooden sign stuck in the ground next to an old fieldstone wall. The driveway curved gently through plantings of shrubs and trees as they drove steadily uphill, with his house visible now and again. As they pulled into an open area, the tires crunched onto pea stones. Before them stood the six-bedroom house built of gray stone in 1890, with later extensions added of cream-colored stucco. From here was a wide-sweeping view of the town below, as well as a glimpse of the shimmering blue sea at the horizon. Next to a nearby tall yew hedge, Tilli noticed a small sign indicating a coastal walking path.

Jim pulled the car right up to the south-facing terrace, with borders full of colorful garden flowers—just like the ones in Tilli's bouquet. As soon as Jim shut off the engine, and before they'd had a chance to get out, the house door flew open. Two Cardigan corgis barreled towards them. Just behind the dogs came three children—Tilli's grandchildren. Vicki, Jim's wife, appeared, straightening her hair with her hands; she waved from the doorway, patiently waiting her turn.

"Maezie, Chloe, Thad, mind yer manners?" The girls giggled as Thad squirmed.

"Oh, not so formal." Tilli smiled. "Here: meet your aunts, Mel and Lyn. And you can call me Tilli." The children politely reached out their hands to shake, but Tilli gave each a hug before stepping aside to let Lyn and Mel do the same.

"Vicki, come on; your turn!" Jim motioned his wife over and put his arm around her shoulders, kissing her on the cheek.

Vicki was girlishly petite, with auburn hair and gray-green eyes. She laughed as she warmly hugged these new family members. "Been expecting ya for so long; glad yer finally here! Let's get inside. Hungry? Thirsty? I've made lemonade. Come wash up. Maezie, Chloe, Thad heft a bag; help 'em with their stuff."

Chloe, Maezie, and Thad toted the luggage upstairs and showed them to their bedrooms. Lyn and Mel's room had twin beds with a slipper tub in their bathroom. The windows faced uphill to a broad pasture where several horses grazed. Soft cream-colored wool throws were folded neatly at the foot of each bed, and there were several pillows to choose from. Cabbage rose wallpaper added to the comfiness of the room. Across the hall was a double bedroom for Tilli, which included her own bathroom. Her windows overlooked the terrace with its flower borders, the sweeping lawn that faced the town of Llandeilo, and the distant sea. This cozy room was painted duck-egg blue, and the chintz coverlet on the bed coordinated with the draperies, which hung neatly down to the soft cream-colored carpet.

As he set Tilli's suitcase onto a stand, Thad said, "Mummy had this oldest part of the house renovated, and she worried the workmen wouldn't finish before you came."

# On the Terrace

After freshening up, they headed downstairs amid laughter coming from the terrace. Jim and his family were outside with the corgis. It was a perfect summer afternoon with the fragrance of roses, lilies, and garden phlox perfuming the air.

"What are the dogs' names?" Mel asked, reaching down to stroke one's silky fur.

Vicki replied, "They're sisters from the same litter, and the one you're patting has more brown fur; she's Pokey. The one next to Jim's chair has more black and tan fur; she's Lila. Pokey is friendly with everyone, but Lila is definitely Jim's dog."

Vicki had made lemonade with freshly squeezed lemons, served with sprigs of mint picked from their garden. She passed a platter of scones, a dish of homemade strawberry preserves, and some clotted cream.

Maezie, Chloe, and Thad saw their opportunity to disappear and ran off laughing in the direction of the horses while the adults settled into cushioned chairs around the table, under the shade of a large market umbrella, to get to know each other.

So much to talk about! In between seemingly endless questions and answers, Vicki or Jim would refill glasses, and from time to time, they'd pause, sit still, and just breathe in their peaceful surroundings, happy to be together.

Lyn asked, "Jim, when did you learn you were adopted?"

"Oh, I knew right from the beginning; maybe I was two or so, I don't even remember. My parents were very forthright. I'll never forget my father telling me that to be adopted was special because when you're adopted, you are the *chosen* child: you are the *one* who is *always* wanted." Jim let these words settle in on his new family before continuing.

"I used to go to Boston Children's Services with my father when I was young. I knew my birth mother had given me up for adoption there." He paused to look at Tilli and reached for her hand. "My father was a medical doctor actively engaged at BCS for many years, as you know. I had a wonderful childhood, loving parents; I've been blessed with a good life. As I was growing up, I'd have fleeting moments when I'd wonder who my birth mother was, where she was—those kinds of thoughts—but I'll admit that I really didn't dwell on this, and certainly never thought about whether or not I had siblings. I was my parents' only child.

"So, when Mrs. Anderson, the social worker at BCS, wrote to me, I was taken by surprise—in a good way. At the same time, as you know, Mum was very ill with cancer. Fortunately, she didn't suffer long. When she died, it came as a shock because I'd hoped she'd overcome the odds, but in such a short time, she was gone. With her living in Florida and us over here, it was difficult. After my father died, Mum would come to Wales and spend the summers with us to get away from the Florida heat and to see her grandchildren. We all miss her greatly."

Tilli sat next to Jim and reached across to lay her hand

on his arm; she kept it there. "Until you lose someone you love more than yourself, you can't know how much grief will fill your heart and days. How lucky you were to have been loved and to have loved so deeply. We want you to know, even though we've only just met today, that from now on, we want to be part of your life—all of your lives—and we love you."

Jim smiled, patted Tilli's hand, and continued with his story. "My father passed on about three years ago. He was incredibly intelligent, a wonderful doctor, and a loving father and husband. It was tough watching his memory fade until Mum and I became strangers to him. About a year before he died, they had moved from Boston to a retirement community in Florida. The community had four levels of care, so as residents' needs increased, the necessary accommodations were there."

Vicki interjected, "Jim and I met in Cardiff, where I grew up. I was working at the Cardiff School of Medicine at the University Hospital of Wales when, one day, into my office walks Jim asking if I knew about volunteer opportunities."

Jim added, "I told Vicki that I was a pediatrician and graduate of the Cardiff School and that I'd been adopted as a child and wanted to volunteer my services at a children's home if possible."

Vicki added, "One thing led to another, and we hit it off!"

Jim laughed. "Yes, we did! And Vicki got me on the adoption board of the St. David's—he's the patron saint of Wales—Children's Society in Cardiff, where the board meets monthly. We review the qualifications of potential adopting parents to be sure children are placed in loving homes.

"My medical practice is in Swansea, but I have a once-a-week office here in Llandeilo. I've taken vacation time for this whole week, so if you like, we can drive into town tomorrow, and I'll show you around?"

Vicki interjected, "Jim and I have something fun planned for each day."

"I saw a sign along the drive as we came up. Is there a walking path nearby?" Tilli knew that Mel and Lyn would love to join her for walks.

Vicki replied, "Oh, yes, of course, that path connects with others; you can go for miles on foot. We used to have a map, but since we know the paths so well, I have a feeling that map's disappeared. Jim can pop into the visitors' center tomorrow and get a fresh one. If you go into town after breakfast to look around, you'll still have time for walking in the afternoon. I've got an appointment that I can't cancel but will join you at lunch.

"Oh, my, look at the time!" Vicki peeked at her watch. "Perhaps we should move inside. I've made a traditional dish for supper, Welsh summer cawl, and I know you must be getting hungry. I've taken that long train ride from London, and if you ate on the train at all, I know the food was just passable.

"For sure, you're all probably wondering what cawl is." Vicki looked at their puzzled faces. "It's stew, and since it's summer, I've adapted the recipe by adding lots of fresh local vegetables, some from our garden and some from the farmer's market where we go on Saturday mornings. It's got bacon, fava and green beans, leeks, fresh peas, and tender lettuces in it, with crusty rolls on the side. How does that sound?"

# Dinnertime

Corgi toenails clicked on the sandstone-tiled floor as Lila and Pokey hurried to their feeding dishes. While washing up at the sink, Chloe, Maezie, and Thad were nudging each other good-naturedly. Vicki was at the stove filling soup plates with the summer cawl.

"Oh! I almost burned the rolls—again—Jim, please open the oven *now*!"

Tilli, Mel, and Lyn were sitting politely in the dining room—as they'd been instructed to do—listening to what was going on in the kitchen. The flowers Jim had given Tilli at the train station were in the center of the table; silverware gleamed, and crystal glasses held spring water.

A pair of French doors stood open onto the terrace, and on both sides of these doors were floor-to-ceiling windows with linen draperies gently swaying in the breeze. A large oil painting of a sailing vessel hung over the mahogany sideboard, while six botanical prints were above the antique inlaid cabinet, with various bottles of spirits lined up atop the butler tray.

"Here we are!" Jim and Vicki carried in bowls while the children brought the rolls and butter, and a dish containing condiments.

During dinner, Tilli looked in Chloe's direction. "We've had some hours to get to know your parents, but haven't really spent any time with the three of you."

Chloe immediately stopped spooning cawl into herself

and giggled, her braces showing. "I'm in level six at St. Teilo's school in town."

"I saw horses behind the house. Do you ride?" Tilli included all of them with her question.

Maezie cut in with, "I'm in level eight at St. Teilo's. We all ride, even Mummy and Daddy."

"Perhaps I should have asked you first, Maezie." Tilli could tell that not only was Maezie the eldest, but she was definitely the leader. Maezie was certainly the tallest, with long sandy brown hair. Had she taken ballet? Her posture was excellent.

Maezie continued, "I take dressage and have earned ribbons at the summer fair—blue ones!" She beamed.

"Well, I'm impressed! What about you, Chloe? What do you like to do?"

Chloe pursed her lips, giving this a thought. She was petite, like her mother, but had her father's eyes. "I like helping Mummy in the kitchen. We bake things: breads, rolls, cakes. We made these dinner rolls."

"She bakes all our birthday cakes!" Thad blurted. "Sometimes they're lopsided but tasty, especially the buttercream icing. I get to lick the bowl!"

"Thad, tell me what you're interested in. Are you at St. Teilo's also?"

He nodded. "I'm in fourth. Play football—*not* the *American* kind—I play footie. Smoky is my horse: he's a gelding. I've jumped over three feet with him." Thad paused, then added, "Sometimes I have to tap Smoky with my crop so he won't stop before the jump. A couple of times, he's sent me tumbling over without him, but the floor inside the riding ring has lots of sawdust, so it doesn't hurt."

Everyone smiled while Thad blushed.

Mel had sat silently watching her mother during this conversation and then interrupted, saying, "Here we are, gathered with a whole new family. It's simply wonderful! And you've all been amazing. So welcoming. I'm pinching myself to be sure it's real."

Lyn added, "We can't thank you enough."

"You know, Jim and Vicki," Tilli said and spread her arms wide to include everyone, "I've wished for decades for this to happen, wondering if it would come true, certainly never expecting it to be like this. I was hoping to find my son, and here we sit with you and Vicki and three *grandchildren* I never even imagined! Connecting with all of you is far above anything I could have wished for."

Jim stood up, saying, "Let's move into the snug and have a toast. The kids are cleaning up. Vicki chilled a bottle of local wine—yes, Wales does have vineyards; we're at the very edge of the European wine-producing map—it's from Llanerch Vineyard in the Vale of Glamorgan. The wine label *Cariad* is the word for love—appropriate, don't you think? We have some bara brith, which is sort of like fruitcake, to go with it. And liqueurs from Cwm Deri estate in Pembrokeshire, if you'd rather."

# Next Morning
## A Bit of Wales

Jim parked the car just after crossing over the Tywi. They paused with him to look at the scenery: the river, cobblestone streets, colorful houses, and a single-arch bridge in the distance.

Jim was excited to be their tour guide. "We can thank the Afon Tywi, or River Towy as it's known in English, for creating some of the most fertile farmland in Wales."

Jim spoke with pride, "The Tywi is a total of sixty-eight miles long, and it's the only river that courses the entire length of this country. It rises in the Cambrian Mountains, then travels through the wooded forests before it disappears into the Llyn Brianne reservoir. From there, it emerges and leisurely meanders through ancient market towns—such as Llandeilo—until it flows into the salt waters of Carmarthen Bay."

Mel looked around at the stone walls and terraced landscape. "Did the Romans ever make it here?" She wanted to share some Welsh history with her students in September, and Mark would be curious, too.

"Vicki reminded me before we left this morning that I was not to get too long-winded; I've a habit of rattling on." The MacInneses chuckled, shook their heads, and told him not to leave anything out!

"Well, here goes! When the Romans invaded Britain in

43AD, they made a beeline for the Tywi Valley. Here they discovered not only rich agricultural land and an abundance of game and fish, but also gold in the hills at Dolaucothi! The Romans turned this area into one of the largest gold mines of their empire. Many more Romans invaded and settled. It wasn't long ago that archaeologists uncovered traces of two Roman forts under a field in nearby Dinefwr Park. Though the Romans left Britain for good in 410AD, they abandoned Wales much earlier."

"I'm ashamed to say," Lyn interrupted, "that we don't learn much about such things in American schools." Though she'd done a bit of research while planning for this trip, she was eager to learn more.

"Well, it's all relative, isn't it? I grew up in Boston, and it wasn't until I settled here after medical school that I delved into Welsh history and culture and learned some of the language. I'm always learning! These days, Maezie, Chloe, and Thad come home from school and, at the dinner table, share what they've learned. But let's walk a bit and have a look; I'll answer your questions as best I can."

"Jim, could we pick up a brochure somewhere? I'm sure I'll never remember all you're telling us, and I need some text to go with my photos."

"Mel, when we get to the top of Crescent Road, we'll stop at the visitor's center. As we walk along, I'll fill you in on how the town of Llandeilo got its name."

Tilli stopped to catch her breath. "Residents must be in good shape to navigate all of these hills."

Jim responded, "Oh, yes, the hills play a big role. We don't need to hurry. Just let me know when anyone wants to pause; we've lots of time!

"Like Llandeilo, the first communities in Wales were

small, scattered, and usually clustered around an old church. Each was a basic Welsh social unit called a *llan*; the nearest English concept would be 'Christian enclosure.'

"This *llan* system possibly dates from the post-Roman missionary activities of churchmen from Ireland; Llandeilo—St. Teilo's Llan—dates from around the mid-sixth century. This site is typical of sites throughout Wales in terms of its secluded location on a wooded hillside. These were meeting spots for country folk and their earliest markets.

"Well, these hills have created problems since medieval times. I see that Mel has already noticed terraces where early residents grew their crops." Jim paused so they could rest while he pointed. "Terraces were built for the road, the houses, and yards. In earliest times, traffic had to negotiate steep and tortuous routes—this was an uncompromising landscape. And then, of course, there's the river, which created other problems, at times washing out banks and even taking out our main bridge." Jim pointed downhill. "It's a single arch bridge now, but further downstream, you'll notice abutments where an earlier one with two arches stood.

"After the Romans left, Llandeilo was associated with a commercially minded monastic community with large agricultural estates. They exerted a dominant ecclesiastical influence on the neighborhood, establishing Llandeilo as a trading center. The old churchyard was where they had their market, selling animals and produce. In the thirteenth century, the wares of the merchants were displayed right on the gravestones!

"When you look at a modern map, you'll see this town

is located at a junction of several main roadways—the cart paths of earlier times—making for excellent access from all directions. And in the eleventh century, when the Normans entered the valley of the Tywi from the south, they consolidated their military hold with a string of motte-and-bailey bridgeheads along the northern banks of the river. For the next four hundred years, Llandeilo was on the front line of most Anglo-Welsh skirmishes and major military confrontations.

"Mind you, I've learned much of this from the children, who repeat at the dinner table what they've learned in school. Vicki and I continue to be astounded by this area's long and varied history."

After picking up maps, brochures, and a few postcards at the visitor's center, they continued on their walk, with Jim occasionally stopping in front of an important building.

Lyn asked, "I've read that the United Kingdom has hundreds of castles. Would there be one in Llandeilo?"

"Lyn, would you believe that Wales has more castles per square mile—a total of six hundred—than any country on earth? And Llandeilo might seem like the perfect place to have built a castle or fortress, but a separate military settlement was established at Dinefwr, about one mile west of here, adjacent to the parish of Llandyfeisant. The bridgehead and major east-west route were controlled from there. We'll visit Dinefwr next weekend when the children can join us. For now, I think we'll pause at Ebenezer Chapel and then see one of the oldest buildings in town before visiting St. Teilo's Churchyard. By then, I think you'll probably have heard enough history for one morning." Jim put his arm around Tilli's shoulders and gave her a hug.

"The site of St. Teilo's Churchyard encloses a hill that physically still dominates the old town. The church was an important scholastic foundation—a Celtic illuminated manuscript used to be kept here—and was regarded as the 'clas' or mother church of the surrounding district of Llandeilo Fawr. It lost this dominance in 1100 when it became a parish church. The role of 'clas' was taken over by Tally Abbey. The manuscript is now in Lichfield Cathedral. There are four stone crosses in or near our town dating from the seventh to the ninth centuries. Two of these originated from this church and churchyard.

"When the parish church was known as Llandeilo Fawr—in pre-Norman times—it was an important church estate and an early center of learning. Just over there is St. Teilo's school where the children go." Jim pointed and continued, "One of the manuscripts describes St. Teilo as the son of a king of Ireland. He played an important part in the consolidation of the Welsh church in the latter part of the fifth century.

"Today, Llandeilo is a place of pilgrimage, probably because Teilo died here. And there's St. Teilo's baptistery." They stopped to see the spring, which rose out of a bed of sand and was set into an alcove inside the churchyard.

Jim continued, "This spring was an unfailing water supply and an important physical factor for the siting of the original settlement. Until 1860, the spring was the community's principal source of water, and about thirty hand pumps were added throughout the town."

After walking mostly uphill, they now turned and headed down Church Street towards the bridge where Jim had parked the car. The day was sunny and comfortably warm. Tilli listened to the cheerful babbling of the river as it splashed and tumbled over the smooth rocks on its journey to the sea. As they continued along, she thought about how lucky she was; not only had she found Jim and his family, but she had the stamina to take strenuous walks and go on trips. What would *Bertie* have made of all this?

Jim broke her reverie. "Just a few words about the Tywi: the river has never been navigable above Carmarthen, too many shallows. But the local fishermen—until recently—used a round, skin-covered basket-boat called a *coracle*, with which fishing families caught plentiful salmon, sea trout, eels, and lampreys.

"You must be getting hungry; I certainly am. Vicki planned fish for lunch. The children will be let out early today—some sort of teacher conference this afternoon."

Driving back to Restful Haven, Mel saw a sign:

*Croeso a mwynhewch.*

"Jim, please tell us something about the Welsh language; it's so different from English. I can't make heads nor tails of it, like that sign back there."

Jim laughed. "The sign reads: Welcome and enjoy! I'll tell you what. The kids are learning Welsh in school, so I'm going to let them tell you about the language."

# Later

After a delicious lunch of baked fish, the children were in the kitchen cleaning up while Tilli, Mel, and Lyn joined Jim and Vicki in the snug. The family room was furnished with a Chesterfield sofa and several comfy chairs. A built-in bookcase filled one entire wall with shelves holding framed photographs, *objets d'art*, and an assortment of books written in English and Welsh. The fireplace was surrounded by a red leather cushioned fender, and nearby stood a large wicker basket filled with split oak logs ready for the first cold day.

Mel was curious about what kinds of books were on their shelves and went over to have a look. A copy of *The Literature of Wales* by Dafydd Johnston was next to a book on the ancient poetry of Taliesin and Aneirin, and a collection of Welsh tales, *The Mabinogi*, was next to an old leather-bound volume on the novel *Rhys Lewis* by Daniel Owen. Mel remembered reading that Owen was the first recognized novelist of the Welsh language, back in 1885. Other more modern works, such as *Tolkien and Wales: Language, Literature and Identity*, by Carl Phelpstead, nestled next to ones about King Arthur and Welsh tales in English.

"Who in your family is interested in ancient Welsh literature?" Mel asked as they settled down in the snug.

"Oh, my degree at Cardiff University was in ancient and medieval literature of Wales," said Vicki, "and the children are learning Welsh as well as the history of our literature in school. Taliesin and Aneirin were poets who wrote heraldic poems in a meter unique to Wales. *The Mabinogi* is a collection of medieval stories, not just ones from Wales. And the name Rhys Lewis comes up many times when learning about the history of Wales, particularly our area. I think there's a book on one of those shelves with a selection of Welsh literature translated into English. I'll find it later, and perhaps you'd like to look through it."

"Oh, I saw that title," Mel interjected as she went over to the bookcase to gently ease it from the shelf.

"It's a good introduction. Perhaps something for reading in bed?" Vicki suggested.

Jim patted the seat next to him on the sofa, indicating Tilli should sit there. "But right now, we'd like to look at something else with all of you—our family photographs. I've pulled aside some from my childhood and thought you'd enjoy these especially."

"Oh, you know we'd all love to see them."

Before Tilli appeared the missing years—ones she'd wished she'd shared as he grew up—his firsts! Jim showed them photos of learning to walk, peddling his red tricycle, getting on the yellow school bus to begin kindergarten, and even a picture of him struggling to tie his new shoes. More milestones followed: birthdays, family vacations, graduations, proms, and a few photos from Jim and Vicki's wedding.

After Jim closed the album, everyone sat quietly for a few minutes reflecting on the years of Jim's life that had unfolded now in a little over two hours!

"Oh, Tilli, we've prepared a little gift for you. Just a sec." Jim opened one cabinet in the bookcase, returned to the coffee table, and placed a wrapped package in front of her.

Everyone waited while she untied the red ribbon and slowly removed the flowery wrapping paper. Tilli couldn't imagine what was inside. "Oh, my! How very thoughtful of you! I will cherish this forever."

She got up and hugged and kissed Jim and Vicki before opening the compact photo album containing pictures of Jim at various stages of his life. Some of the pictures they'd just seen, while others were new to her. The final picture in the album was a recent one of Jim and Vicki with their children—a family portrait.

Tilli pointed to one more—an empty page. "Jim, did you mean to put a photo here?"

"Ah! I left that blank for a reason. Patrick, a long-time friend of ours and the professional photographer who took that family portrait, is coming by tomorrow afternoon—after the children return from school—to take pictures of all of us together."

At this point, Maezie, Chloe, and Thad walked in. The corgis, Pokey and Lila, looked like they'd been running; they arrived with tongues hanging out. Lila immediately found Jim's place and flopped herself down, spreading her hind legs out behind her, with her tummy flat against the carpet.

"We've just finished looking at family pictures," Tilli told the children.

"Oh, great! We helped Daddy and Mummy choose which ones to put in." Maezie sat down on the arm of Vicki's chair and leaned over to rest her head on her mother's shoulder.

"I put the one of us building the igloo in there. Daddy

helped. We had lots of snow one winter. Pokey and Lila didn't like it when we put them inside!" Thad laughed.

"Mummy brought out hot chocolate, and we sat—shivering—in the igloo and drank it. That night, Thad and his friend Sam slept in there!" Tilli could tell that Chloe had wanted to be next to her mother, but Maezie had beaten her to it.

"Chloe, why don't you come here?" Tilli patted the cushion next to her, and Chloe came right over.

"Even with down sleeping bags, we only lasted 'til midnight. Sam told me he wanted to sleep in my room, so we headed for the house. Brrr! An igloo isn't warm!"

After the children had settled down, Mel thought it was a good time to ask about the Welsh language. "We're curious. We don't understand Welsh. Most signs are written in both English and Welsh, but we're clueless about pronunciation. Your Daddy told us you're all learning Welsh in school. Who wants to start?"

Maezie looked from her Daddy to her sister, then to her brother, hoping one of them would take this up, but Chloe wouldn't make eye contact with her, and Thad sat on the oriental carpet pretending to study its pattern.

"Oh, I think you might find this boring, Aunt Mel."

"Oh, you know I won't. I'm a teacher, remember? And my students will be interested. Which makes me ask: do any of you have a pen pal? Perhaps my schoolchildren and the three of you could write to each other? They'd love hearing about your life here, and you'd learn about theirs. Something to consider. Oh, please go ahead."

Seeing no one else was going to rescue her, Maezie began. "Well, the very first thing we learn is the proper name of the Welsh language: *Cymraeg.* It's from a

Germanic word, something like 'foreigner.' *Cymraeg* is from a subdivision of Celtic. It's an Indo-European language that came from central Asia, where it was first spoken. It's sort of like Breton and Cornish.

"We've also learned that at the start of the twentieth century, about half of Wales spoke Welsh, but by 1991, only about nineteen percent spoke it. Where we live—the Swansea Valley area of Wales—it is still fluently spoken. We even have our own dialect.

"Early Welsh was born as its own language in the sixth century, and it's the oldest living language of Great Britain. And it's one of the oldest languages in all of Europe."

"I have a quick question," Lyn said, asking Maezie to pause. "Is the Welsh language like Gaelic?"

"No, Aunt Lyn. Though they're both Celtic languages, they come from different subdivisions." Maezie looked to see if anyone else had a question, even hoping they were bored so she could stop, but she saw only encouragement.

"So, when Henry the Eighth became king, Wales was taken into the English state. He commanded only English could be used in the courts of Wales. If people used the Welsh language, they wouldn't be able to hold public office. The Welsh Language Act did away with this just in 1993.

"By the twentieth century, the schools in Wales were forbidden to teach Welsh. If a child spoke Welsh in school, a big piece of wood, attached to a leather strap, was hung around his neck. This piece of wood was called a *cribban*, and it was passed from one child to another if they were caught speaking Welsh. At the end of the school day, the last one wearing this *cribban* was beaten. There are still old people living in Wales today who remember this. No wonder Welsh was spoken less and less.

"After 1993, the speaking of Welsh slowly went up, but mostly among younger people. Today, children all over Wales are once again learning Welsh—in school."

Seeing Maezie had finished, Vicki broke out in a big smile and proudly added, "The survival of our Welsh language is truly a remarkable story when you consider that the heart of English culture and language—with its worldwide expansion—lies right next door."

Mel stood up and gave Maezie a hug. "As a teacher, I'm giving you an 'A' for your presentation. Bravo!" Everyone clapped while Maezie blushed.

# A Bit More of Wales

Every day, Jim and Vicki, at times with the children, took their new-found family exploring. At nearby Garn Goch, they stood on the hillside to gaze at the barren landscape covered with bracken, trying to imagine what was no longer visible: those settlements and forts of long ago.

Jim broke the silence. "Archaeologists recently discovered that Garn Goch was settled as early as the Bronze Age, 2000 to 1400BC, with forts built during the Iron Age, around 500BC, and into the Roman period. They chose this location because of the broad and long view."

Tilli asked, "Jim, what does *Garn Goch* mean?"

"It means 'red hill' in English. See all this bracken?" He swept the air with his arm. "It's gorgeous in the fall when it turns red."

Another morning, Jim and Vicki drove them to Dinefwr Park, the location of Dinefwr Castle, a place of paramount importance in Welsh history, a place where myth, legend, and history were woven together.

Vicki told them: "It was Lord Rhys, *Rhys ap Gruffudd*, in the twelfth century, who secured the role of *Dinefwr*"—pronounced as Dynevor—"in the history of Wales. Dinefwr Castle came to symbolize the historic might of medieval Wales. He is one of the most admired leaders in the history of this country. If you want to learn more about this amazing man, there's a book on the shelf at home that will give you lots more information about him and the Dinefwr family. After five centuries of continuous ownership by the Dinefwr family, the estate was dispersed in the middle of the twentieth century."

Vicki continued, "Today, Dinefwr is about seven hundred acres in size. In 1992, the herd of rare White Park cattle, which had been sold, was brought back. And, in the year 2000, the Dinefwr Project was initiated, by the National Trust and the South and West Wales Wildlife Trust, for restoration and public access."

Jim gave Vicki a moment to catch her breath while he explained, "This site, like at Garn Goch, was most likely also inhabited much earlier: the Neolithic times, the Bronze Age, and by the Romans."

From the rocky crag of Dinefwr Castle, the view was commanding. Looking out over the wide Tywi Valley, they thought about its significance as a medieval center of religious and political power.

"So much history!" Mel was absorbing every morsel as she jotted down notes.

Lyn added, "Jim, I'm beginning to see why you and Vicki settled here; the landscape is magnificent, and there are many interesting historical sites."

Tilli was admiring the scenic beauty around them. "And will you look at all these magnificent old trees!"

"Ah, the trees!" Jim shook his head. "Yes, some of them—limes, oaks, and sweet chestnuts—didn't get cut down for bridge-building by the Romans. Entire forests were cut down to clear battle sites. Later, warships were built from oaks; whole swaths were cut down in the eighteenth century during the Napoleonic wars with France. Tannins for hides was one of the heaviest uses of the trees, when the bark was stripped off oaks—very sought-after

Welsh oaks—and shipped away by boatloads. The list goes on; it's amazing any trees remain!"

Vicki added, "Some venerable trees today are over four hundred years old! Ancient woodlands now stand protected. 'The history of the landscape is the history of man, and the history of man embellished within the landscape.' That's a quote from Greg Howes, a historian with roots in the Tywi Valley. Wales, especially this area where we live, is staunchly Welsh, even though we are part of Britain. The learning of Welsh history begins even before children start school."

For one precious week, Tilli, Mel, and Lyn visited with Jim and his family—didn't the time fly?—what with leisurely hours spent getting to know them, combined with strolls down the coastal path by the house, oftentimes with the grandchildren leading the way, and longer excursions to historic, beautiful, and interesting places all around. The day arrived when it was time to leave for Scotland.

"No tears!" Tilli told herself and them. "We shall see each other again."

In Swansea, Jim walked with them to the gate where their train departed for Glasgow, Scotland, and just before parting, he reached down and whispered something into Tilli's ear and gave her a long hug.

Aloud, he said, "I'm hoping, Tilli, that you'll come and spend some weeks with us *every* year from now on. And you, Mel, and Lyn are always welcome. Our family is tiny. We want to stay connected, and the children need a grandmother and aunts. Vicki's parents are no longer living, and she doesn't have much contact with her younger brother. So, please, let's keep as close as we can."

"We'll telephone when we get to Lochaline," Mel called from the open window of the train compartment while Tilli waved her handkerchief as they inched down the track and out of the station. With wheels screeching, they rounded a tight bend, and soon Jim was no longer in sight. Lyn reached up to latch the window.

# Scotland

Glasgow was where they spent one night before continuing to Lochaline. Lyn had chosen a hotel in the city center, a stone's throw from the central train station, and with a car rental agency nearby. The next morning, over a second cup of coffee, they relaxed while Mel walked over to pick up the Vauxhall Astra, a medium-sized sedan with automatic drive. Mel wasn't familiar with driving on the left-hand side of the road and decided that a car with a standard shift would only add to the stress of driving.

Once on their way, Lyn helped Mel navigate the unfamiliar roads and was prepared with a map of Scotland open in her lap; they headed north in the direction of Stirling.

Mel pointed, "wow, what are those?"

"I don't know, but let me look." Lyn reached into her door pocket and pulled out a brochure. "Hmm, these one-hundred-foot-tall horse heads are sculptures depicting the kelpies, shape-shifting water spirits from Scottish folklore, supposed to haunt rivers and streams. They're in a new park in Falkirk. We must be close to the Forth and Clyde Canal."

Tilli chimed in from the back seat, "What do you say we keep driving? We've miles to go; started out rather late." Tilli thought that if they stopped here, the girls would want to stop everywhere, and they'd never get to Lochaline and the MacInnes castle. She considered the days when Lyn was planning for this trip to the United Kingdom and how their itinerary had kept growing. If she hadn't put the brakes on, they'd be undertaking a roller coaster of activities. Besides, she was still reminiscing, in the backseat of the Vauxhall, about the wonderful days with Jim and his family.

By the time they arrived in Callander, which was at the boundary of the lowlands and highlands of Scotland, and just before more dramatic scenery began to unfold, they were ready for a break. Here were several restaurants and food shops to choose from, and they purchased lunches to go from Mac's Deli. Mel continued driving to Loch Lubnaig, where they stopped to have a picnic.

"If this spot is any indication of what we're in for ..." Mel began.

"So relaxing," Tilli added.

"I can't remember the last time we enjoyed a picnic by a lake." Lyn sighed.

"I can't remember the last time we enjoyed a picnic— period." Tilli smiled.

A granite bench, warmed by the sun, was the perfect place from which to admire Loch Lubnaig's crystal clear water and calm surface, with the green hills hugging the far shore. Two swans paddled in circles, and coming ever nearer, they repeatedly dunked their heads, at times caressing each other with their long necks. Though near to town and road, this scene presented an unspoiled canvas.

Continuing out of Callander, they stopped at the woolen shop where Highland *coos*, cows, munched in the pasture. Among a wide assortment of undyed, hand-knitted woolens, Mel didn't think she'd find the MacInnes tartan.

The sales associate showed them a sample of the Mac-Innes colors from a swatch book: blue, green, and black plaid with a thin red line running through. "I'd have to order it fer ye, but if yer headed to Lochaline, that'd be the spot to find yers in stock."

Mel chose a warm, cream-colored hat with a narrow brim, while Lyn bought a soft gray scarf with matching gloves.

"You girls will be toasty next winter, but I'll wait 'til Lochaline—something wooly made with the MacInnes plaid."

On the road to Glencoe—"Girls, look at that mountain. It's just like a pyramid!"—Tilli didn't miss much from the comfort of her back seat.

Lyn picked up the brochure and read, "It's called *Buachaille Etive Mòr*, and we're now looking across a vast, fifty-square-mile, uninhabited wilderness called Rannoch Moor."

Lyn continued, "It also cautions that we—not the driver, unless we're stopped—should turn around and have a look at the backside of this pointy mountain."

Amid scenery featured in many photos of Glencoe, they saw a totally different view after rounding the bend: nestled among the broad fields of bracken sat a solitary small white cottage called Lagangarbh Hut.

"Oh, please stop, Mel; I want to take a few pictures."

"Mom, of course; it's a wee bit remote but very picturesque," Lyn was already aiming her camera as they started walking towards the mountain hut.

Not long after, they arrived at the National Trust for Scotland Glencoe Visitor Centre where they signed up for the next morning's ranger-guided Land Rover tour. After much driving today, Mel was especially eager to be able to have a look around and discover the glen's history, wildlife, and geology.

While moseying about at the visitor's center, they paused to read about the dark side of this beautiful area. From colorful murals and other depictions, they learned about what happened on February 13, 1692, when the Campbells accepted hospitality from the MacDonald clan.

After inviting the Campbells into their midst, thirty-eight members of the MacDonald clan were massacred. Members of the Campbell clan had been under orders of the new King William of Orange, who had deposed King James VII of Scotland. Apparently, the MacDonald clan's chief had not pledged his allegiance to the new monarch by a specified date. Perhaps a blizzard kept him from responding on time, or perhaps he was still loyal to the old King. For whatever reason, the MacDonald clan's chief had not responded. This event marked a turning point in Scotland's history: the new monarch did not represent both nations equally. To this day, ill feelings between the MacDonalds and the Campbells continue. It was the Campbell clan's violation of the rules of hospitality that was most unforgivable.

After reading the captions under the pictures on display, Tilli shook her head. "I'm puzzled as to why people cling fiercely to past grievances. I mean, *three hundred years*! All of the Campbells and MacDonalds involved in this tragic event have long ago died—generations have come and gone—those alive now had nothing to do with this, and still, there's no forgiveness."

"Hmm, those alive today are the blood relatives of the ones who committed the crime. History is not to be forgotten, certainly. Makes me pause to consider how countless historic battles fought and won or lost—world-wide—continue to affect people today."

Lyn looked around, saying, "Let's go to the café; I'm parched." They selected a small round table on the terrace, one in the shade, then ordered tea. Surrounded by shrubs and colorful annuals blooming in the borders alongside the museum, it was a pleasant spot to pause for a while. "Shall we pay a visit to the Glencoe Folk Museum? We won't get to it tomorrow."

"That sounds great, Lyn. What about you, Mom?"

"I've never been inside a traditional thatched-roof cottage. Let's do it."

After this museum, and tired from the day's activities, they headed to the Clachaig Inn, a stagecoach inn that spanned centuries. Up a narrow stair, down to the end of the hall, they were shown to their cozy rooms with beamed ceilings. After setting their luggage down, they stooped to peek through the small, curtained windows at an uninterrupted view of the mountains.

"Oh, I'm popping down right now on this bed for a *wee* nap."

"Okay; then Mel and I will go downstairs and make dinner reservations for this evening. See you in a half-hour, Mom."

"When you're a *wee* rested," Lyn started to say.

"Oh, will you two please stop all this *wee* business!" Mel tried to sound annoyed but laughed. "Everything is *wee* this and *bonnie* that."

"What about the *coos*? So much nicer than 'cows,' " Tilli added.

A couple of hours remained before dinner, time

enough to walk the circular trail beginning right outside the Clachaig Inn. They had to cross over a bridge spanning the River Coe, which roared and pounded through the gorge, free and wild. From some distance, they could still hear its thunder as the trail continued through An Torr woodland, now with views of Signal Rock and across Clachaig Flats.

"This is where the massacre of the MacDonald clan happened"—Lyn pointed to Signal Rock—"and this very site played a role. Hard to imagine now, isn't it?"

Old walls with lichen-covered rocks meandered through the forest; a couple of shaggy horses grazed in a nearby pasture. Mountains sprung up, seemingly out of nowhere. They reflected on this tragic event while walking along the smooth path.

"So peaceful, isn't it? Jeez! Now, these annoying midges." Mel began swatting at nearly invisible flies.

As the insects attacked them from out of nowhere, they ran. "Bug spray is definitely in order for tomorrow's adventure," Tilli hollered.

Heading to dinner at the Bidean Lounge, located inside the Clachaig Inn, they approached the door, and Tilli stopped to point at a weathered sign. "How come we didn't notice this before?"

*No Hawkers or Campbells!*

Mel frowned. "Guess the Clachaig Inn is doing its part to keep history alive."

Tilli ordered the Scottish Angus beef for dinner, which was served with a local cheddar and a tomato chutney, while Lyn felt adventurous and decided on the haggis, neeps, and tatties, which was a hearty meal and quite good. Mel selected something she recognized: the venison burger.

The night was still young, and the summertime sun wouldn't set for a couple of hours. Sounds of live music wafted from the direction of the Boots Bar, a historic Highland watering hole, where many ale taps ran from one end of the long bar to the other. Empty bar stools beckoned them to sit a wee and sample from the two hundred single malt whiskies in stock.

After they'd each chosen a beverage, Lyn reached over to clink Mel's glass: "To the MacInnes Family!"

The next day, they continued driving from Glen Coe to Glen Etive, which is located between Glencoe and the Bridge of Orchy in the north of Argyll, not far from the Glencoe Mountain Resort. Feeling more adventurous—thanks to the ranger-led Land Rover tour they'd experienced earlier that morning—they decided to explore on their own. By now, Mel had grown accustomed to the roads, and the traffic was light.

The woman at the Clachaig Inn reception desk had told them to look for a signpost pointing southwest onto a minor road, noting that it would seem like it was running into the wilds of Scotland for absolutely no reason.

Mel turned onto this twelve-mile, single-track road, where they found one of the most beautiful places in Scotland, with views of the area where the James Bond film, *Skyfall*, was filmed. Ian Fleming grew up not far from here. They certainly were off the grid!

The first highlights were the "Herdsmen of Etive," two enormous mountains that totally dominated the landscape and which were among the most-photographed mountains in Scotland. The road continued along the River Etive all the way to its final destination at Loch Etive.

"Lyn, do the brochures tell you anything about those yellow shrubs that seem to be blooming everywhere on the hillsides?"

"Mom, they're called gorse, and it says here that it is 'a thorny, flowering evergreen plant associated with Britain and growing wild in many locations.' It's in the legume family."

They stopped several times along the way for picture-taking and to breathe in the clean mountain air. About four miles from the initial turning point, they arrived at Etive Mòr waterfall. Mel shut off the engine, and they got out to stretch. Within arm's reach were a few wild deer busily nibbling; they lifted their heads to stare, and obviously not minding people, went right back to browsing.

"Let's unpack our lunch and picnic here. I can't imagine a lovelier place." Tilli already had her eye on a flat rock perfect for sitting. Nature was pure, raw, and unspoiled. Across the expansive moorland, gorse bloomed among the bracken, and the sweet smell of the tiny yellow flowers wafted toward them. They imagined themselves as the only people in the world—it was so quiet that the bees were the only ones making noise! Perhaps a half-hour elapsed before one car came along to break the silence; a family pulled over briefly to take pictures.

After lunch, Mel turned the car around, and they continued towards Glencoe Mountain Resort, where a twelve-minute chairlift ride took them up effortlessly to the Eagles Rest. At the mountaintop, they got off the lift and walked a short distance to take in the fantastic panoramic views down Glen Etive.

By late afternoon, they were headed back to the Vauxhall, where Lyn studied the map. "Well, not much farther to drive today."

Fort William, the largest town in the Highlands, wasn't far away. Lyn had booked two nights at the Inn at Ardgour, which overlooked beautiful Loch Linnhe, and was close to the ferry landing. Though they were only about seventy miles from Lochaline on the Morvern peninsula, where they would visit the MacInnes castle, there was much to explore in the Fort William area.

"We're in no hurry." Tilli sat sipping wine at the dinner table that evening. "Who knows when or if we'll return to Scotland, what with all the visits we'll—or that is to say—I'll be making to Wales!"

"Speak for yourself, Mom. I know Mark would love it here. I'll be back for sure."

For dinner, they all had the fisherman's pie, with creamy seafood laced with garlic and herbs and topped with gratinated creamed potatoes and seasonal vegetables.

Lyn had reserved tickets for the next morning for the eighty-four-mile round-trip Jacobite Steam train, one of the world's most beautiful rail trips. Mel was especially excited since she knew that many of the schoolchildren in her class were Harry Potter fans and that they'd love to see her pictures and hear about this train, known to them as the Hogwarts Express.

Though the train made a couple of stops, they stayed on 'til the end of the line at the fishing port of Mallaig. At Glenfinnan, the train crossed the twenty-one-arched viaduct, also made famous by the Harry Potter films. After crossing this viaduct, the train stopped so passengers could look back and take pictures of it and their magnificent surroundings.

All along the journey, they enjoyed views of Ben Nevis, a dormant volcano and the United Kingdom's highest mountain. Lochs and impressive natural features were all around them. Once in Mallaig, there was time to walk about the town and take in the seaside atmosphere before returning to Fort William. After an outdoor lunch of fish and chips by the wharf, they shopped for postcards.

The next morning, over breakfast, Lyn announced, "We can't leave Scotland without visiting at least one whisky distillery, so this afternoon I've booked us for a tour with a tasting of three different whiskies at the end. And, since Ben Nevis Distillery is one of the oldest in Scotland, and right here in Fort William, we're heading over there at two o'clock."

"What else have you planned for today?" Mel wondered.

"I'd like to go for a walk somewhere. This scenery is awe-inspiring," Tilli added.

"Okay." In between sips of coffee, Lyn looked at her notes. "We could drive over to the Neptune's Staircase, which are eight interconnected locks on the Caledonian Canal, just north of here. Within four-hundred-and-fifty meters, ships travel up or down about twenty meters in height. We can walk along the towpath to watch. Oh, and there's a café with great views of Ben Nevis."

"That sounds like fun. Any other options?" Mel wanted a hike. "Waterfalls? Nature?"

Lyn finished her coffee and looked through her notes. "Hmm, we're right in the heart of the Lochaber Geopark. Could do a guided tour, using our own car, where we'll learn about how the glens and lochs were formed, the mountains built up, and the types of rocks, or we could just go on our own. Maybe hike to Steall Falls, just south of here.

"It's only one of the places within the Lochaber Geopark territory and the second-highest waterfall in Britain. I wrote down that the walk is about two miles long through Nevis Gorge, taking us past ancient woodland and alpine meadows. If there's been rain, we need to be cautious as it can be slippery. Oh, my goodness!" Lyn had just read something surprising. "There's no way I'm going to cross that gorge to get up close to those falls. You have to balance your way on a single wire while holding onto two upper wires to get over! Can you imagine? Believe it or not, it gets so popular that people actually queue up to do this!"

"We certainly don't need that, but it would be fun to watch! Why don't we walk as far as we like and then turn around?"

"I like your idea, Mom. We've got plenty to explore today." Pushing back their chairs, they got ready to drive to Neptune's Staircase.

The next morning, with the car packed, they headed to the ferry landing to cross over onto the Morvern

Peninsula, one of five West Highland peninsulas at the very edge of Scotland.

As Mel drove south, the roads became narrower and less traveled. They followed the contours of the land as the scenery unfolded around them—unspoiled landscapes, stunning seascapes, rolling green hillsides, rivers chasing downhill towards beautiful lochs, and wide expanses of heather moorlands. They drove through tidy towns—really only clusters of buildings—and passed by small farms. More farm animals than people lived on the Morvern Peninsula.

"Sheep!" Lyn called out. Mel swerved the Vauxhall to the left-hand side of the narrow, winding, and hilly road with hedgerows on both sides. She had grown accustomed to driving in Scotland, but wished her sister and mother had adjusted as well.

Tilli had confidence in Mel's driving. It was these roads she questioned. Ready for a head-on collision at any moment, Tilli kept hitting an imaginary brake, with her right foot thumping the floor in the backseat. She hung onto—at times white-knuckled—the ceiling strap next to her window.

"Mom, please try to relax; you, too, Lyn." Mel didn't mean to sound angry, but their stressing out didn't make her driving go any easier. Why weren't they enjoying the scenery—scenery she'd had little opportunity to take in since *she* had to keep her eyes on the road? Mel shut off the engine, took her hands off the wheel, and relaxed her shoulders. "And don't just shout, Lyn, when you see something. Geez, it's upsetting!"

For several minutes, they sat and watched as the flock of bleating black-and-white sheep came around the bend to completely surround their car. These animals were in no hurry. A lone sheepdog brought up the rear and did its best to keep the flock moving. Though the young shepherd constantly scanned his flock to be certain there were no stragglers, he managed a smile and a wave.

"I know we don't have far to travel today, but these roads! Well, I just close my eyes when other cars come in our direction. And what about those who suddenly appear behind us? I don't know how these people can drive so fast." Tilli laughed nervously.

"Lyn, do you want to drive?"

"Nunnno! Mel," Lyn said and shook her head. "You said you'd do the driving."

"Well then, ladies, please allow me to do my job." Mel restarted the engine.

Lyn studied the map in her lap. "No GPS in this car. Imagine that. Isn't this the twenty-first century?"

"Not here, Lyn." Tilli considered the rolling countryside, occasional stone houses, sheep, and more sheep; probably not much had changed in a hundred years. Perhaps the only difference today was that this road was paved.

By mid-afternoon, they entered the town of Lochaline—home of the MacInnes clan. Tilli tried to absorb the scenery that unfolded around them, wanted to capture the essence of Lochaline through her very pores, never to forget how she felt at this moment. She reflected on the wishes in her diary entries; while some had been amended a few times, others—like visiting here—had remained constant. Except, when she had written about coming here, she had imagined it being with Bertie. Oh, why hadn't *he* pressed her to come years ago?

"I can feel your father sitting right here beside me," Tilli said while patting the seat next to her.

Mel looked into the rearview mirror. "I know Daddy's spirit is with us."

"He's been with us this entire trip," Lyn added.

Driving through Lochaline, they passed by the Whitehouse Restaurant. It had won multiple awards of excellence with rave reviews for its scrumptious meals made with locally sourced ingredients. They would come here one evening for dinner. The ferry landing, where ships left for Fishnish on the Isle of Mull, was straight ahead.

Mel took a right-hand turn and continued through the sparsely settled village; its white-washed stone houses with their steeply-pitched roofs and dormers were nestled into the green hillsides and surrounded by the sea. Everywhere they looked was lovelier than they'd imagined.

"Take the next right, Mel." Lyn had the directions in hand to Wee House, their rental for the next few days.

Mel swung the Vauxhall onto a narrow dirt drive, which led to a three-bedroom, white-washed stone cottage only a short walk from a pebble and sand beach. Lupines, hollyhocks, and climbing roses bloomed next to the house, and the salty air was refreshingly brisk on this July day.

At Wee House, they would have leisure time to relax and also take the ferry over to the Isle of Mull for a day, as well as venture out on a sea kayak tour, where they'd paddle and explore the indented, rugged coastline to see otters, white-tailed sea eagles, seals, herons, and many red-footed guillemots.

# Two Days Later

"Lyn, how did you ever arrange this? I mean, the Mac-Innes Castle is a private residence; it's not a museum open to the public." Tilli would have been satisfied to view the castle from a distance. Maybe take a few pictures, but this?

Unbeknownst to Tilli and Mel, Lyn had written to the new owners of the castle months before they had left Hamlet. To her surprise, the owners had replied quickly, even including information about the castle, so they could learn about its history before coming—to afternoon tea.

Mel allowed plenty of time for the drive to Kinlochaline castle, as it was located in a remote spot. By now, she knew that wherever they wanted to go, there was no direct way to get there, as the coastline, with its endless coves and inlets, made traveling circuitous and the distances longer than anticipated.

Though in modern times the castle's site seemed remote, in its day, it had secured a prominent spot at the confluence of the River Aline and Loch Aline, providing the MacInnes clan with direct access to the Sound of Mull, a major trade route that connected them to a much wider region.

The castle fortress was built in the fifteenth century, but it sat on the site of an earlier fortification and was in the hands of the MacInnes clan no later than the twelfth century.

The site was both an economic benefit as well as a

defensive risk, for it saw regular Viking attacks. In 1164, it faced ruin from these raids, so the MacInnes clan allied themselves with Somerled and remained associated with his descendants, the powerful MacDonalds, Lords of the Isles, for two hundred years.

In 1368, a bitter feud started with John MacDonald, who ordered his kinsman Donald MacLean to murder the MacInnes chieftain. Donald duly obeyed and slaughtered both the MacInnes chief and other prominent members of the clan at a different nearby castle. Kinlochaline Castle then passed into the hands of the MacLeans, and they rebuilt the castle in the form of a tower house in the late fifteenth century.

The structure was modified in the early seventeenth century with the addition of angle turrets plus a corbelled parapet. The castle was attacked again in 1644 by the forces of a Royalist-Irish general, who arrived on the Isle of Mull, and from there, took four hundred men to attack Kinlochaline castle, which they captured and burned.

Kinlochaline Castle was repaired. It was again attacked in 1679, this time by Archibald Campbell, Earl of Argyll, as part of a regional feud and extensively damaged. By 1690, it had been abandoned as a residence. Before 1730, it had become a roofless ruin. The castle stood derelict until the 1890s, when some inaccurate restoration work was undertaken. Serious efforts were made in the twentieth century to restore the site. It was in the late 1990s that extensive rebuilding took place, which included the addition of a building on top of the battlements.

Tilli looked out of her car window as Mel drove through a forested area, then across a single-lane stone bridge over a small river, and finally up a rocky knoll towards the square, four-story limestone structure. Before them rose Kinlochaline Castle on Rock Morven, once the seat of the Chief of Clan MacInnes.

"Mom, this doesn't look like Daddy's picture hanging over our fireplace. This castle isn't a ruin; it's in perfect condition.

"And Mel, look up. See that structure? A house was built right on top of the castle's flat roof. New windows. And the stonework is perfect."

The MacInnes castle was aglow in the rosy afternoon sunshine. The unfurled flag, up on the ramparts, ruffled gently in the wind; on it were the thistle and the bee.

Mel drove slowly over the fine yellow pea stone, which scrunched under their tires, then she parked the car close to a short flight of stone steps. They paused before going up and stood quietly before continuing to the rugged wooden entry door.

"I'm pinching myself to be sure this is real." Tilli beamed with her pleasure.

Set into the mortar above the door was the symbol of a salmon. For a moment, Tilli wondered about the significance of this salmon. And what about the castle's flag with its thistle and the bee?

They'd barely knocked when the new owners opened the door widely and greeted them warmly. Entering the great hall, they saw the MacInnes coat of arms, a bow and arrow with the MacInnes motto, *Ghift Dhe Agus an Righ*, which translated from the Gaelic as "By Grace of God and King."

An elevator quickly brought them up to the roof, where on the terrace, with views in all directions, a table had been prepared with delicious food and tea. From the young family, they learned that they'd purchased Kinlochaline Castle from Historic Scotland, which oversaw the renovations in the 1990s, when the house-like structure was permitted to be added to the top.

After a relaxing visit, they returned to the ground level, where the family graciously invited them to look around the great hall. Above the main fireplace was a carving of a clan woman holding an object in one hand. The carving had been freshly painted by the new owners in the style it may have had originally. This clan woman, believed to be the Lady of the Black Veil, had paid the architect of the castle in a large amount of butter; it was assumed this object was what she was holding in her hand. The castle is known in Lochaline today as *Caisteal an Ime* or the Castle of Butter.

They peeked into the dungeon large enough to hold two people. As the owners walked them about, they learned that the walls were ten feet thick and that the massive limestone blocks in these walls actually contained rare fossils. The owners told them that the castle's limestone walls still held so much water from centuries of neglect that it would take more centuries for the inside to dry out.

Just before they were to leave, the owners presented Tilli with a book, *Stories of our Clan*, compiled and illustrated by Mary A. Faulk. The book contained lots of information about the MacInnes clan.

After their return to Hamlet, they had time to read and talk about Clan MacInnes. They learned where the family name came from—Gaelic: *MacAonghais*, son of Angus— referring to the Pictish King Onnust, who died in 761. They read about the importance of the thistle and the bee, how the salmon saved the clan, and other stories. From this book by Mary Faulk, they discovered that the Mac-Innes family's descendants emigrated to Canada, New Zealand, and other English-speaking countries.

# Home Again

A few weeks after their return from Scotland, Tilli sat at the old desk in the den. It was almost midnight when she finished her entry in the diary. Padding softly over to the bookcase to slip the journal back into place, she paused and reflected upon her experiences, especially those golden hours with Jim and his family. And she and the girls had discovered that the MacInnes castle—the one in the painting that hung over the fireplace—was no longer in ruins but restored and alive with a happy, growing family. "Oh, Bertie." She smiled. "We had a once-in-a-lifetime trip; so glad you came with us in spirit."

# Acknowledgements

My gratitude goes to the first reader of *Five Wishes*, my daughter Elizabeth, who gave me editorial direction that helped shape the story. Mary Mackie pointed out a significant flaw in the text which I corrected. Special thanks to my beta reader Nancy Horton for her suggestions and comments that led to further improvements. I extend my appreciation to everyone at Atmosphere Press for their efforts to make this novel a reality. Thanks to editor and proofreader BE Allatt for polishing the manuscript until it shined. Art Director Ronaldo Alves designed the perfect castle image for the cover. Special recognition goes to my personal proofreader, Emil, who has shared his love, support, and encouragement for over fifty years.

# About Atmosphere Press

Atmosphere Press is an independent, full-service publisher for excellent books in all genres and for all audiences. Learn more about what we do at atmospherepress.com.

We encourage you to check out some of Atmosphere's latest releases, which are available at Amazon.com and via order from your local bookstore:

*Icarus Never Flew 'Round Here,* by Matt Edwards

*The Chimera Wolf,* by P.A. Power

*Umbilical,* by Jane Kay

*The Two-Blood Lion,* by Nick Westfield

*Shogun of the Heavens: The Fall of Immortals,* by I.D.G. Curry

*Hot Air Rising,* by Matthew Taylor

*30 Summers,* by A.S. Randall

*Delilah Recovered,* by Amelia Estelle Dellos

*A Prophecy in Ash,* by Julie Zantopoulos

*The Killer Half,* by JB Blake

*Ocean Lessons,* by Karen Lethlean

*Unrealized Fantasies,* by Marilyn Whitehorse

*The Mayari Chronicles: Initium,* by Karen McClain

*Squeeze Plays,* by Jeffrey Marshall

*JADA: Just Another Dead Animal,* by James Morris

*Hart Street and Main: Metamorphosis,* by Tabitha Sprunger

# About the Author

Karin is a graduate of Harvard University with a degree in Humanities. She wrote the first guidebook for the historic Gloucester area, *Cape Ann & Vicinity: a Guide for Residents and Visitors*. Her first children's book, *Flora Has an Adventure* (ages 4-8 years), was published in 2019. She has written short stories published in *Hawaii Pacific Review* and by the Kurt Vonnegut Museum in Indiana, in their anthology honoring the 50th anniversary of *Slaughterhouse-Five*. She lives on a Christmas tree farm with her husband and a flock of friendly chickens. *Five Wishes* is her first novel.

Printed in the USA
CPSIA information can be obtained
at www.ICGtesting.com
LVHW091231011123
762288LV00002B/12